SCREENSAVER !

Beth Porter

COPYRIGHT
First published in England October 2017

Copyright © 2017 Beth Porter trading as Womenstuff Publishing

All rights reserved. No part of this publication may be reproduced, stored in a retrieval system or transmitted in any form or by any means without the prior permission in writing of the publisher, nor be circulated in writing of any publisher, nor be otherwise circulated in any form of binding or cover other than that in which it is published without a similar condition including this condition, being imposed on the subsequent purchaser. Some passages of this publication may not be suitable for children.

ISBN-13: 9780957627260

DEDICATION
For his friendship and support over the hills of goodtimes and the valleys of despair, and for showing me that dreams and reality are the same, I dedicate this book to Howard Schuman.

Acknowledgements

I've gestated the idea for ScreeenSaver! over many decades and in several forms. My gratitude goes to a number of very supportive people who have encouraged me and helped me to achieve this protracted birth, with especial thanks to Judy Rains, Alan Stafford, Alec Reid, Bethan Owen-Lee, and Yvonne Coolbear.

CHAPTERS

LEVEL 1 - PROLOG   4

CHAPTER 1	7
CHAPTER 2	19
CHAPTER 3	26
CHAPTER 4	32
CHAPTER 5	38
CHAPTER 6	55
CHAPTER 7	65
CHAPTER 8	80

LEVEL 2 - CHAPTER 9   99

CHAPTER 10	110
CHAPTER 11	126
CHAPTER 12	138
CHAPTER 13	150
CHAPTER 14	161

LEVEL 3 - CHAPTER 15   171

CHAPTER 16	182
CHAPTER 17	200
CHAPTER 18	210

BONUS LEVEL 223

ABOUT BETH   227

PRE-PUBLICATION REVIEWS   229

LEVEL 1 – PROLOG

Who wants some once-upon-a-time? Okay, this story begins with a series of graphics… inked and partially coloured frames, like an action-based comic book, complete with the written declarations of an androgynous Narrator. Just picture it… Frame One shows a newborn baby in a cradle on a cloud - with rival space-ships firing missiles at each other in the background. The spacecraft fighters transcend time, blending rocket launchers with BenHur chariots.

Speech bubbles float above the Narrator. "Brynthila - born to a universe at war. Tumbling through time and space."

The following frames, some skewed at angles, others larger than the rest, depict Brynthila's fatally wounded Mother slumped over an empty up-ended cradle - baby Brynthila falling through the skies - Brynthila landing in a full washing basket - and the astonished face of a humble Washerwoman.

The Narrator weaves the images into the story. Frames show the cowering Washerwoman entering a lavish castle - presenting the Baby to Lord Cassemar - who angrily gestures her away.

"First parentless - then homeless - her young life was saved by a lowly servant of the evil Lord Cassemar, the most devious, malicious, malevolent lord around - and not in a good way - who ordered the infant to be put to death! But the kindhearted Washerwoman secretly brought up Brynthila as her own daughter."

The frames now show the Washerwoman surreptitiously hiding the Baby in a small storage annexe. The Narrator reveals the passing of years, as the Baby grows into a Toddler, then a young Girl. When Lord Cassemar discovers the maiden, he snatches her away from her foster mother and confines her to the turret room of his castle.

From a full view of the sinister-looking gothic citadel nestled into a dense wood, the next frame focuses on one turret, where Brynthila, the young maiden, stares forlornly out of the mullioned window. Subsequent frames flood with an almost blinding celestial light which shadows the distant hills. The statuesque form of a giant goddess floats into Brynthila's vision.

The Narrator appears in a corner inset of the frame to explain. "Until one day the Goddess Gevreen made her a solemn promise: You must venture far before you can find your way back home. If you can escape from Lord Cassemar's castle, cross the River of Timewasting, do battle with the five-headed Pentangle monster and cut off each of its heads: Porbo, Morbo, Worbo, Gorbo, and Lorbo - if you stop the war, collect all your assigned treasure trove, find your imprisoned soul-mate, set him free and escort him back to your homeland without falling back to where you started through the Trapdoor of Doom, then and only …"

At this point the graphic artist has begun running out of space, and the words of explanation are squeezed smaller, tighter, barely fitting into the frame. On the soundtrack, the Narrator is running out of breath. He inhales and continues, "… only then can you reclaim your birthright as Brynthila, The Venerated Goddess of the Maze of Life. And win the game."

The next frame shows Brynthila transformed from a two-dimensional drawing into a full colour, fully-rendered 3D CGI adult woman with long flowing blonde locks. Her garment combines medieval princess with warrior goddess - but too flimsy and revealing to be practical.

The Narrator declares, "Brynthila has come of age! The adventure has begun!!"

On the final word "begun," there is a distorted flicker in the picture. The image toggles back and forth between incomprehensible programming code, and the frozen image of Brynthila crouched in mid-attack.

The picture is overlapped by a sotto voce woman's whisper. "Told you we should have put it on a memory stick," she says.

Chapter 1

Well, well, well! So, we're not in an animated fantasy, after all. Nope. We're in an office, staring at a computer screen.

Behind the desk sits 30-something Max Checkman, almost dapper in a three-piece suit. You know The Checkman, right? No? You're double-joking, I thought everyone knows Max… tinge of TOWIE, not as rich as he pretends to be? *Bluebell's Magic Garden*? No? I'm guessing maybe you're not into vid games for tots and teens.

Fair enough. So anyway, welcome to Max's office. Like his expanding waistline, it's big. Like his life, it's deceptive, and suspiciously sparsely furnished.

Along one wall are framed photographs of him with various celebrities. Prince Harry, Johnny Depp, Adele. They're all inexpertly photo-shopped. In one he holds up a trophy. And that's actually real. But in pride of place is a framed diploma of sorts, issued to Max just a couple of months ago. It's from the Village Hall Marketing and Yoga Seminar.

A room divider marks off a small reception area. Propped against it is an over-sized cardboard blow-up of an anthropomorphic bluebell with a cutesy face, wearing a gingham pinafore. Away at the far end of the room, the London eye, the Shard, the Gherkin, all define the iconic skyscape through the window-frame.

Max studies the frozen Brynthila in mid-crouch. "Yo, Denny? Jo? What's this … uhm, split code?"

Max glances up at the young man and woman hovering behind him. They exchange a look over his head; it's a rolled eyes moment. True to form, the boss hasn't a clue what he's talking about.

Both are in their early 20s and have learned to tolerate, and even to humour him. After all, he does pay them. Denny, short for

Brenden, could charm proverbial birds from their nests, and his black velour pullover sets off the brooding Welsh/Italian good looks of his ancestors. Fit enough to be a male model, he's actually a digital artist.

You know how body language doesn't lie, right? Well, by the way every molecule of Denny's pulls away from Jo, it's either a shared, albeit very repressed passion... or they really do loathe each other. But both smile bravely at Max. He taps vainly at the keyboard, focused on the digital woman still immobile on the screen.

"Code?" he asks again.

Denny suppresses a laugh as Jo pulls a clownish face. He tries to calm Max's anxiety. "Battery... it's the battery."

Max turns to Jo. "That right?" Games programmer Josephine Hawker-Meade, recovers her composure, and nods maniacally in agreement.

There's no polite way to say this, but Jo's a mess. Some women truly suit a tousled mop of natural curls. Hers is a dull beige tangle, spiraling down her neck. She attempts to hide the wreckage brought on by a pizza and doughnut diet under a baggy pullover. Her glasses frame clings on with a blue plaster across the bridge of her nose.

Never willing to admit to dodgy code, she says, "Battery. Definitely."

"Okay," says Max, " then let's run the disc on my machine."

In the uneasy silence, Jo and Denny look daggers at each other. They both start speaking simultaneously. Jo's emphatic "No!" is topped by Denny's not all that helpful explanation that the demo disc still needs vital hard drive input, but they promise that's a simple fix, not to worry, and everything will be right as rain for his meeting with Mr Money, and that's a double promise. Jo readily agrees, adding this morning's viewing was simply to confirm, after all, they're on the right track.

They glance over at Max. Has he bought that? Well, he's been listening patiently, his face set to poker mode. They still need his approval. Denny braves the silence. "So, Max? Apart from the... Was that... er? Did you... uhm?"

Jo and Denny daren't move. Eventually Max cracks a smile. A big smile. "Brilliant. Perfect. Flawless. Almost. Obviously, this is just the promotional screensaver for the real game, but I knew I was right to get you two dudes working together again."

He holds up a DVD game cassette. The cover sleeve reproduces the perky human-face flower on the blow-up leaning against the wall. Across the flower is the game's title: *Bluebell's Magic Garden*. Max fingers the games cassette with an almost paternal pride. "Bluebell was a winner, and we will triumph again with... with... what's 'er name ..."

Jo and Denny speak in tandem, drowning out any doubt. "Brynthila."

"Right. Cool," says Max. "*Brynthila: The Maze of Life*. Provided you can get that demo fixed on time."

Before Jo or Denny can reply, Max calls over in the direction of the room divider. "Fiona?! Where's the ..."

But Fiona doesn't need the whole question. It's not just that she's Max's exemplary PA. From the time their parents brought him home from the maternity hospital when she was ten, she's always been able to predict her baby brother's thoughts even before he thinks them.

She calls out, "Sideboard behind you."

Max turns to find a bottle of champagne, which he opens. He pours out the bubbly into mismatched mugs and passes them over. "A toast. Jo. Denny. And, of course, to Bryn... uhm... thila."

Parroting the toast, Jo and Denny look visibly relieved. But as they sip, Max's smile fades. He loosens his tie and sits back behind the desk. "So, let's talk changes."

Denny drains his cup. "Of course," he agrees a tad too readily. He looks for a place to put down his mug, then hands it to Jo.

She tries not to take it, but can't find room on Max's desk, so stands holding both cups. She's not so eager. "Changes?" It's half a query, half a challenge.

"A few," Max cautions. "Just a few." He tries to remember the correct technique for Managing Change he learned at the seminar.

Denny grabs Jo's arm to silence her unspoken "But." She hands him back the cups, and pulls away. Max has started pacing about the office. Both Jo and Denny recognise this as his signal to pontificate, usually about something which, let's just say, wouldn't be his specialist subject on Mastermind. As he's about to hold forth, his phone rings.

He calls out to Fiona, "Take a message."

But loyal Fiona knows when to interrupt. She sticks her head around the office divider panel, looking like a puppet in a sea-side amusement. She also looks remarkably like her little brother. "Take the call." It's more a soft command than a suggestion. And Max meekly obeys.

He tries to regain authority. "Sorry, dudes. Gotta take this. Chat among yourselves."

As Max talks into the phone, Denny steers Jo over to the window, stopping along the way to set the mugs down on the sideboard.

Now, here's an odd thing. As they near the window, the view is definitely not the London skyscape that might be visible from a posh City office. Instead, the urban vista has been painted onto a huge window blind. When Denny opens it, the window actually overlooks the shops of a tidy village High Street done up in Mock Tudor façades.

Jo mutters, "I wish he wouldn't call us dudes."

"I wish I was dating Rihanna."

"I wish you'd fall into a bottomless pit, and…"

Denny tries to get back to matters in hand. "Oh, shut up, Jo. How are we going to make changes if we can't even get this demo working?"

"Well, whose fault is that?"

"You're not helping."

"Oh, please, I've been programming my buns off, including all the sound effects. You just muck about with a paint program." They both know this outburst means she's worried about the computer glitch.

The window pane fills with the drops of a sudden shower. "Bugger!" says Denny. "I left the top down on the car."

"And I suppose that's my fault, is it?"

Denny isn't exactly contrite. He brings Jo back to their dilemma. "Yeah, well, I still say Brynthila is too… too… I don't know the word."

"Ah, the limits of a comprehensive education."

"And you know everything, do you, little miss self-taught. What I do know is that I designed Brynthila to be sharp, ready for action, and you programmed in some cutesy kitten you probably saw on Lol-cats!"

Jo is about to give as good as she gets, when Max calls them over.

"Yo, Dudes! Chill! Listen, that was the money on the phone. Good news! Tomorrow's meeting's put back till the evening, before their trip. Which means …"

He does a little "chair dance," far more excited than a grown man should be... "Which means I get to stay in a posh hotel." And he calls over to Fiona, "I need..."

But she's way ahead of him, as usual. "I just made the reservation."

Max recovers his composure, "Can't have a money meeting in a tatty B and B, can I?" He slips further into 'boss mode,' looking from Jo to Denny, "So, changes. Deal? Or no deal?"

And, while Denny says, "No problemo!" Jo wants to know, "How many did you have in mind? I mean you haven't actually said what they are, yet."

Max replies, "It's conceptual!"

Which Jo doesn't think is all that helpful. "Well, conceptually... what time is their train?"
"No, no. Plane, not train. It's an airport meeting... in the airport hotel. The money dudes are headed for the Big Apple. Where the Big Money is. They're very big on face-to-face."

Did I mention Jo is big on protecting the planet? Well, she is. She sighs her disappointment, "Ah, another flight on Air-pollution Airways. So good to know we're helping the environment."

Denny's less altruistic. "Give it a rest, Jo."

Jo mouths "naff off" and turns back to Max. "What about you? I hope at least you're taking the train to Contamination City." He ignores her. The Village Hall Marketing Seminar didn't cover this.

A thunderclap echoes from afar. Through it, Denny says,"Why don't you talk us through the changes, Max."

Max is convinced that the Seminar has provided him with all the jargon he needs to deal with what he's learned to call Bigger

ScreenSaver!

Picture items. "Market. Think market. It's a market matter. What's your games market? The teenage boy, right?"

Denny nods in vigorous agreement while Jo reminds them, "And girl. Remember? You asked us, no you begged us to come up with something to capture the... what did you call it?... the growing tween girl market."

Max knows he's on thin feminist ice. "Sure, sure... but teenage girls stop after nineteen. Whereas your teenage boy continues well into his thirties... and beyond."

He looks over at Denny, hoping for confirmation. But Denny's long ago learned not to get drawn into any kind of argument with the boss. He taps away at his keyboard.

Jo has been taking her glasses off and putting them back on. Several times. It's one of her nervous habits. Right now, she's very nervous. She wants to control her exasperation, really she does. And why isn't Denny helping? She protests, "But this is a game for women too. I thought that was the point. It empowers them, it ..."

Max half-jumps in his seat. "Empower! Good word. I like it! Good selling word! Fiona," he calls out, "write down empower for my meeting notes. She has power! She's a wower!"

"Hello boys, she's in the shower." Jo's whisper of irony isn't quite low enough to elude Max.

He takes it all-too seriously. "I like it - a shower scene! Uhm... no, well, I mean... a tasteful shower scene."

Jo hisses at Denny. "You promised you deleted that shower stuff!"

But Denny hasn't been following and looks baffled. Max tries to calm Jo down. "Jo, Jo. Jo-Jo! Give and take. Take and give! You've got your girly hero. She just needs a pinch more... how can I put it? Plasticity. Think market."

Jo is steaming with the righteous red rage of principle. "I knew it, I knew it! You say 'plastic,' but you just mean action-boy in a skimpy frock with big, plastic... [she does the classic mime for big breasts] airbags. You're back to your old ..."

Max looks to Denny for some 'locker room support', but he's too absorbed at the computer screen. "You're exaggerating," he tells Jo.

She can't help it, she explodes. "Well at least I don't do it anatomically! Remember when you wanted to put our sweet little Bluebell in a bikini! A bluebell in a bikini! I give up, Max... don't make me part of your Donald Trump fantasy. You..."

"Whoa!" Max tries to regain control. "Chill little lady I just meant..."

She says, "I am so NOT your 'little lady,' and I'm perfectly chill! We talked about this, remember?" She looks to Denny, "Didn't we?" She fiddles with her glasses again; they're a bit lopsided when she replaces them.

Finally, Denny can see things getting out of hand. He'd hate to admit it, but he needs this gig, no matter what it takes. He focuses on Jo's stream of angry logic.

She continues, "We all... All... agreed on an intelligent, athletic heroine who uses her brain to solve problems as well as conquer demons. What are you saying now? Just because Brynthila is intelligent and athletic she's less... uhm, relevant to men?"

Max is willing to dismiss Jo's outburst as creative temperament, but he's reaching his limit of tolerance. He tries another tactic. Calm and reasonable, which is what he learned at the management seminar. Be Reasonable, he recalls, came just after Take Control.

"No," he says, "not less relevant. Not at all. As I say - the whole concept is fine. Just needs a few cosmetic improvements."

ScreenSaver!

Jo still expects Denny to back her up, but he leaps in to agree with Max. "Know just what you mean, Max. The looks don't quite reflect the character. Too soft. Too Hello Kitty. Needs more attitude."

"Like it!" says Max. "Cat with attitude."

And as if on cue, they both say, "Catitude!" And Denny continues, "In fact, I've already been working on a few ideas along that line. Jo hasn't seen these yet."

Jo has been adjusting her glasses again. She gives Denny a withering glance. He holds up two fingers, just as Jo's glasses frames snap in two.

I am very sorry to report that Jo's composure snaps as well, and she cannot stop the tears of exasperation. She rounds on Max, who's now standing alongside Denny.

"Oh, for… that's it! It's perfectly obvious he doesn't want to work with me. Well, that's cool. I'm not bothered!" She sniffs back the tears, but doesn't catch that snot-bubble forming from her left nostril. "And may I remind you again, Max, you came to us. [sniff] I never wanted… I mean, you approved our idea… [sniff] you promised us the moon, you …" [sniff] She salvages a torn tissue from her pocket, and dabs at her nose.

Denny nods in agreement. "She's right."

"I am?" Jo is suddenly hopeful. Until Denny says, "Yeah, I never wanted to work with you." But he offers her a clean handkerchief, and she gives her nose a mighty blow that might rouse an elephant herd in the next village, if an elephant herd had heard it.

"Stop!" Max commands. With a sense of determination, he roots around in one of his desk drawers and pulls out a folder stamped with a logo. He skim reads some stapled pages tucked inside, finds what he was looking for and smiles at Denny and Jo. He's grateful his management seminar was so thorough. Any situation can be sorted.

First analyse the problem, then apply the solution. Simple!

He reads aloud from one of the bullet points: "Heat of battle, dah-dah-dah… deadlines looming, dah-dah-dah… staff revert to playground behaviour." He turns to them. "Right. There's only one way to deal with this. Now stand still and shut up."

Both Denny and Jo are startled into silence by this new persona from Max.

"Mouths," he says, "open!" And they do. From the seminar pack he unwraps two baby's teething dummies. He approaches Jo, pops a dummy in her mouth. Both the residual tears and her broken glasses put Max out of focus. He speaks directly at her.

"Jo, you're the cleverest programmer in the Home Counties. And Denny…"

Max turns to him, and pops the other dummy in his mouth. He drapes an arm around his shoulder. "Denny, you're the most original digital artist I've ever met. You're my winning team, dudes. You're almost there. So very almost. Just think movie star. I mean, that's how I'll pitch it tomorrow. First the game, then the movie spinoff. Or, wait! Maybe the movie first. Wotcha reckon? Who'd play Brynthingy? Online viral campaign. Downloads, ringtones, tee-shirts. The lot."

Still wary, Jo starts to speak, oblivious to the dummy; the result is gibberish, until she removes it. "But, it will still be our game, though, won't it? Our Brynthila?"

"Totally, dude. Your Brynthila. But more real. More honest. Just bursting … with…"

Denny has turned his laptop screen towards Max. There's the old look Brynthila. But one keystroke and a downward screen-swipe reveals a sexed-up Brynthila with noticeably more cleavage. Max is distracted by the image on the screen.

"… Just bursting out of her… her… out of …" Max gives Denny a discrete thumbs up of approval, unseen by Jo. Denny keeps sucking his dummy, perhaps a tad too enthusiastically.

Max continues. "… out of the screen. So just get me that demo disc Pronto Tonto and leave the selling to yours truly!"

Denny whips the dummy out of his mouth. He and Jo try not to let their panic show. And Denny's keen to check the water damage to his car. They start for the door. But Fiona's voice stops them from behind the room divider. "Stunts!"

"Wait!" Max commands. Denny and Jo return to the room as another clap of thunder rolls above the High Street. "Fiona's right; we need stunts. I'm talking Jackie Chan, I'm talking Bruce Willis, I'm talking …"

"Bollocks." Max only half hears Jo's whispered comment.

"Who?"

"Bullock. Sandra Bullock. Unless you want to turn Brynthila into an aging bald kung-fu guy."

"Funny! So, Denny, what have you got in the stunt box?"
Jo echoes with mock anticipation, "Yeah Denny, show us your stunt box."

"Actually, I have been working on a few… Of course, it's Jo's programming. But…"

Jo gestures obscenely to Denny, who immediately wipes the sexy Brynthila off screen. He presses a few keys, and a new image reveals a CGI Brynthila on the castle battlements, throwing a rope with grappling iron onto an impossibly distant stone archway. The supporting stone pillar morphs into an animated giant warrior. Above the clouds a space-chariot rolls by, shooting out lasers. Brynthila redirects a laser beam, decimating the giant.

"Ta-dah!" crows Denny.

"Wicked!" Max's eyes widen. "That's what I'm talking about. Plasticity!"

Max high-fives Denny. He's done what he can with programming previously supplied by Jo, so there are some weird gaps in the action. No one can quite explain that bathtub in the tree-top. Or why Brynthila attempts to grab a rubber chicken out of a moat. But the animated scene plays out, with our agile heroine swinging through the air seen from constantly changing angles and perspectives. She teeters on a narrow cliff ledge, which starts to crumble away.

Max says, "Just clean that up a bit, and stuff it into the demo. Deal?"

But before they can answer, suddenly the picture flickers, then freezes. Denny casually taps a key. It makes no difference, so both he and Jo tap more frantically. They smile awkwardly at Max, who glares fiercely back. "Just get it sorted."

None of them notices Brynthila's face on screen. Her mouth opens to cry for help, her eyes blink like a mechanical doll at warp speed. Look a bit closer. If she weren't a digital figment of imagination, you might say she looks genuinely terrified.

Chapter 2

Denny's hard at work in his minimalist, ultra-tidy flat. A job-lot of Perspex and chrome. It's not quite as opulent as he's convinced is his destiny, but as much as he can afford. At the moment, he's too pre-occupied to beat himself up about it.

The late-afternoon sunlight filters through near-by trees into the ground-floor windows of a square room and open-plan kitchen. Denny's work desk supports a meticulous filing system housing thousands of digital images, all neatly labelled. His feet are crossed on the desk, an open laptop resting on his lap. He locates a contact sheet of thumbnails, and clicks through rendered snippets of jumps, arm positions, hair combing, smiles. Having chosen some ingredients, he removes his feet from the desk and leans forward to concentrate on the screen. He cuts and pastes some bits to form Brynthila into a combination of sexy space adventurer crossed with medieval Princess-Warrior. He leans back in his chair to admire his work. I have to admit, despite his arrogance, he's very good.

Grabbing the empty coffee mug from his desk, Denny heads for the high-tech kitchen. A gleaming espresso machine perches on the counter, into which he measures some dark beans and water, and waits for the aroma of Kenya's best to fill the room.

. Meanwhile, in a very different part of town, Jo's in faded jeans and a t-shirt which reads 'Programmers Do It For Clicks.' She's devoid of make-up, curls tangled like an abused floor-mop. She types furiously, obsessively, occasionally consulting calculations written on her arm in ballpoint.

It's difficult to assign a function to Jo's turret quarters, defined by its rounded walls. The only purely decorative item is a large rectangular photograph of a vivid forest landscape. Mounted under glass, it's hung next to one of the room's two windows. At first glance it might be a painting, the colours deceptively lit from within, like an enchanted forest. It was a gift from Jo's mother who worked as an events photographer before she married Jonathan Hawker-Meade. Jo loves it.

The room is immersed in a chaos appreciated solely by its occupant. A solid oak desk follows the curve of the walls; it's overburdened with a scanner, two huge computer units, a pile of freshly ironed clothes, a collection of remote control units, and an open pizza box. Perched atop a dark oak boarded dowry chest layered with the patina of centuries, is a thick pile of lined paper scribble pads headed 2- Do List. It's anchored by an elegant carved wooden apple paperweight.

Naked mother-boards, a games controller, and other mysterious electronics litter the un-made four-poster. Coils of cables trap a cluster of trackball and optical mice, while handwritten equations and technical scrawls on post-it notes decorate the walls. One reads "My CPI is faster than your CPI."

Best not examine the floor too closely, if you know what I mean. Peeking from under the bed is a serving tray full of unwashed plates, cups and half-eaten take-away remnants still in their delivery cartons. Nestled into one corner of the generous room sits a superlarge television monitor. At first glance it looks like an old-fashioned console unit, but if you're into the techno-future, you'll know this is the real-deal.

Remember that blow-up promo of Bluebell in Max's office? Jo has one, too, along with another of Denny and herself each holding either side of a trophy. Easy to see this ain't your typical girly bedroom.

Jo's wireless phone is on speaker, so when it rings, she's jolted from her typing to hear her own voice on the message announcement. "In the words of Magritte, *ceci n'est pas moi*, so leave me some words for later."

The caller does just that. His message is introduced by the throaty bark of a dog. The human voice is male, though hardly audible, charitably described as soft-spoken, a notch above whisper on the

ScreenSaver!

Mohs scale of mineral hardness.

"Jo? You there, it's Kurt." Jo's too absorbed at her computer screen to answer, and lets the message continue. "Are you cool to dog sit Lovelace tomorrow? Need to pick up that Linux Sys Utility for you. Ring me."

Jo completes a run of entering computer code which resolves itself onscreen. She pushes her fist into the air with a triumphant whoop. Like Denny she leans back to admire her calculations, idly reaching for a slice of cold pizza from the open box beside her. She licks congealed sauce from her fingers and wipes her hand on her t-shirt.

She looks around this room which she loves. It's been hers since childhood, and it's her safe place. The woodlands adjoining the house offer protection, but from what it's hard to say. Looking in from the outside, her life appears charmed. So why is she plagued with bouts of rage and anxiety? But peering beyond the indoor mess Jo can conjure a more perfect image of whatever home means. It's a resolution she can construct, in the same way that she can process runic programming code and turn it into a matrix for coherent pictures.

You've seen those split screens sometimes used by film-makers for parallel action in separate locations, right? Okay, here's Denny on one side and Jo on the other. Each of them carries on working. Jo sends Denny a mail attachment with instructions how to incorporate her new code. He tries out a series of new actions for Brynthila, and loves the result. He replies to Jo's message with a huge grinning emoji. In her room, Jo blushes, pleased they're on the same wavelength. At work, that is.

Denny responds to a ping from the espresso machine on his kitchen counter. He carries the steaming coffee back to his desk, accompanied by the zinging jazz riff of his ringtone. It's Ella Fitzgerald's *April in Paris*. He checks the caller I.D. "Hi Max." "Can't get through to Jo. How's it going? Finished yet?"

Denny tries his best to sound fresh and perky. "Nearly. We'll ring you, okay?" As he speaks, Denny opens the door of his flat and peers along the corridor leading to the front entrance. There's another flat door opposite and a staircase headed to the floor above. He checks his watch.

Across town Jo takes a break from her monitor full of computer code to gaze at the afternoon mist from her diamond-paned mullioned window. She can see some of the driveway, a circular rose garden in full bloom, and a small copse separating the grand house from the town. Her turret tower graces one wing of the extraordinary fourteenth century residence known as Falcon Lodge. Not that Jo is in any position to appreciate the history at the moment, but the house has been part of the Hawker-Meade estate since it was first built as a hunting lodge for visitors from the Court. It looks remarkably like the castle of Lord Cassemar on Brynthila's demo disc.

Jo succumbs to a giant yawn, interrupted by the phone ringing. It's Denny. Again. This time she picks up. "How's it going?" he says.

"Much the same as it was last time you rang - ooh, five minutes ago."

"Cool. Yeah, I mean, it's just Max keeps … I just want to make sure… I mean, we've still got to program in some background music and atmos. We're nowhere on that, are we, and we've got to make that deadline, Jo. Vital. Uber-importante."

"But not quite uber enough for you to come round and help."

The tone starts to shift. Denny says, "Not my area. You're the techno-nerd."

"Not a smart thing to say to someone with access to a Delete key."

And you can see just how fragile this thin conversational ice can be. But Denny tries again. "All right, all right. Truce. And, straight up, I really liked that new code snippet. Did you get the latest artwork? That stuff I've been slaving over all day?"

"Give me a minute," she says, and goes back to her desk where she fires up the computer that houses her eMails. With some slight distaste, she clicks through attachments of various sexed-up images of Brynthila. She starts to object, but Denny says, "Just substitute the version we had before you started getting prissy."

"I merely observed - as she's constantly looking for clues - it could be a design fault if she can't even see her own feet."

"Like I said 'Prissy.'"

"Oh, come on, Denny, how many times have we had this conversation? What interests me is Brynthila's character. She can look like a couple of balloons tied to a matchstick for all I care. Give me a minute, I just have to …"

Jo clicks on the new compromise figure of Brynthila and sets her walking round her castle room. She sighs. "Well, I admit, it's an improvement. And I like her new cloak… But… but… we'll…"

"Hey, you're not crying, are you?"

"No! Maybe. Oh, Den, we're never going to have this ready for Max's big meeting. Are we?"

"Depends how fast you work… and see what's causing those glitches, will you."

But fragile Jo is looking for a tad more support. "Do I get a please?"

Denny turns on the charm. "Oh come on, Ms. Josephine, ma'am, you know how I value every little thing you've done. And then some!"

Jo laughs. "So you should, Brenden, so you should. Any partnership will only sustain a maximum of one superfluous person."

Denny's not quite sure what she means, but he's distracted by a buzz on his doorbell. Still talking into his phone he heads for the door. "Right. So, about those glitches?"

Exasperated, Jo spins round in her chair to peer out the window, leaving Brynthila on the screen behind her. "No way," she says. "It's your clapped-out laptop that's the problem. She's working fine on my machine."

Denny opens his front door. He's now totally focused on the beautiful young woman, posing against the door-frame. Her stunning evening dress is held up with spaghetti straps, just supporting her ample chestal substances. "Well, hello Lauren," he says. She's the closest Denny has to a regular girlfriend. He beckons her inside.

Jo can tell he's distracted. "Pardon?... Denny? Brynthila... I said she's working here on my monitor."

"Uhm, yeah. Are you sure?" he says.

Jo says, "Positive." But behind her, Brynthila's image on screen goes through a digital paroxysm of freezing and juddering.

"Ergo, definitely your laptop," she repeats. "You really should update that steam-powered model ... trade it in."

Denny watches Lauren strut around the room, as though on a cat-walk. She tosses her head, making her thick black hair swing back into place with its expert cut. Giggling flirtatiously, she lowers one of the dress straps. He motions for her to be quiet as he carries on talking to Jo.

"Got it, right, new model. Update... I intend to."

"It's well known for crashing," says Jo.

. Lauren embraces Denny from behind. She tickles him. He tries not to laugh. "Lauren... I mean, law unto itself, that thing."

"I know," Jo says. "It needs a hammer taking to it."

Denny rounds on Lauren, grabbing both her wrists in one hand. He leads her toward the bedroom. "Mm," he says to Jo, "or maybe just a bit of tender loving care." He drops the phone, kissing Lauren as they sidle toward the bed.

Jo says, "Den? Denny?" And she turns to face her monitor of betrayal.

Chapter 3

A very tired Jo, even more dishevelled, returns to her computer with a mug of coffee. She starts tapping away to produce a screen full of computer code. Finally, Jo presses a key-combo which brings up an image on another monitor of Brynthila, grappling hand-to-hand with a hideous slavering multi-headed beast. Jo types in a phrase of text and the label 'Pentangle Monster' pops-up underneath the monster.

Meanwhile, Denny and Lauren are enjoying a more amorous tussle on his bed. If you wanted to, you might compare their progressive canoodling to Brynthila's sparring with the Pentangle Monster.

As Denny's evening sizzles, Jo struggles to stay awake in front of her screens. She's just aware of the dark rose sunset outside the window before her head gradually lowers until it hits her arms. It's not long before Jo's snores blend into the roars of the monster shadow boxing with Brynthila on an action loop. Suddenly the loop pauses as Brynthila turns her head to see Jo deep in dreamland. She gestures to the monster to keep the noise down. And sleep settles over the turret suite.

If this book had a soundtrack, now would be the right time for the chiffon strains of Grieg's Morning Song. If you don't know it, Wikipedia's got an audio of the intro.

The dawn cracks gently, sunlight creeping through the turret room onto Jo's curls. The Helios chariot of fire rolls on across town where Denny's asleep next to Lauren. They both jump when the phone trills *April in Paris*. Denny gropes groggily to answer it, as Lauren burrows under the pillow. "Max!" he says through a yawn.

Denny juggles the phone as he pulls on his snug Calvin Kleins, and makes his way to the kitchen. He continues speaking with Max as he prepares the espresso machine, setting it to XXXStrong.

ScreenSaver! 27

"Wait ... no, please... Max! ... Forget?! As if! ... No, uhm, the disc is... Well, almost ready ... last night? ... I know, sorry, we should have rung you... Yes, perfectly good explanation ... Uhm... Road accident ... Not me, Jo. I know, rotten luck, eh? ... Whose car? Uhm, Jo's actually ... yes, she, no, you're right, she does, she does ride a motorbike. Jo's bike. Did I say car? No, I meant a car hit her bike... she was on her way to ... what? ... No, not hurt, just shook up...Well, what time's your meeting? ... That's hours away ... Yeah, sure, no problemo ... on my way to her now ... you bet, we'll ring you."

As he rings off he notices Lauren, still fast asleep. "Bugger!" The espresso machine sighs its whoosh-hiss. Denny sticks his head under the kitchen mono-tap, and shakes his hair dry. He pads over to the bed and prods Lauren, head still under the pillow. She produces a grumpy note of incomprehensibility. "No, Lauren. Up. Gotta get up and out, baby."

He rips off the duvet and picks up her underwear and evening dress from the floor. As if he's pulling clothes onto a store mannequin, Denny finally manages to get Lauren dressed. He sits her up in the bed and goes to pour a cup of coffee. She falls over, trying to stay asleep. He tries not to spill the coffee as he steadies her upright, and holds the cup to her lips. The dark mud-like drink scalds her mouth, but at last she's awake. And in some pain.

"That hurt!" She's pouting, wanting some TLC. But Denny's all out. "No, gotta get up and out." He drags her off the bed, stooping to pick up her high heels. "Up. Out." He pushes her out of the flat and tosses her shoes after her. "I'll call you," he says as he closes the door and finishes dressing himself in double-quick time.

Lauren's leaning on the low brick wall in front of Denny's house, struggling sleepily to do up the strap on her heels. The house, like the others on the street, is an achingly average semi-detached conversion. What a contrast to Denny's stylish interior. Clutching his laptop, Denny barrels out the front door and jumps into a red convertible parked near the kerb. He uses the Starsky and Hutch method of entry, deft, ready for adventure, and leaving a rumpled, puzzled Lauren watching him peel away. After half a block, he slams on the brakes and calls back to Lauren. "C'mon, I'll drop you at the bus stop."

About twenty minutes later Denny approaches the turning into Falcon Lodge. From the very first time he beheld the place, he knew that even if he could afford such a grand house, he'd never quite feel at home. Forever a visitor. The imposing ancient gates, modernised with an impenetrable security system, mark the divide between insiders and invaders. An heraldic crest has been incorporated into the heavy metal, depicting a falcon perched atop a castle tower. Denny pulls up at the gates, stretching over to the entry buzzer. He waves at the camera, and the gates slowly open inviting him into the grounds. He slows his speed along the private drive lined with ancient oaks.

The Lodge's current matriarch is Elaine, Jo's mother, up early and hard at work dead-heading roses with secateurs. She's as refined as Jo isn't, and this morning she sports a trug, colour-coordinated gardening gloves and hat, and a designer smock with butterfly motif, neat and tailored enough for a spread in *Country Life*.

She looks up at the sound of flying gravel as Denny's convertible pulls into the drive alongside Jo's pristine motorbike complete with sidecar. There's definitely been no accident.

In her turret room, Jo, too, is roused from sleep by the car's engine. She's still head down at her desk, and has been there all night. She yawns loudly, fishing around the loose cables for her glasses. She looks blearily at her watch, sits bolt upright and peels off the slice of pizza stuck to her cheek. She almost throws it away, then takes a bite.

Downstairs, Denny disentangles himself from his car and greets Elaine. She smiles warmly, fumbling to remove her gloves while still holding the secateurs. "Denny! What a lovely surprise." As he approaches, she offers her hand to shake. He reaches to take the basket from her, and she realises her hand still clutches the secateurs. It's a bit like a music-hall routine. She laughs at the confusion; he blushes.

"Uhm... Morning, Mrs. Hawker-Meade."

"Elaine. Please."

Normally master of any situation, Denny always feels intimidated amid all this old money, but Elaine is confident enough for both of them. She pats him on the back, and ushers him into the house. Waiting in the side entrance hall is the ever-loyal family butler, who relieves Elaine of her flower- filled trug. "Thanks, Osborne," she says. "Will you put these in water, please." She places her gloves and garden hat into the trug and turns her attention to Denny.

Before Denny met Jo, his experience with domestic servants was nil, and he's never quite sure whether or not to say hello. But by the time he decides he should, Osborne has vanished around a corner. He tries to recover his composure. "Uhm... Jo upstairs?"

Elaine calls up the staircase. "Jo! Josephine! Denny's here. Shall I send him up?"

Jo rubs the sleep from her bleary eyes, and opens her door a fraction. Trying to keep the panic from her voice she says, "No! I'll be right down!"

She stumbles into her walk-in wardrobe, where she's met by a row of empty hangers. Next stop, the laundry basket. Rummaging through, she pulls out a random selection of underwear, sniffing crotches and armpit areas. She chooses the least offensive candidates and sprays everything with cologne.

Meanwhile, downstairs, Elaine engages Denny in small talk. "So, how's the... er... space invaders thingy going?"

Denny's baffled. "Space invad...? What's Jo been telling you?"

"Not much actually, she's in her own little world up there." She sighs wistfully. "I mean, we love her to bits, her father and I, but we wanted a daughter who'd join the pony club, get engaged in Tatler, you know, all the usual, and we've produced a girl who speaks in binary code. Shall I have Osborne set an extra place for lunch?"

Denny's tempted. "I'm not sure how long we'll … "

He's interrupted by the sight of Jo at the top of the stairs in a shapeless cardigan. She rolls up her overlong sleeves, trying to keep a casual tone. "Hi Denny. Come on up."

As she rolls up the second sleeve, a pair of large underpants falls out and lands at Denny's feet. Jo reddens with embarrassment, as Elaine deftly scoops up the item. "Have fun, you two," she says.

In the turret room, Jo flops down on the floor, amid a snake pit of cables, elbows propped up in front of that huge, I mean a really huge television monitor. On the screen is a continuous loop of a scene from the game, featuring Brynthila at her athletic best, dodging a trio of armoured assailants and laser-powered missiles as she frantically seeks refuge.

Denny removes his v-neck and lays it carefully on the floor before lying down on it next to Jo. He likes what he sees. "Brilliant! That should shut Max up."

"You think it'll be 'plastic' enough for him? Mr Plastic Max. Mr Dirty Plastic Macs."
Denny chuckles. "Cool. But what about the glitches?"

"Oh, come on, Den, we've been over this. I told you. It's not the disc… it's your clapped- out …" Which is the moment the screen freezes. Denny refrains from voicing his smugness. "No!" wails Jo. "Jesus, not again!" She starts tapping keys furiously.

Denny looks heavenwards. "Jesus? Mohammed? Buddha?! any of you guys know how to fix computers?"

"Oh, please, just shut up and help! I'm rebooting. Keep hitting F8 and I'll check the connections."

Denny half-crouches, tapping away at the keyboard, while Jo crawls under him to get to the cables.

Outside the turret room, Elaine knocks discreetly, then edges the door open. She speaks before entering. "Would you two like ... " She's faced with Denny's and Jo's upturned bottoms... "some tea?" And she makes a discreet exit, the very paragon of *sang froid*.

From beneath the tangle of wires and equipment comes Jo's plaintive voice. "That's it! I'm ringing Kurt."

Denny's surprised to hear the name. "What... Mr Hardware? You're not still seeing that loser, are you?"

Jo locates her wireless phone inside an empty pizza box and speed dials Kurt's number. It rings inside his van. He's at the wheel, sharing a similar hair-style with the fluffy dog beside him. He flicks the phone to hands-free, his voice still set to Incoherent Mumble, which Jo has learned to interpret. "Mr. Hardware here. Speak to me."

"Kurt, we're in trouble. Can you call round? Preferably with the Linux unit." But even before she's finished speaking, Kurt executes a daring u-turn.

Chapter 4

Kurt's van is parked along side Denny's convertible in the driveway. A mobile phone number is painted beneath the Mr. Hardware logo, which depicts a cartoon computer with a smiley face, and stick arms and legs.

Inside the turret room, Denny paces impatiently. Kurt's adorably scruffy dog nuzzles his leg, and he brushes it away, checking for shed hairs. Jo rushes to the dog's defence, giving it a cuddle.

"Don't do that... she's not an insect. Are you Lovelace?"

"No? Well, I bet he's home to a few. What a stink!"

Jo sniffs the dog, which licks her face. "He's a she, and she doesn't stink. Do you Wovewace? No you don't."

"Well, something does," says Denny, looking pointedly over at Kurt who currently has Jo's demo computer in bits. He wields a soldering iron in one hand and a joint in the other.

Jo shushes him. "Kurt's cool. He's a friend. A dear friend."

"Kurt, dear friend, you going to be much longer?"

Kurt mutters. And Denny replies, "Sorry? Were those actual words? *Sprechen sie Deutsch*? *Parlare Italiano*? Jo, he does speak English, doesn't he?"

Kurt throws an unwanted bit of computer over his shoulder. It narrowly misses Denny. The dog rushes to pick it up and drops it at Denny's feet. Denny's shocked. "He aimed that at me!"

"'Course he didn't. How's it going, Kurt?"

Kurt mutters, Jo translates. "He says, nearly there."

"Oh, where's that? Effluent creek?"

Kurt mutters more forcibly, and Jo relays, "It'll be ready when it's blah-blah ready."

"Well... Fan blah-blah tastic!"

Kurt lobs another bit of computer at Denny. Denny approaches him, fuming. "Listen mate, if that's not back in one piece in an hour we're dead. And I do mean 'we.'"

Kurt picks up another discarded piece of computer and brandishes it threateningly. Kurt growls, Lovelace growls. In an effort to avoid a punch up, Jo steps between the men. She thrusts Denny's laptop into his hands. "Break! Lunch break. Come on. I could do with a walk. Kurt... Mummy's working in her dark room today, but just ask if you need anything."
Kurt mumbles and gives the thumbs up as Jo ushers Denny out. Kurt lights up another joint. He watches from the turret window as the pair walk up the driveway, clearly arguing. They amble past Denny's convertible parked between Kurt's scruffy van and Jo's motorbike. Inside the room, Lovelace picks up Denny's v-neck sweater and shakes it in her jaws. She and Kurt play Fetch The V-Neck.

Denny and Jo soon reach the town's high street and find a table at a local pizza place. While Jo goes to the counter to order, Denny sets up his laptop. He selects the scene in the demo where Brynthila battles a scaly creature with purple eyes.

The restaurant fills up as Denny and Jo pick at their meal and try to figure out what's going wrong. Their common dilemma has brokered a truce. "But it can't be both our computers," Denny reasons. "It has to be the disc."

"Maybe your 'puter gave my 'puter a virus."

"No," Denny plays along. "Not on the first date. Seriously, Jo, if we don't get that demo to Max we're both toast. I mean, I know it doesn't matter much to you... you've got the colossal mansion, and I've got the colossal mortgage, but even if I find a comfy cardboard box with mod cons... I'm no good in shop doorways. And I sure ain't going home to me mam."

"Why not?"

"You haven't met my mother, have you?" Jo shakes her head. "Just count your lucky stars."

Jo's trying to see things from Denny's perspective. "Honestly, the main problem is we keep fiddling with it. Look, it's fine in demo mode. And that's all Max is going to do. Turn it on and let it run. Besides, anything more strenuous would land him in intensive care."

"You know and I know, if that disc crashes his machine, we'll all be in intensive care."

Jo tries to think positive. "Come on, don't be such a drama queen. Kurt will fix it. Don't forget, he's Mr Hardware. You want any pudding?"

Denny shakes his head, and Jo rethinks her calorie intake. She picks at bits of leftover pizza.

Denny says, "Where'd you meet that geek anyway?"

"Jealous? Come on, relax, will you. Coffee?"

Denny glances anxiously at the time display on his laptop. "Okay, but we need to get back."

And, over at Falcon Lodge, Kurt has reassembled the main computer unit on the desk. As he turns it on, the huge monitor on the floor flashes into life. He taps a few keys and Brynthila appears in vivid close up.

Kurt whoops in triumph and gets down on all fours alongside Lovelace. He mumbles at the image, his face almost touching the screen. Brynthila appears to pull away from him. Lovelace nuzzles into Denny's v-neck.

The dog is immediately tail-wagging and alert as Kurt stands, ready to go out. She tries to follow him, but obeys the mumbled command to stay. Kurt loops her lead around a leg of Jo's desk chair and heads downstairs. He turns the van down the grand drive and into the High Street.

Inside the restaurant, Denny laughs at the scene on his laptop screen as Brynthila follows a cute little piglike creature, imitating its waddlewalk. "He's definitely my favourite."

"Who? Oh - Pixmag."

"Yeah. The way he moves." Still seated, Denny tries to imitate the waddle. "How'd you come up with the name?"

"Oh, you know, just another anagram. Denny, we really should…"

"Anagram, eh? No, wait, don't tell me …" He starts doodling on a napkin, rearranging letters. He mutters as he doodles. "Mixpag. Gaxpim. Xagmpi."

Jo laughs. "No, much simpler. Think 'pig' and 'Max.'"

"Oh, yeah. Better watch it," warns Denny.

"He'll never notice. Come on, help me choose a few more scenes for the demo. Maybe we should record a voice-over."

But as she drags and drops Brynthila into a bed-chamber, Denny's intent on his napkin doodles. One of them evolves into a woman, sort of like Jo, sort of like Brynthila. While on the laptop screen, a digital kitten claws its way up to the four-poster bed.

"Denny?" repeats Jo. "Voice-over? Or not?"

ScreenSaver!

A few blocks away, Kurt pulls Mr Hardware into a parking spot on the High Street. He jumps out and starts walking, just killing time. Maybe he'll bump into Denny and Jo. Maybe not. He enters a take-away.

Meanwhile, Denny and Jo review Brynthila's onscreen antics. They're laughing away just as Kurt walks past the window outside, munching a take-away pasty. He pauses to scan the menu on display, and Jo spots him. Uh-oh, why isn't he back at the house. Denny waves frantically, and Jo taps on the window. Finally they catch Kurt's attention. Denny calls through the glass. "What about the computer? The computer! Have you fixed it?"

But Kurt doesn't understand. Denny points to his laptop. Kurt smiles, and holds up his watch. Then he gives them the thumbs up. But Jo looks around for the dog.

"Where's Lovelace?" she says, miming a begging dog. "Your dog!" she shouts.

Kurt smiles and enacts an elaborate mime to show the dog is back in Jo's room, tied up by its lead. Over this mime Denny asks, "Why would he name his dog after a 1960s porn star?"

"What are you talking about?" Jo says.

"Duh! Lovelace… Linda Lovelace?… Deep Throat? Don't you know anything?"

Jo's exasperated. "Lovelace," she explains patiently, "Ada Lovelace was an early pioneer of computing. Don't you know anything?"

By this time, Kurt has attracted the attention of other diners, who assume he's a street entertainer and applaud his feat of mime. He takes a self-conscious bow, then strolls off, while Denny tries a mime of his own. He ties a piece of imaginary rope around his own neck, pulling it upwards and hanging himself, his tongue lolling out. A child at the neighbouring table looks horrified. Jo notices, nudges Denny and tells him to stop.

ScreenSaver!

Chapter 5

Did you know that a dog's olfactory receptors are nearly fifty times more efficient than yours or mine? I just mention that for general information.

Up in the turret room, Lovelace sniffs the air. She tests out the play of her lead. Lying flat out on her stomach, she avidly watches the huge monitor. As she edges herself closer to Brynthila's image, she drags the chair along, which bumps against the desk. The computer tower wobbles precariously, but rights itself. Lovelace whines softly.

Two things are capturing her attention: the computer animation of Brynthila's metallic DigiKitten scampering onto the canopied bed in an extended loop, and the remnants of a Chinese take-away, its carton discarded next to the huge monitor. Between the food and the screen, an empty coffee cup supports Kurt's soldering iron, its red light still glowing. As Lovelace strains forward, the chair topples over, releasing the dog and crashing against the monitor casing. Lovelace whimpers and hides under the desk, pretty sure she shouldn't have done that.

The chair has pushed the coffee cup closer to the screen, and the red-hot iron now burns a small hole into the plasma. After a moment the dog returns to the monitor, sniffing furiously and still whimpering.

Lovelace is more than surprised to feel a hand patting her head reassuringly. The hand belongs to the digital onscreen image of Brynthila; but it's attached to a humanoid arm which squeezes out through the widening hole in the screen. The dog jumps up, totally baffled and further knocking the monitor. The soldering iron fizzes against the screen causing a small flash of light and mini-explosion. When the smoke clears, Brynthila stands in the middle of the room, apparently as real as you and me. She looks around in bewilderment. Lovelace creeps closer, wagging her tail in tentative friendship.

At the pizza parlour, Denny and Jo nurse their coffees, still

ScreenSaver!

discussing strategy for their meeting with Max. Denny's doodles litter the table, but both he and Jo are studying the static frames of the demo screensaver.

"Yes, I like it! Good choices." Jo swigs the remains of her coffee.

Denny turns the screen back to face himself. "I reckon there's plenty here to keep the money-men quiet. Complete animated screensaver... *Voila*! Plus - provided 'dear friend Kurt' actually fixes the drive - they get the added bonus of those brand-new action scenes. Job done!"

"I suppose so. I hate to admit it out loud, but that new stuff's terrific." And Denny has to admit - if only to himself - that he likes it when Jo likes his work.

She says, "Bring up that fight again with The Pentangle Monster, will you ..." Denny presses a few keys and turns the laptop around to face Jo, "... because that might be a good point to, you know, introduce a clue about the trapped Prince, and he... and he, he ..."

Suddenly Jo screams, turning the heads of the few remaining diners. Neither Denny nor Jo can believe their eyes. "What the ..." It's not what they can see, but what they can't! Because, as Jo frantically presses keys changing from one scene to another, there's the perfect background artwork, there's the foreground, all beautifully rendered. But Brynthila is nowhere to be seen.

Jo moans, "Where is she? She's gone." She converts the program to a screenful of incomprehensible programming language. She grabs one of Denny's doodle napkins. Denny really doesn't want her to see that sketch combining her and Brynthila, but he needn't worry, because she doesn't even give it a glance. She just turns it over to note down some of the screencode. "She's gone," she wails. "Our Princess! She's been abducted."

A concerned diner at the next table leans over. "Shall we ring the police?"

Jo grabs Denny's phone and presses in Kurt's number. "Voicemail," she says ringing off.

Denny tries levity to hide his bewilderment. "Maybe she eloped with Osborne."

But Jo's panic is rising. "Shut up, we've got to find him. Kurt. No, wait, you find him, he can't be far. I'll run home, and you …"

Denny interrupts. "Take the short cut."

"What shortcut?"

Denny explains, "You know…" But Jo shakes her head. "… that concealed path behind my house that leads through the woods to your front drive …"

His mobile rings with Ella's jazz riff. He checks the caller I.D. "Max! How's it hanging?"

"Don't tell him we're here in town," Jo whispers, adding that Denny needs to reassure him. He tries.

"Couldn't be better … Sure, we're on schedule. When's that meeting? … No problemo … Yeah, just some finishing touches … Uh-huh .. Mm-hmm."

Denny gives Jo a thumbs up, and shoos her toward the door. She tears down the street but pauses to look back through the restaurant window at Denny, still on his mobile. He throws some cash on the table and runs out in the opposite direction from Jo.

Denny races along the High Street to find Kurt. He sticks his head into the doorway of a newsagent and a chemist, before he finally spots the Mr Hardware van a few blocks away. He runs up to it, and nearly collides with Kurt opening the driver's door.

Meanwhile, Jo negotiates a narrow side street as it transforms into an overgrown lane. The lane curves toward the back of Denny's flat, into a small copse. She disappears into the woods. There's only one path, and she follows it as quickly as she can, battling brambles and stinging nettles, until the undergrowth blocks her way.

Deciding she can't go all the way back, Jo tries to clamber over a fallen log, but retreats when she's hit in the face by a clump of brambles. This disturbs another, heftier branch which bops her on the head, felling her to the ground. She crawls on all fours, over knobbly roots and strange furry stems of vines, trying to ignore her stinging scratches.

Finally she emerges into the middle of the grand driveway that leads to Falcon Lodge. As she approaches the imposing residence, she rubs the bump on her head, pausing only for a mini-moment to appreciate the magnificence of the place. And, as she has so often, to wonder why it never makes her feel like a princess.

The thought of princesses brings Jo back to reality. She sprints on, eager to find Brynthila. Noting how unfit she actually is, Jo pants audibly as she races round to the garden entrance, nearly bumping into the unflappable Osborne. He's carrying a tray of crystal tumblers, deftly adjusting his weight to steady them as Jo rushes past.

"Hi Osborne," she says, as she flashes past toward the turret stairs.

"Afternoon, Miss." The very soul of discretion, Osborne refrains from comment on Jo's bloody encounter with the trees, and watches her bound up the stairs.

She reaches a wide landing, where the staircase divides, and takes the narrower flight, winding up to her turret suite. She stands in the doorway, catching her breath, and taking in the scene. Lovelace approaches, hoping for forgiveness with a waggy tail. Jo starts to put two and two together from the knocked-over furniture, the soldering iron, the smell of burning, the huge hole in the monitor.

She examines the hole more closely, poking a cautious finger through. When she turns round, she's confronted with the real life Brynthila. Apparent flesh and blood. Right there in front of her. She screams. Brynthila screams. Lovelace barks, picks up Denny's v-neck in her mouth and runs past Jo and down the stairs. The dog finds refuge in Denny's convertible.

In vain, Jo tries to form a coherent sentence. "Where did you... how did you ..."

"Greetings," says Brynthila. "I am Brynthila, Venerated Goddess of the Maze of Life. And you are?"

"Stop that! I know who you are." Jo feels more baffled than ever. "What are you doing out in the... out of the... out!"

Brynthila takes in this strange creature. Looks familiar, but so dirty and bloody and dishevelled. Must be a servant, she reasons. "Fetch me a trencher of meat, wench, 'tis time to sup!"

Jo speaks to the ceiling. "Please tell me I'm dreaming." She pinches the skin on her wrist, then cautiously pokes at Brynthila. Brynthila presumes this is a greeting and pokes back, unleashing a succession of pokes, prods and pinches.

"Right." Jo rubs her bruised arm. "I'm not dreaming. So. I must be mad!"

"Are you?" asks Brynthila. "Are you Mad Marian, the Washerwoman said beguiled by woodness. The kind woman who became my foster mother and raised me in the castle hidden from evil Lord Cas ..."

"Woodness? No, of course not! I am Jo, who created you out of binary code."

"Created me?" And Brynthila flings her arms around a startled Jo. "Mother! I thought never to see thee again! I bethought thee dead!"

ScreenSaver!

As he and Kurt head along the rural road in the scruffy van, Denny can't hide his discomfort. He fidgets, reaches beneath him and pulls out a chewed bone, still glistening with Lovelace's drool. Kurt chuckles and mumbles. Denny glares at him.

He's jolted half out of his seat when Kurt brings the van to a sudden stop. In front of them is a complicated set of road-works. They can only join a stationary line of cars, and wait for the traffic to inch forward.

"Great," says Denny, "that's all we bloody need!" Kurt, mumbling, hands him a joint.

Back in the turret suite, Brynthila keeps repeating, "Mother, mother."

Gently but firmly, Jo pulls her away, holding her at arm's length. "I am so NOT your mother."

"Then," Brynthila murmurs with some degree of awe, "then … then… if you are my creator but you are not my mother, then you must be Gevreen, the Great Goddess." She lowers her head in reverence and bobs a curtsey. "My lady."

"No, no," says Jo. "I'm not your mother and, well, do I look like a goddess? I mean, look at me! Unh-uh, one of us is loopy. Unless Kurt put weed in my tea."

Brynthila's confused. "Who weed in your tea? I will avenge…"

Jo interrupts. "I don't know how you got out, but …" She holds Brynthila's shoulders as she peers at her, then at the really huge television monitor with the really huge hole, then back to Brynthila. Suddenly, she shoves Brynthila backwards and attempts to push her head first into the screen.

Brynthila yelps. "Ow! If you truly created me why do you seek to harm me? Is this my Level One Loyalty Test?" She claps her hands in glee. "'Tis, verily, is't not? Wait, of course! I know! You crave presents. Here! Look! I have gifts. Gifts for a Goddess!"

As she speaks, Brynthila reaches behind her through the hole of the monitor. She pulls out an intricately filigreed silver satchel and rummages, at last producing an ornate hand mirror. She presents it to Jo, who fails to take it. She's been rendered totally speechless... for a moment anyway.

"No, no!" says Brynthila, only momentarily dejected. "What was I thinking?! That's for the Guardian Goat of the River of Timewasting." And back she dives into the satchel. But Jo knows exactly what she's searching for.

"And I don't eat live rats, either." At which declaration Brynthila freezes in midsearch, and delivers a hard slap to the squeaking, scurrying, scampering lump in her satchel... all goes very quiet.

"Aha!" crows Brynthila. "So, I see... you know everything I do before I do it. Double Aha! You are the old Seer Woman who foresees the future. Uhm... are you not?"

"Steady on... a bit less of the 'old,' thank you. Look, if you are who I think you are... and you seem to be, even though that probably means I've gone stark staring mad... IF you are truly Brynthila, then as I told you, I created you. You're a programme. A digital algorithm. I command, you obey."

Brynthila takes a moment to process this data. "You created me. I'm a programme. Well, fie upon thee, Madam!"

"What?!"

"If you hold my welfare so dear, why must I travel the Ice Field of Farrah dressed in only the skimpiest of garments? I was freezing my chips off!"

"Not my idea. That was Denny's doing." Jo points to the blowup of Bluebell flanked by her and Denny. Brynthila is instantly smitten with Denny's image and kneels before it as though the photo were real.

"Are you my Prince?"

Jo pulls her up. "Oh, please! That's not real, it's just a blow-up. A photo. See?" She pokes a finger at the cardboard figure. "What is it with that boy... women even fall for his two-D image! Look, Denny might think he's god's gift, but he's not anyone's prince! Where is he, by the way?" Jo checks the time, as Brynthila pounces on a phrase.

"Gift of the gods, eh?" she says.

Meanwhile, at the road-block, the line of cars has started to move at last. Mr Hardware navigates the traffic cones and heads for Falcon Lodge. "Step on it," says Denny. Then, "I always wanted to say that!" And as he passes the joint back to Kurt, they share a stoned smile.

Inside the turret room, Jo's getting increasingly desperate. "Look, Brynthila, please. You've got to get back inside the game. It's really, really important. Besides you don't belong out here. It's dangerous!"

Brynthila turns into a stubborn toddler. Metaphorically. "Not so! Marry, I woulds't meet Prince Denny."

"Marry?! No way!" says Jo.

"Yes way," counters Brynthila. "'Tis my destiny. Besides, thou art but a programming slave. And well I wot that a Prince ranks higher than a slave."

"Well you... what?"

"Yes, thou cans't not part us."

Jo realises she has to employ more cunning. "Look, trust me, you can't... you so cannot meet him because he'll... he won't... he... he... aha! No, because first, first you have to find the magic potion so that he won't drop down dead when he sets eyes on you."

Brynthila's eyes narrow. She almost believes Jo. "Well... mayhap, but prithee... where be this supposed elixir?"

"Back in the game." Jo gives her a tiny push toward the screen.

"No!"

Jo momentarily takes the fierce tone of a commanding officer. "Get back in there!" Then she instantly reverts to pathetic begging. "Please!" But all the commanding, cajoling and pleading fall on deaf ears as Brynthila strokes Denny's image and stands firm. Suddenly, Jo has an idea.

"Okay, here's the new plan. You stay here in case Denny ..."

Brynthila interrupts, "Prince Denny."

"... in case Prince bloody Denny rings. Meanwhile I'll go down to check the uhm, battlements, and see if I can hurry him up. But I'll have to lock you in. What did I do with my key?" Jo races around, lifting knick-knacks and food cartons, checking pockets, flipping through computer manuals, trying to find the key.

Brynthila's scared. "Lock me in? Oh, I see your shallow plan. You are in league with evil Lord Cas..."

"No, no. Not at all! It's just... it's just... there are monsters out there.... on the stairs." Jo does a feeble impression of a monster, trying to curl her fingers to represent claws. "Grrr! And I must protect you. Now help me find that key. Come on. If you find the key, you'll get to the next level."

That's all Brynthila needs to hear. With a quick "Gramercy, my lady," she whizzes around the room at warp speed, and in a heartbeat, appears in front of Jo, holding out the key. Jo is impressed. "Good work! Where did you find it?"

"Just there, inside the door lock."

Jo can't believe she's missed the obvious and chalks it up to exhaustion. Brynthila lingers, expecting some kind of praise or acknowledgement, but Jo just snatches the key and exits, locking her Princess in.

A bewildered Brynthila tries the door. Wistfully she wanders over to the photo blowup of Denny. "I thought it would be easier to spot the enemy," she sighs.

Jo flies down the staircase, out through the garden entrance and onto the gravel drive. Seeing that Kurt's van is still not there, she ambles up the driveway a bit aimlessly, still trying to come to terms with her encounter with Brynthila. It can't be real. But it is, it's really real.

She heads back to Denny's convertible and tries to jump into the passenger seat. But she needs practice in the coordination department and lands face down and bottom up. As she rights herself, she notices Lovelace, paws on the steering wheel. The dog licks her hand.

Upstairs, Brynthila peruses the books on Jo's shelf. She's particularly attracted by a succession of computer manuals covering a range of hardware and software topics. Gently, almost discreetly, she tears a small piece of print from one of the pages… and pops it into her mouth. She chews thoughtfully, trying to analyse the flavour.

Meanwhile, Kurt guides the van up the long and winding driveway to Falcon Lodge. Seated next to him, Denny rings Jo.

Brynthila's diverted from her reading by a telephone ringing. She imitates the sound perfectly, as though she were answering a bird-call. Eventually, she tracks the ringing to Jo's desk, removes a misplaced wash-cloth, and gazes in rapture at the marvel of the phone. Then the answer machine clicks on.

Brynthila is amazed to hear Jo's recorded voice apparently

ScreenSaver! 48

coming from nowhere, announcing its invitation to the caller. Before she can follow Jo's orders to 'leave some words,' Denny identifies himself. What bliss!

"We're on the drive right now. Where the hell are you?" he says. Brynthila can't imagine what she's done to displease him and starts to reply, but the message continues. She returns to the big cardboard blowup of Denny as though it were the source of his voice. "Max just rang... again! He's like some demented alarm clock. Lest we forget, the money-men are flying out to the Big Apple tonight, and he's going to check up on us every hour. We've got to crack this or else!" Aha, thinks Brynthila. New orders. New task list. New challenge!

Downstairs, Jo spots her mother near one of the flower-beds, consulting with Osborne. Her camera is slung around her neck. Elaine waves to her. Suddenly Kurt's van pulls into view, crunching gravel. Jo races over.

Up in the turret room, Brynthila has been trying to decipher Denny's message. She's discovered the large ornamental paperweight, carved in the shape of a wooden apple. "Most excellent! One big apple," she says, as though it were an ingredient for a spell. She tries to bite into it, then spots one of Kurt's screwdrivers and tries to open the forbidden fruit. When that doesn't work, she picks up the discarded wash cloth, and begins to polish the apple vigorously, as though it were Aladdin's lamp.

She's keen to work out the rest of the clues. "Now, all I need do is 'fly out' and 'crack this.' Fly where? Yes, of course!" she trills in triumph. "As The Goddess Gevreen decreed: 'I must go far before I can return home.' But what is't must be cracked?"

She weighs the apple in one hand, looks at the window, then back at the apple, and back again at the window. Her dazzling smile of enlightenment floods the room.

On the driveway, Denny and Kurt stride back towards the house with Jo between them gesturing wildly. Trying to explain what she's seen up in her room, she points to the turret window. They all three look up. Lovelace looks up. Elaine and Osborne look up, as well. Elaine's instinct kicks in as she points her zoom lens and clicks off some shots of this dramatic turn of events.

As though framed in a portrait, Brynthila peers down to the garden. She sees the upturned faces, recognising Denny from his photo. She smiles and waves. She wants to run down to him and disappears from view to test the door again. It's still locked. With no other choice, she turns back toward the window. Her concentration rivals a determined cricket bowler as she starts a windup.

Below the window, everyone still gazes up. Suddenly, the wooden apple smashes through the leaded window, showering glass shards. The onlookers jump back to avoid being hit. And there, standing on the balcony ledge is Brynthila, a breeze rippling her ankle-length caster.

Denny fears the worst and yells, "Don't jump!"

Brynthila feels around behind her and rips the curtain from its railing. She secures it through a hole in the balcony corbel, and slipping the silver satchel over her head, she prepares her descent. Inspired by Denny waving at her, she sends a message skyward.

"Thank you for your gift." She closes her eyes, spreads out her caster-cloak like wings, and floats down gracefully into Denny's arms. The force, however, is still enough to knock them both to the ground. Brynthila looks idyllically happy. Denny is mystified, cautious and embarrassed, but he can't help noticing this is one hot babe! The others are beyond words. Lovelace jumps into Denny's car and snuggles under his v-neck.

Denny tries as delicately as he can to lift Brynthila from his chest. The others help them up. Elaine hands Osborne her camera and sends him inside for some water.

"Are you okay?" Denny says. "Are you ... uhm... who are you?"

Jo half-whispers, "I've been trying to tell you. Meet Brynthila." Brynthila curtsies before her Prince.

But Denny rounds on Jo. "Very funny... who is this, some look alike for Max's launch party? Sorry, Miss ... whoever you are..."

"No," Jo protests, "I told you, she came out of the computer."

But Denny misunderstands again. "Honestly, we have a deadline - with the emphasis on Dead - and you're hitting the chat rooms? And you blame me for... !" Exasperated, he turns back to Brynthila. "Sorry, you've had a wasted journey, Miss... uhm...Ms... Missus?"

Brynthila speaks. "Good morrow, sire, the wench speaks true. I am Brynthila. And you are my Prince. Prince Denny." She curtsies. "I am pledged to rescue you from... from... from danger," she concludes, hoping that will cover all eventualities.

"Well, you've certainly learned your lines. What is that, Method Acting?"

Brynthila turns her gaze on Elaine, who's standing dumbstruck next to an equally gobsmacked Kurt. Elaine holds out her hand to shake. Brynthila approaches and sniffs it.

Nothing fazes Elaine. Well, almost nothing. "Hello. I'm Elaine. Will you stay for tea?"

Brynthila is disappointed. "Well, you are clearly not the Piquant Gorgon of Zola." She moves on to Kurt and sniffs, wrinkling her nose in disgust. "Aha!" she says. "'Tis you!"

Quick as a flash, Brynthila reaches in the silver satchel, pulls out some rope and proceeds to tie Kurt up. His joint burns steadily between his lips. In some weirdo way, he's clearly enjoying the attention. Jo tries to pull Brynthila away from Kurt. "No, stop that! Denny, help me get her back upstairs."

Denny is avoiding reality by meticulously plucking every minute speck of grass and dust from his clothing. "Just send her home. Call a cab."

"Don't you get it? She is home." Jo tries to steer Brynthila into the house. But she's having none of that. Elaine tries to get hold of her, but she races across the lawn toward the rose-garden. In her flight to freedom, she turns and beckons saucily to Denny.

Jo pleads, "Denny, please. Fetch her back. Trust me, she'll listen to you. I'll explain later."

Denny hesitates, then runs after Brynthila. But as he passes his convertible, he clocks the dog. And his v-neck top. He tries to tempt Lovelace out, but she thinks it's a fun game and keeps jumping back again. Denny gives up and continues to chase Brynthila.

Meanwhile, Jo's close to tears. Elaine puts a comforting arm around her daughter.

Denny's lost sight of Brynthila, but he knows she can't have gone far. As he approaches a flowering shrub, Brynthila's arm reaches out and pulls him close to her. He's wary but attracted. He's also breathing hard from running, compared with Brynthila who isn't winded at all.

"You're certainly fit, I'll give you that. Do you work out?"

"I have worked out 'tis you! 'Tis destiny!" Brynthila has become a strange mix of dominatrix and flirt. If Denny thought he knew women, he's got to admit he's never met any like this one. He's surprised at her strength as she pulls him over to a tree. "Hey, steady on!"

Brynthila commands, "This is the spot. Start digging."

"You what?"

In reply, Brynthila pulls a dog-eared hand-drawn map from the satchel. She points to an X marked in red. "'Tis for your own protection. Here, right here is where we find our next treasure. Invisibility potion I think. Dig!"

Denny is now totally convinced she's a loony - but hot! "Invisi... ? Look, you're doing a great job, but ..."

Brynthila repeats more forcibly. "Dig!"

Denny's mind races to come up with a way to get out of this. "I can't. Because... because, uhm... No spade!"

Brynthila accepts this rational explanation. "Look," Denny cajoles, "why don't we go back upstairs. We can find a spade, Jo can pay you what she owes and, if you're not busy later maybe we can ... well, let's play it by ear. Okay?"

Back at the house Elaine dabs the tears from Jo's cheeks. "Oh, darling, don't cry. I'm surprised at Denny. How insensitive to bring his girlfriend when you're working so hard."

Jo blows her nose and looks around for somewhere to dispose of the sodden tissue. To save her daughter's embarrassment, Elaine takes it back. "She's .. quite pretty, I suppose, in an obvious sort of way."

"She's not exactly what she seems."

Elaine misunderstands. "Yes, well, in this day and age who is?!" She fiddles with Jo's clothing and tries to smooth her hair. "But just say the word, because I know this lovely little man in Harley Street who works absolute magic. Snip. Tuck. Not that you need it, darling."

"Thanks, Mummy. I'll pass."

"Well, think about it. I've got to be in town next week and we could make a day of it. Bit of shopping, bit of pampering, you know…" She hates seeing her daughter in such distress and hopes some light-hearted chatter might divert her. She dabs again at Jo's watering eyes. "Did I tell you the publishers are keen on my train idea?"

"No, what… sorry, Mummy. Remind me."

"Well it's just frippery I suppose. A glossy, over-sized book of my photographs of gorgeous landscapes as seen through the windows of a premium rail journey."

"Wow, Mummy, that is so exciting!" She hugs her mother and turns to Kurt. "Hear that, Kurt. Isn't it…"

But they're suddenly aware of Kurt's mumbled whimper. He's been trying to spit out the lit joint, but the thin paper is sticking to his lips. It's also perilously close to burning his mouth. Jo and Elaine turn to help, just as Osborne appears carrying a tumbler of water. With no small degree of disguised delight, he flings the water over Kurt's face to douse the joint. Ever-prepared, he hands Elaine a small pocket-knife. She frees Kurt, who glares at Osborne and mumbles something incomprehensible. Jo grabs his hand and pulls him into the doorway, calling back to Elaine. "He says thanks… and congratulations!"

Across the lawn, Jo spots Denny leading Brynthila toward the house. She looks at her watch.

At the very same moment, on the platform of a lifeless suburban train station, Max also checks the time. He's sitting next to the trusty Fiona. "I thought you said they'd be here by now." It sounds as though he's blaming her, but she smiles reassuringly and pats his hand. He snarls at her. She snarls right back.

Meanwhile, Jo pushes Kurt inside the house. "Let's go, they'll catch us up." Lovelace jumps deftly out of Denny's car and pads after Kurt.

But, unseen by Jo, Brynthila pulls away from Denny. Half-skipping, half-running, she leads him up the garden path. "With a hey and a ho, and a hey nonny-no," she sings.

Chapter 6

Up in the turret suite and well-guarded by Lovelace, Jo and Kurt search frantically through a gallery of game characters. Only Brynthila is missing from her digital display plinth. Kurt tries a different combination of keys, mumbling incoherently. Jo reminds him, "Yes I know you fixed it. But if that weirdo downstairs really is Brynthila then bang goes every known law of science. You are aware of that, aren't you?! And where the hell is she, anyway... her and Denny?!"

Kurt mumbles again and offers Jo a toke on his joint. She brushes it aside. Her voice rises in desperation. "Well, you may be living in a parallel universe, but in this world we've got to get her back in the game and get that disc to Max. You can write it all up for *Computer Weekly* later. Or the *Fortean Times*! Now, get busy. Please!"

When Kurt starts to reply, she continues, "And no, there's no time to rebuild her from scratch." Suddenly she has an idea. "But wait a minute! Maybe... just maybe... we can do a slight makeover." She winds a stray handful of curls obstructing her vision, and secures it on top of her head with a metal document clip. Ready for business!

From the display monitor, Jo selects a galumphing male warrior. With a flourish of programming code, she re-renders him into a rough-hewn but shapely version of Brynthila. She overlays the image with a digital gallery of character choices: hair styles, lips, noses, ears, and costumes. After dragging-and-dropping some of the images onto the figure, in just a few minutes, Jo has whipped up a passable version of her heroine, though with a decided tinge of drag-queen.

With a small chuckle, Jo imitates her mother. "I know this lovely little man in Harley Street - works absolute - magic!" Triumphantly she shows off her work to Kurt. "Ta-dah!"

Lovelace barks approvingly as Kurt re-lights the joint. He

kisses Jo on the forehead. He mumbles.

To which Jo replies, "Patronising git! Where the hell is Denny?! And that bimbo!"

Max and Fiona are still playing a waiting game on the station platform. Fiona pours Max a coffee from the thermos flask in her hold-all. He, meanwhile, texts obsessively on his mobile. He doesn't quite catch a tannoy announcement and asks Fiona to repeat it. "Train's been delayed... leaves on the bloody line. Typical!" She gathers up their things. The handful of other passengers do the same and exit the platform.

Max berates the entire universe. "Thwarted at every turn!"

Fiona tries to calm him down. "At least they've put on a replacement bus service. Station car park. Come along, chop-chop."

Denny and Brynthila sit under a sturdy tree. He has his mobile at the ready and asks, "Don't play coy. What's your number?" But before she can answer, a blast of the jazz riff from the phone frightens Brynthila. She clings on tight to Denny, and, conflicted by her proximity, he switches off the phone.

"Prithee, what maketh this din?" she says, maybe a smidge too timidly.

"Oh, just some big bad man."

She looks everywhere for a big, bad man. Nothing. She concludes 'he' must be invisible, and quickly reverting to her guardian role, she declares, "Though I am pitchkettled quite, and cannot fathom these sounds mysterious, I shall protect thee, sire." Without further ado and quite unexpected force, she pushes Denny to the ground, undoes her cloak, and flings it over him, covering his face. He struggles with the heavy cloth and sits up sputtering.

Back at the station car park, Fiona waits in the queue with Max to board the replacement service bus. He's furious and glares at Fiona, trying desperately to find a way to make it all her fault. All his plans are slipping away. It's started to rain, and several passengers in the bus queue unleash their umbrellas.

Max throws his mobile to the ground... on the verge of a toddler tantrum. "I'll never get there in time. In China, they think early is on time... and on time is late!" His voice rises another octave. "They'll jet off to the Big Apple, and I'll be left with the pips! And to top it off, Denny's only gone and turned off his phone. At a time like this, he's turned off his bloody phone!" His high-pitched whines have deflated into defeat. "Doesn't he know... I... can't, Fiona! I just can't!" He stamps his feet, burbling unintelligibly. Other travellers in the queue try to be discreet.

Fiona's seen it all before. "Just stop it, Max! Calm down! This is exactly what you used to do when you were a little boy." She holds out her arms. "Oh, all right. Come here!" as Max snuggles into her. "And who was always there to get you through? Was it your big sister Fiona? Was it?"

The rain plasters Max's hair to his forehead, but he wails as though he's being water- boarded. "Yes! But, what am I going to do if they don't deliver the discs and I miss the meeting? Or, even worse, if I'm late?! You know what they do in China if someone is late for a meeting?"

She shakes her head and tries a reverse reality check. "Firing squad?"

"Yes!!" says Max. "I mean, no. I don't know, but it's serious!"

Fiona holds out a hanky. "Blow," she orders.

"What am I going to do, Fi?"

Fiona retrieves his mobile from the ground and hands it over. "Well, first of all, we're going to get out of the bloody rain. Back to the car, hurry up. We'll wait for the disc. I'll drive you to London." They break away from the bus queue and try to dodge the rain over to

Fiona's car. As they settle in, she hands Max some paper towels from the glove compartment. "Now, dry your hair, ring Jo, tell them to bring the demo here... and stop crying!"

A few minutes later, Jo is on the phone with Max, trying to get a word in edgeways. "Yes, Max ... No, Max ... I'm sure he ... I'll get right on it. Pronto Tonto!... What accident?... No, I told you everything's fine. Raring to go... Car park, got it. Be there before you know it."

She rings off and turns to Kurt with an executive decision. "Enough faffing, Kurt. We have to go. Pronto Tonto! Copy the new stuff on a disc and I'll get Denny. Rev up the van."

She grabs her motorcycle helmet from a hook on the back of her door. As she starts for the stairs, Kurt's mumbles point her to the strange digital incarnation of Transgendered Brynthila Mark 2 on the monitor.

"Oh, don't exaggerate. She... she's doing a stunt, she's bound to be a bit... rumpled and crumpled."

Down in the rose garden, and looking every bit as dishevelled as her resurrected digital incarnation, Brynthila leans seductively against a small tree, surrounded by blossom. It's a fairy tale moment. With deliberate semi-modesty, she doesn't quite adjust a bit of cloth over her cleavage. Denny leans over to kiss her, but the magic is spoiled by the revs of Jo's motorcycle. Brynthila, terrified, cowers from the approaching metal monster. She screams "Dragon!"

Jo manoeuvres the bike up to the rose garden entry trellis. She points to the sidecar. "Train station. Now!"

Feeling strangely rescued, Denny immediately pitches in to help and drags the reluctant Brynthila closer to the bike. "Get in the naffing sidecar! Chop-chop."

Now Brynthila's terrified and confused. "Chop ...?"

ScreenSaver! 59

Denny gives her a shove. "That's it, into the chopper." Finally, he pushes Brynthila into the sidecar and hops on behind Jo, holding her around the waist. Brynthila notices and is not happy. She assuages her anxiety by grabbing onto Denny's thigh. A bit too tightly!

Jo yells over to Denny, "She's back in the demo, don't ask!" She points to the live Brynthila. "But we better take this one with us." She steers the bike back to Kurt's van in the forecourt, and cuts her engine. Denny and Jo lift Brynthila out of the sidecar, and everyone piles into the van. Lovelace barks a cheery Woof. "Got the demo disc?" Jo asks Kurt. He gives a thumbs-up. At last they're off!

Max and Fiona are still waiting in the station car park. Fiona demists the windscreen as the replacement bus pulls into the car park. She gestures to the overnight bag nestled on the back seat. "I packed you clean knickers." To cover his embarrassment he asks whether she's also packed a copy of the itinerary for the money-men. She turns around in her seat and retrieves a neatly-typed travel schedule.

"Have you seen this, Fi? New York, Vegas, Comic Con in San Diego! Only the bigtime for these guys. What a life!"

Fiona pats his hand. "You'll get there, Maxi. Now, breathe two, three, and out two three. And breathe two, three and... what are you doing?"
Max is trying to divert his anxiety by ringing Denny again. Fiona notices the perspiration on his forehead and hands him another clean handkerchief. Talk about be prepared! They both watch the replacement bus pull out of the car park onto the main road.

As the bus disappears around a bend, it crosses with Kurt's van, headed for the car park. Mr Hardware screams to a stop beside Fiona's car. Max fairly rips open the car door to take possession of the demo disc.

The rain thickens into hailstones. From his seat Max tries to peer into the van as Jo and Denny argue with Kurt. Kurt searches frantically through all his pockets as well every nook and cranny in the van. Brynthila tries to help, but sees it's hopeless. She appears to go into a kind of trance.

Max braves the weather, forcing himself into the back of the van. He notices Brynthila for the first time and asks Denny and Jo. "Who's this?"

"A surprise. Tell you later," calls Jo.

Denny rounds on her. "You said he had the disc." Then to Kurt, "Do you? Don't you?! Well, where is it!" Kurt mumbles. "Jo, I swear, hold me back before I do him an injury."

Jo's on Denny's side this time. She's completely lost her cool. "Where's the bloody disc, Kurt?!"

Max tries to stay calm. He catches his sister's eye. She gives him an encouraging thumbs up.

Suddenly, Brynthila's eyes flash and she emerges from her trance. She confronts Kurt, whispering something in his ear. Immediately, he stops in his tracks. For the first time in living memory he utters a distinct and comprehensible English phrase. "I know where the disc is!"

Denny and Jo are astounded. Lovelace jumps up and licks Kurt's face. She licks Brynthila's face. She starts to lick Max's face, but he brushes her down and calls over to Fiona. "What now?" She dodges the hailstones, joining the others in the van.

Kurt's back to mumbling, so Jo explains he's accidentally left the disc in the machine after he copied the new action scenes. Decisive as ever, Fiona takes charge. As she taps away on her tablet she conveys her plan to the others.

"Right, listen up. It is what it is. Local heliport's just minutes away. We'll never make it by car to Heathrow through the rush-hour. So, *voila*! Max is booked on the next chopper. Freight flight. Just takes minutes." She performs one further digital transaction. "And his room's now confirmed at the airport Hilton." [Other hotels are available.]

Jo rolls her eyes at this evil addition to global warming, but Fiona defends her brother. "It'll give him a chance to calm down, have a quick wash and brush-up before his meeting. Okay with you? Assuming you and Denny do actually want this job. And the dosh."

She turns to the others who are in awe of her management skills. "Well, what are you waiting for. Go get that demo disc and deliver it ASAP. We'll be in the Biggles Bar." And so, the brave little band double back to the house to make things right.

"And don't be late," Max calls after them. "It's just like my management course," he says to Fiona, not for the first time. "Where there are problems, there are solutions." Fiona strains every sinew to remember her promise to her parents always to protect her brother... and never, ever, to bash him over the head.

As Fiona drives with determination to the heliport, Max is more than happy to leave all the solutions to her. As usual. He rings his money contacts to confirm their meeting. "Coolio," he tells Fiona, "they've reserved one of the conference rooms."

"Who was that strange woman?" Fiona asks.

"I think they said she's a surprise."

"I'll say!"

Once more, Kurt pulls the Mr Hardware van onto the gravel entry drive outside the house. He tells Lovelace to stay and joins Jo, Denny, and Brynthila as they head upstairs. They pass Osborne on the wide landing, and Jo says "Hi Osborne." The others chorus, "Hi Osborne."

In the turret room Jo extracts the demo disc from the computer drive. "You promise this is the one?" Kurt nods. They have to trust him as there's no time to lose.

Once again they pass Osborne on the stairs. "Bye Osborne, " says Jo. "Bye Osborne," echo the others.

Fiona and Max sit side-by-side on stools at the Biggles Bar. She sips a mint tea, and he nurses a beer. "Don't drink too much," warns Fiona. "You need a clear head."

"This better work," he mutters. "What time's take-off... I mean lift-off?"

She fiddles with her ticket for the short-term car park "Calm down, they'll be here."

But as the minutes tick away, she's not so sure. When Max begs her to try ringing Denny, she can't get a signal. "Typical!" Taking an executive decision, Fiona gathers up Max's bag and all the bits and pieces. Then, just before they leave, she hands a message to the bartender folded around a fiver, in case Denny and Jo do turn up. "Okay, troops," she says to Max, "march out."

Mr Hardware careers into the tiny air field, and follows the road around to the modest Departure entrance. Kurt barely has time to pull up the handbrake, before Denny, Jo, and Brynthila pile out and race for the automatic entry doors. But through the van widow, Kurt bellows something incomprehensible. He holds out the disc. Jo dashes back, grabs it and rejoins Denny and Brynthila. "He says he'll wait for us out front."

As they run into the terminal, Fiona leads Max outside and around to the heliport where a 'copter stands at the ready. Emerging from a small hangar, a sprightly man wearing a vintage leather flying jacket extends an arm in greeting. "All points London, is it?" he grins.

"If you'd be so kind," says Fiona.

"I'm Rafe," he says, starting to take Fiona's large handbag.

"No, you're all right, Rafe; here's your passenger. Mr. Checkman."

Max is trying to keep from turning green, and Rafe's familiar with the signs. "First time in a chopper, sir?"

Max nods imperceptibly. Rafe relieves him of his overnight bag and guides him in through the 'copter door.

"Not to worry. This flight's mainly freight, so you get to sit up top. Great views!"

By this time, the trio are dashing through the building, on the lookout for the Biggles Bar. They push past other passengers who are intrigued by Brynthila's outfit. In turn, she's fascinated by such 'alien' surroundings and keeps stopping to examine luggage on wheels, the information booth, ticket machines.

They finally locate the bar, only to discover no Max and no Fiona. Brynthila is intrigued by the bartender, because she can only see him from the waist up. She leans over to investigate his nether regions, but Denny grabs her arm and pulls her back. "Hiya, mate, you haven't seen a woman with a short pudgy dude…"

The bartender waves a folded note at Denny. "Yeah, she said you'd probably get here… eventually."

Denny reads the message and hands it to Jo. "Thanks, where's the helicopter place?" The bartender gives Denny directions. "Can't miss it. Only machine out there. Ask for Rafe," he says helpfully.

Denny, Jo, and Brynthila approach the heliport area just in time to see the plane's rotors begin spinning around for lift-off. Fiona stands well back from the down-draft and waves to Max, high up in the plane. She turns as Denny, Jo and Brynthila race up. Braving danger, they're trying to stop the pilot. Jo brandishes the disc, screaming "Wait! Stop!" It's hopeless. The rotors completely overpower her voice.

Fiona's still fuming. "Nice of you all to drop by."

A couple of uniformed men hurry out from the hangar,

knocking over a propped-up sign advertising flight times and flying lessons. The men try to restrain the trio. Jo is still screaming. "Stop that helicopter! It's a matter of life and death!"

Brynthila responds to the blatant challenge and grabs the disc from Jo. The 'copter's rotary wings gain speed, creating even more wind around the perimeter of the plane. The guards are powerless as Brynthila faces the spinning blades.

"Wow!" Denny's impressed. "She really does take her acting seriously."

From his window seat on the top deck, a frustrated Max examines a screenshot of Brynthila on the case of the demo. He opens it - empty, of course. But he can't give up now, it's his reputation on the line. He rehearses several scenarios of the excuses he can offer the money-men. As he glances out the window, his face freezes. Looking back at him is Brynthila on the other side of the glass, mere inches away. The rotor blades whip her long hair into abstract tangles.

Incredulous and terrified, Max turns back into the plane to find he's all alone. He looks back out the window, but Brynthila has vanished. Then, suddenly, up she pops again, smiling and waving as the 'copter prepares its vertical lift- off. She holds up the disc - then disappears, and reappears again, bouncing up as though on springs. Finally, she thrusts her arm straight through the window - shattering the glass - and hands over the disc to a now gibbering Max.

An ear-splitting alarm goes off in the cabin. It's joined by a chorus of alarms all over the airport. The helicopter rotors reverse to a halt. The plane judders. All hell breaks loose. The last thing Max remembers thinking before a first-aid kit hits him on the head is "that's impossible."

Chapter 7

About an hour later, a handful of airport staff have hustled and bustled in every nook and cranny to soothe nerves and clean up the damage. Denny and Jo accompany Brynthila, all under guard for questioning. They really have no idea the trouble they're in.

Loyal Kurt has parked the Mr Hardware van on a double yellow, just outside the apricot pink departure terminal - just where it shouldn't be. Whenever anyone in uniform wanders by, Kurt pretends he's about to leave. He signals to pull away, then drives around for a few minutes before resuming his vigil. In the passenger seat, Lovelace whines that she'd like to go outside, please. Kurt mumbles and follows her out. While she sniffs around for the right place to do what a dog must do, Kurt decides he probably should lose the joint he's been toking on.

Meanwhile, out on another runway, a shiny four-seater jet begins taxiing. Seated inside, and still visibly shaken after his recent ordeal, Max is quietly hysterical. A solicitous flight attendant fastens his seatbelt, giving the buckle a reassuring pat. Max is not reassured. He clutches the precious demo disc, resisting all efforts by the stewardess to stow it more safely. As much to blot out reality as anything, he nervously slides down the black-out panel in front of his window and succumbs to the hypnotic hum of the engine. He scarcely feels the moment of take-off. Fiona will take care of everything, he tells himself.

Tucked away behind the heliport is an unassuming maintenance shed which is being used as an interview room. Brynthila, Jo, and Denny sit around a table as instructed. They're waiting for the airport security investigator to return. He's been questioning them about aircraft sabotage. Denny is doubting his own sanity, since Jo seems so convinced about the reality of Brynthila.

He burbles at Jo. "Never mind her... Are you for real?" Jo nods confirmation. Denny burbles on, flicking his glance to Brynthila. "You really think she's who I think you think she is? And you really think she just popped out of …" Jo keeps nodding; she's beginning to look like one of those noddy dogs people put on their dashboards.

Unaware she's the subject of their confusion, a bored Brynthila gets up from the table and wanders around, examining everything that isn't nailed down. She was programmed for action, not waiting around. She flicks through a rotorcraft maintenance manual, and an illustrated copy of rotor & wing magazine titled The Safety Issue. She surreptitiously tears out a page… and pops it into her mouth.

Jo tries to keep tabs on Brynthila's explorations. She turns to Denny. "By the way, what happened to Max?"

"Hitched a whistle-stop to Heathrow on a Cessna Mustang, lucky sod."

"Mustang? Isn't that a horse?"

"You're joking, right?" Jo shrugs. "It wouldn't surprise me if your father had one."

"What, a horse?"

"I give up… it's a private jet."

"Oh. Well, I think I'd know if we had a private jet. Or a horse."

"Whatever… Max is up in the air. Fiona knows the pilot."

"She's such a fixer. We should write her into the game."

At which point the investigator returns juggling his clipboard with a carafe of water and a stack of plastic cups. After re-locking the shed door and pocketing the key, he deposits his armful on the table near a tape recorder. He smooths the already tidy moustache perched under his nose. Denny catches Brynthila's eye and motions for her to sit back down between him and Jo. She picks up a handful of Air Accident Investigation Bulletin reports and complies.

ScreenSaver!

Jo pours out some water and swigs it down. "Thank you, Mr Wallace. Very kind." She offers to pour him some too, but he shakes his head and adjusts the security identification badge clipped on the lanyard around his neck.

Methodically, he straightens his yellow hi-viz jacket and settles in opposite the three suspects. He consults the paperwork on the clipboard in front of him, lines up a brace of pens, and checks his watch. Then he switches on the tape recorder, leaning forward slightly to identify himself. "Will Wallace. Interview re-commencing at 15.48." Although he's clearly intrigued by the animated images on Denny's laptop, he tries to ignore them. He looks at Denny in anticipation. "Well, Mr da Vinci... picking up where we left off, you and Ms Hawker-Meade have declared yourselves guardians of... " He consults the clipboard. "Ms Bril... uhm, Ms Thyl... so, as those jointly responsible, I repeat, did you or did you not commit..."

Denny's laugh is as hollow as a dead tree. "Vandalism?! I can assure you, Mr Wallace... can I call you Will?... nothing could be further from the truth. We're... we're... what we are is... journalists." And, with a series of verbal contortions, he launches into a convincing pretzel-twist of explanation. "Investigative journalists. Working undercover. Investigating. Brothers-in-arms to yourself, actually, because, much like yourself, we're investigating to protect the public. Aren't we, Jo?"

Jo nods furiously. "Much like yourselves."

The officer indicates Brynthila, the epitome of innocence. By contrast, his own face muscles tighten in an effort to keep calm. "She put her fist through the aircraft window, Mr da Vinci. Exactly how is that protecting the public?"

Not quite as prepared as a boy scout, Denny tap-dances his way through the barrage of questions. He tries to capture the initiative. "Are you aware, Will," he demands, "how many injuries are sustained every year due to weak stress points in aircraft windows? No, I didn't think so."

Suddenly, Brynthila stands and holds up a copy of The Air Accident Investigation Branch Annual Safety Report. She breaks unexpectedly into a spiel that leaves everyone jaw-dropped and dumb-founded. "Actually, Mr Wallace," she says, adjusting her voice to the timbre of a very well- primed school-girl, "we know from the pioneering work of Deborah Hersman in assuring United States aircraft safety standards as adopted and echoed by our own UK Department of Transport, and not without reference to some elements pertinent to the incident at Stapleford in 2015, that your own department may have questions to answer. For example, if a mere weak maiden such as myself can push straight through the cabin window of a rotary craft... Well, how can said window possibly be meeting the demanding polymerisation standards of single-layer acrylic laminate to DTD-5592 requirements?"

She sits and returns to her study of another technical manual. Double takes all round. Flummoxed to the max, Mr Wallace turns to Jo and Denny. "Yes... well, whether I might or might not know the answer to... what she said... you still haven't explained what any of it has to do with this computer game?" Inadvertently, the investigator has led them into familiar territory. Denny types in a succession of keys to demonstrate various scenes of the game while Jo plays along, trying to busk her way through. She addresses the officer as though she's giving him a private masterclass.

"I'm glad you asked that, actually, Mr Wallace. Because we take a very... uhm... interactive approach to aircraft safety. As my colleague is demonstrating, we've created an entertaining game that can teach your staff lessons by example." She checks the scene on Denny's screen showing two mini- trolls peering precariously over a cliff-edge. "Yes... just as an example... here... as you see... here, we've put these chaps in an extremely dangerous situation, and the heroine is about to come along to explain the standard health and safety protocols to ..."

But Mr Wallace has had it. "Enough!" He jumps up, taking a moment to turn his security clearance badge the right way round. "I've been on duty since six this morning. We're short staffed, it's been a pig of a day, and I'm due to finish early tonight. My wife is cooking schnitzel. It's my favourite. I do NOT have time for this nonsense."

ScreenSaver! 69

He circles the table speaking to each of them in turn. "Now, everyone empty your pockets." The trio create small piles on the table in front of them. Jo's stack includes a pocket screwdriver, half a slice of dead pizza, and a photo of Denny which she shoves underneath the pizza before anyone sees it. Denny's treasure trove contains keys, comb, mini-tube of hair gel, and one of the doodles of his 'napkin woman.' Jo sees it and exchanges a look with Denny. Her blush tells him she's flattered.

Mr Wallace points at Brynthila, then at her filigreed silver satchel. "You! What's in there?"

Brynthila fishes about inside the case, setting out a bejewelled mirror, a small stunned rat, and a cut glass vial. Jo recognises these items as ones Denny designed for the Level One game inventory. Surreptitiously, she points them out to Denny. He's impressed that this actress Jo has hired, has become familiar so quickly with the persona of her character. But Jo is baffled how the hell digital Brynthila has transformed two-dimensional objects so neatly into the meat-world.

Cautiously, Mr Wallace uncorks the vial and sniffs. "What's this?"

Brynthila holds her hand out for the vial. "'Tis nothing, my liege. Just an invisibility potion. Prithee, what is schnitzel?"

The officer assumes she's a nut-case, wedges the glass stopper back and sets the vial on the table. Brynthila stands, swipes the tiny bottle and surreptitiously eases up the stopper again. Meanwhile, Denny frantically presses keys, which makes Mr Wallace even more suspicious. Both he and Jo now also crowd around the laptop.

"What are you doing now? What's she talking about, invisibility…"

In a dark corner of the shed, Brynthila takes a swig from the vial at the precise moment that her digital image vanishes from the screen saver. They look up to find that she, too, has disappeared, along with the satchel of her possessions.

Mr Wallace gropes the air, trying to find her, when he's suddenly knocked unconscious by an invisible punch to the jaw from the invisible Brynthila. She fumbles the key from his pocket and opens the door. Then, still invisible, she shoves Jo and Denny through it.

"Yes, 'tis I," she says. "Hurry! Methinks this magic won't last long."

Jo and Denny run around the airport roads to find Kurt's van. They're chased by a phalanx of security guards determined to stop them. But suddenly the guards are felled in a heap, as the invisible Brynthila pushes over the man bringing up the rear, and the rest tumble down like a row of dominos.

"Over here," she calls to Denny and Jo, and leads them though a door marked Private, into the terminal building.

Kurt's van is still parked out front, but it's empty. It's also becoming the object of suspicion by a patrolling traffic warden.

Jo and Denny emerge from the terminal entrance and spot the van. Jo climbs into the front passenger seat and Denny gets in the back. The door appears to close by itself. Jo pants as though she's just completed a marathon. Denny is also panting, but in a slightly odd way.

Jo looks around. "Wait a minute! Where's Kurt? Where's Lovelace? Where's Bryn…"

Right in front of Jo's disbelieving eyes, Brynthila slowly materialises. It's clear that Denny's heavy breathing is being caused by her passionate embrace.

Jo shouts "Denny!" as much because she sees the traffic official approaching in the rear view mirror as to curtail his attempts at back-seat romance. The events of the day are also convincing her that she's dreaming and will awake very soon.

She turns Brynthila around by the shoulder. "First we have to get out of here, Pronto Tonto. And then, we've got to find you some new clothes. So let go of him and…"

Brynthila's defiant. "Is this the thanks I get for saving your life?! Fie, Madam, fie on you!"

Jo and Denny decide to ignore her wrath. Denny climbs over into the driver's seat. "Let me drive."

"Sure. Where's the key? Come to think of it, where's Kurt?"

Brynthila's still determined to help. It's just how she's been programmed. "I shall rescue you, my Prince," she declares, clambering into the front, squeezed between Denny and Jo. Then she drops down to figure out the van's mechanics.

Jo completely misinterprets her motivation and looks daggers at Denny, who shrugs. Brynthila meanwhile has been fumbling under the dashboard with nothing more sinister in mind than to hot-wire the van. But as Jo's rating on the jealousy metre pops off the scale, Brynthila holds up her hand and reveals the elusive ignition key. Denny awkwardly extracts Brynthila from under his feet. He grabs the key from her, revs the engine and checks the rear-view mirror to pull away from the kerb.

The traffic warden closes in, but just in time, Denny steers the van toward the airport exit. On the way they pass a couple of airport security guards in high-viz yellow vests on the lookout for them. Brynthila points to a very puzzled Kurt on the pavement, holding Lovelace's lead and trying to wave them down. Without a care for consequence, the dog marks her territory right on the shoe of one of the guards, which successfully diverts his attention from the fleeing van.

"Bad dog!" scolds Kurt, a mumble lost on the guards. Lovelace, however, lowers her head in shame.

At the door of one of the small conference rooms in the airport hotel, Max shakes hands with two Chinese gentlemen. They've each set down their carry-on luggage to bid him farewell. After exchanging safe-flight clichés and promises to keep each other in the loop, the men retrieve their bags and head for the walkway to Terminal 4. Max turns

ScreenSaver!

in the opposite direction leading to the lift. He's already picked up the key to his room when he checked in earlier. He was so afraid to be late for the meeting, he'd only had time to throw his overnight bag on the bed, and splash some water on his face. But now he's ready to indulge. First, though, he checks in with Fiona.

Back in town Denny finds a parking bay outside some shops on the High Street. He and Jo are exhausted, but Brynthila is bouncing with excitement. "Is this the next level?" she asks.

Denny turns to Jo. "Are we or aren't we going to find out what the hell happened here?"

"Yes, of course! Uhm... How do you propose we actually do that... 'cause I haven't a clue!"

Brynthila perks up. "Clues? Oh, fie on me... I left my task list back in the castle. Do I need to bank more clues?"

Denny ignores her. "Well, I don't know about you, but I'd think better with some caffeine." He's half out the van, when Jo asks whether to leave Brynthila locked in. Considering her proficiency with engines, he replies, "Best take her along."

Jo wishes she could clip her creation to a lead as they walk past the shops, each one a new temptation for Brynthila. Like a toddler, she has to be pulled out of every doorway, and both Jo and Denny are getting fed up with chastising her. Finally, Denny bellows, "Just wait till I get some coffee, will you!" Brynthila hides from his rage behind Jo.

Their little scene has caused some passers-by to stare over at them. One young lad points, "Look mummy, that lady is like in my book!" "Must be an advert or something," his mother replies.

"Denny, wait. We can't let her walk around in that gear."

"Okay, yes, I mean no. Just keep her in check for a minute. I've got to get a coffee before I die. You want anything?"

ScreenSaver!

Jo shakes her head as Denny crosses the street and enters a small deli. She barely has time to prevent Brynthila from examining a running shoe displayed on the rack outside a sports emporium, when Denny returns carrying a take-away cardboard cup. He takes a sip through the lid as he joins Jo and Brynthila. "Ahh, that's better. Right. Now what?"

Still puzzled by the row of so-many shoes, Brynthila asks "Are those to shod the multi-footed Decapods of Doom?"

But Denny is plagued by questions of his own. "Come clean, Jo, where did you find this... whoever she is? I mean the magic tricks are awesome, I'll give you that."

"You're just not getting it, are you?! Penn and Teller have nothing to do with this." They stare at Brynthila, now gazing longingly into a bookshop window. She ingeniously fashions her flimsy wimple into a neck-scarf, and tucks up her surcote into the embroidered belt, allowing a display of her kirtle undergarment and soft-leather long-toed poulaines on her feet.

"Do you or don't you agree she needs a different outfit?" Denny nods his head. "Something to blend in, nothing to stand out," Jo continues. "There's that boutique-y place on the next block." And off they go.

Keeping Brynthila between them for safety, they enter the clothes shop, much to the amusement and amazement of the young woman at the till. A beat-box soundtrack stifles any meaningful dialogue.

Brynthila follows her guardians to a rack of casual outfits, and coos over the selections Denny's picked out... filmy cruise wear, sarongs, crop tops. But Jo has been choosing garments from a very different display, aimed at a more conservative market. She snatches back Denny's choices with a firm "No!" Brynthila pouts. Denny can't see what the problem is. "Why not?" he shouts through the music. "Look, she likes them."

"Because she can't draw attention. What's the matter with you... I thought we agreed."

ScreenSaver!

"Oh, right, I see, you want her to look like you." And the music suddenly cuts out just as he adds, "Miss Dowdy from Dowdyshire."

Denny hasn't quite taken in the effect his barb is having on Jo. She turns away in case she embarrasses herself with tears. Recovering her dignity, she returns to the clothes rack and grabs a few knee-length dresses with a marked absence of décolletage. Or waistline. Or any appeal at all.

Brynthila has sensed the tension between "her Prince" and "her creator." She gently takes a glittered tunic top from Denny's hands and returns it to a nearby display counter.

Jo holds four dresses against Brynthila to check the sizes. She starts to usher her into the changing area. "Wait here," she orders Denny.

Summoning courage, Brynthila says, "No, you may wait here, as well, my Lady. I can dress myself." She takes the clothes and disappears behind a floor-length curtain.

The changing room area is guarded by a bored teenager on work experience. Her job entails handing out numbered plastic tags to customers depending on the amount of garments they take in. Well, that's what she's meant to be doing. What she's actually doing is texting on her mobile while she listens to the music banging into her headphones. A sign on the wall above her head reads 'No more than 5 garments allowed in the changing area.'

Brynthila is intrigued by the lizard tattoo around her wrist. "Are you the keeper of the Lizard Gate?"

The trainee ignores her. Brynthila tries again. "Well then, have you got a clue?"

The girl finally looks up, counts the four dresses, and hands Brynthila a plastic tag marked with the number four. Ah, she reasons, this must be my authorisation pass to unknown lands. She ventures further into a corridor of numbered cubicles, and checks her tag against cubicle four. She pulls back the curtain to reveal a startled, half-dressed young

ScreenSaver!

mother whose little girl sits cross-legged on the floor, colouring in a book with crayons.

The young mother screams and angrily pulls the curtain closed. Brynthila opens it again, only to have the woman yank it shut. She wonders if this is one of those competition mini-games to get her to the next level. She hasn't yet received The Rules, but clearly she must claim this territory as her own. She can't let Prince Denny down.

With the dresses still draped over her arm, she fetches out the stunned rat from her satchel and tosses it over the curtain into the young mother's cubicle. There's an almighty screech, the mother grabs her daughter's hand, and holding her clothing tight to her chest, they flee out onto the shop floor.

Denny and Jo have been avoiding eye contact, but each looks round at the sight of a little girl pulling at the skirt of her screaming mother. "I dropped my book, Mummy, I want my book." Suddenly, the colouring book comes sailing through the air and lands in the startled girl's arms.

A smug Brynthila enters the cubicle, retrieves the rat, and stuffs it into the satchel. She hangs up the dresses on the garment rail, and starts to peel off the layers of her costume.

In his hotel room, Max wiggles his toes into the yielding pile of the carpet as he steps out of his street shoes, and attaches the Do Not Disturb sign to the door. The studied cordiality mask he wore at the meeting, turns to unconfined glee. He jumps onto the double bed, springing up and down as though it were a bouncy castle. He pads into the black and white ensuite haven of luxury, envious of the bunny-soft towels and approving the complementary toiletries on offer. He's delighted to discover even the bathroom is fully wi-fi. Oh, yes, he tells himself, he definitely deserves this. After what he's been through today? Definitively definite!

He turns on the bath taps, and heads for the mini-bar. His biggest decision just now is to choose between dining in one of the three restaurants or ordering room service and a selection of in- house cinema on the giant telly. He grabs his iPad.

Neither Denny nor Jo is big on clothes shopping at the best of times. Denny keeps on trend with the latest fashions online, while Jo would happily wear her faded jeans and t-shirts till they disintegrate. But at the moment, they each fight boredom as they're treated to a succession of outfits modelled by Brynthila. Whenever Denny likes one, Jo objects. And the dress Jo favours gets the thumbs down from Denny. I'm trying to be fair to everyone here, but I have to admit that Jo's choices are on the wrong side of flattering.

As they're about to embark on yet another quarrel, Denny's phone rings. Caller I.D. tells him it's Lauren. "Gotta take this," he says edging toward the exit for better reception. Jo can't help overhearing his seductive laugh. "Clubbing? What tonight?" he says.

Jo suddenly decides they've had enough shopping. She turns Brynthila around to zip up the dress and stuffs her left arm into a loose-fitting matching over-jacket. "That's the one," she declares. "Do up the buttons and let's just go." She heads over to the front till. "Get your belongings while I pay."

After exchanging her cubicle tag for a large shopping bag, Brynthila stuffs it with her costume, and replaces all the artefacts from the game into the silver satchel. She approaches Jo waiting her turn in the small queue at the till, and hands her the shopping bag. Denny's waiting in the doorway, and she joins him. "Prithee, sire, what is pay?" she asks him.

"Pay… you know. No? Oh, I get it, you're a foreign exchange student. Well, your accent is perfect! But your vocabulary needs some work."

"I am no gooby nor buffle, sire, therefore prithee do instruct me."

Denny wonders what her game is, but decides to play along. "Let's see, pay. Payment. You know… dosh, quids, folding stuff, dough-ray-me." Brynthila stares blankly. "Look," Denny tries another tack, "suppose you meet someone who has something you want. How do you get it?"

Oh, excellent, thinks Brynthila; this is one of those Question and Answer mini-games. She knows those rules, and asks the first of her allotted supplementary questions. "Is't the kind of something for my inventory?"

"You what? Inventory? No, I mean, I don't know. Just something you want. What do you do?"

"A bout of wrestling, hand to hand? Or...mayhap... we barter?"

"Yes, mayhap... I mean maybe. But what about coin? You know, pounds, shillings, pence."

"Ah, coin! Groats and farthings, angels and half-angels!"

"I guess. You really do stay in character, don't you? Are you a history student?" Denny looks her up and down as Jo emerges from the shop. He says, "I'm no Stella McCartney, but isn't her skirt on the long side?"

Before they can stop her, Brynthila obligingly rips a perfect strip off the hemline to knee-length. Jo rounds on Denny. "Now look what you've done?"

"Well, she does have good legs," he says. And Brynthila's allegiance quickly shifts away from Jo.

"Just shut up, will you." She checks her watch again. "Why doesn't Max ring?"

Jo and Denny flank Brynthila as they walk down the High Street. She compares herself to other young women they pass, and frowns her disappointment. "I favour my own garment best." She tries to pull her game dress from the shopping bag, but Jo stops her.

"Yes, of course you do. But this... this is a disguise. It's very exciting."

Brynthila is intrigued. These are the very rules she needs to learn. But it's only when Denny echoes "Very exciting," that she admits, "Yes! I am very excited!"

Denny's phone rings its jazz riff. Guess who?!

You guessed, it's Max, up to his neck in a bubble bath and sipping from a glass of champagne. His iPad is propped up alongside the tub. Denny greets him, trying to hide the camera image of the naked man from Brynthila.

"You've done me proud," Max crows. "We ran the demo. I was like: what do you reckon?And they were like: we love it! Apart from the five-o'clock shadow on Bryn…thingy."

"thyla…"

"Yeah, thyla. What's that about, dude? Not going trans on me, are you?"

"Uhm.. about that… anyway, so does that mean we get the development dosh?" Denny tries to silence Jo who's flinging a string of questions at him.

"Absolutely, dude! Definitively definite. Plus-a-rama… they're definitely sponsoring a stand for us at this year's Games Fair! I'm like so made up about it, dude! … Are you still in touch with that weirdo woman, the one that sort of looks like Brynthila?"

Denny points at Brynthila and whispers to Jo, "He wants to know if we're still in touch with "that woman" who jumped from your bedroom."

Fearing the worst, Jo tells him to ask why. Denny nods. "Yes," he says cautiously. "Why?"

"Well, I've been thinking… if she wants to help with the marketing, that could be cool. If you can keep her under control. Can you?"

Which is a question Denny has been asking himself all day.

Chapter 8

Denny has followed Jo and Brynthila down a side-street and into a cobbled market square, lined with food and craft stalls. As he relates the details of his conversation with Max, Brynthila wanders away from them, fascinated by the random array of fruit, figurines and crockery on display. She pauses in front of a stall specialising in kitchenalia. Ever alert to a mini-game, she tries to work out an algorithm to collate the items on a silver salver into an elegant mathematical grouping.

Making sure no one is watching, she picks up a silver swizzle stick, and tries to use it as a wand. Recalling her recent dialogue with Prince Denny, this is surely the kind of something she wants for her inventory. She rules out hand-to-hand combat with the broad-shouldered stallholder, currently bargaining with a customer. Nor can she produce coin of any denomination. So she resorts to a third option which Denny failed to mention. Surreptitiously she pops the silver stick into her filigreed satchel, but she hasn't been as cautious as she thought. The stallholder grabs her sleeve.

"Oi! Whatchoo playing at? Give over!"

Brynthila pulls away, searching frantically for Jo and Denny. She reaches into her satchel and blows a handful of invisible dust into the stallholder's eyes. He freezes in mid-grab as though turned to stone. Brynthila spots Jo and Denny through the throng of shoppers and runs to catch up.

The pair are clearly arguing. Again! Brynthila wonders what she must do to help bring peace unto the land. If only she could summon the Goddess Gevreen.

"Look, Jo," declares Denny, "he's the boss, and he definitely wants Brynthila to help."

"If you think about that for one tiny second in your tiny brain, you'd know it's not possible. It's the opposite of possible. It's Im!"

"What's im-possible is that you could ever stop being so stubborn. What's the problem?"

"If you ever managed to take your brain out of your pants for one minute, you'd notice that... how can I put this so even you will understand... she's not the genuine article. She's not bloody real!" And turning about face, she stomps off back to the van. But she's back in a moment, hand outstretched. "Keys. Please." Denny complies, watching Jo walk away with the shopping bag.

Brynthila has overheard Jo's remark and is clearly hurt, which is something Denny does notice. Leaving Jo to her own devices, he tries to comfort the tearful Brynthila. "Now, now, what's all this? No crying allowed on the public highway. By royal decree."

"Sorry, your highwayness." Brynthila bobs a courtesy. "I mean your high... my Prince."

Denny's first impulse is to correct her misunderstanding about his lineage, but he can't help thinking how cool it would be if she assumes he really is a prince!

Brynthila is still confused. "She said I am not the article. Am I? Am I bloody real?"

Instead of a direct answer, Denny holds out his hand, as though to a small child. "I'm heading back home. Wanna come? You can make sure no one's invaded my territory." Brynthila takes his proffered hand and they turn up an alleyway. "Good girl!... and," he adds, "you can tell me how you're pulling off all those wicked special effects."

Brynthila frowns momentarily at the word 'wicked." But Denny's smile of admiration wipes away any doubts.

By this time Jo has reached the van and realises she's alone. She scours the street for a sight of Denny and Brynthila, but they've vanished. After waiting a few minutes, she feels guilty about leaving

Kurt and she tries to ring him from the van phone. But of course he cannot reply as the van phone is his only phone. Well, she tried. The only thing she wants now is some sleep.

As Denny and Brynthila wander down a narrow lane leading out of town, his phone buzzes. Brynthila asks, "Is that the big bad man again?"

But Denny sees it's a text from Lauren, and he turns off his phone. "No, no, you're safe now." He squeezes her hand and leads her into the woods.

Back at Falcon Lodge, the sound of Kurt's van rouses Osborne, who's been napping in a chair in the lingering dusk. He opens the door for Jo and takes the van keys she proffers.

"Hi, Osborne. Can you give these to my friend Kurt if he shows up, please. Tell him I'm really knackered, and I said to ring me before he leaves tomorrow."

"Certainly, Miss."

"Thanks, you're a lifesaver."

Jo's about to scoot upstairs when her mother's voice from above stops her.

"Josabunny! Is that you?!"

Jo is mortified by her childhood nickname. "Mummy!" Jo was really hoping to escape from her bizarre day. Perhaps a short nap will restore everything to normal again when she wakes up.

Elaine appears on the wide landing. She holds out a necklace for her daughter to fasten, and asks, "Will you be joining us for dinner?"

Fearing the worst, Jo asks, "Us who?" Then she has a happier thought, "Is Daddy back from…"

ScreenSaver! 83

"Not just yet. No, I've asked the Thompsons round. And you can put that 'yuuch' face back in the box."

Jo moans. "Don't be like that," Elaine continues. "Teddy Thompson's had a crush on you for years, since playgroup."

"Exactly! He's King Dweeb."

"Josephine! Your father and I did not raise a rude child."

Jo changes the subject. "Actually, when is Daddy coming home?"

"Well, he rang from Accra. Terrible line. But I'm meeting his flight tomorrow. We've both missed him, haven't we?"

Jo can't stop herself, "Chopped down enough rain forest, has he?"

Elaine's tone has frosted in an instant. "Your father is a highly respected asset advisor on six continents."

Jo refrains from an observation about corporate assets on the Antarctic ice sheets, but she knows she has to melt her Ice Queen mother, and does it with a kiss on the cheek. Elaine softens. She smooths Jo's curls away from her eyes. "Now, get in that shower, and I know there are clean clothes in your room… somewhere. Let's try a dress for a change; I don't think I've had a glimpse of your legs since our holiday in the Bahamas!"

Jo knows this attempt at humour means Elaine has forgiven her. "I want you at the table bright and shiny in one hour sharp. And I want to see… well, I imagine lipstick is too much to hope for, but at least I want to see smiles."

Jo offers a grateful,"Yes, Mummy," and starts upstairs to her turret room. Elaine calls after her. "And don't forget your brother's sports day next week. Family support! Honestly, if it weren't for us, I think you'd take root in front of that computer!"

As Jo gets ready for supper, across town, the silky sounds of Sarah

ScreenSaver!

Vaughan fill Denny's flat. A half-empty wine bottle sits on the floor alongside two glasses. Brynthila and Denny lie sprawled out over some floor cushions. He gazes at her and strokes her arm, still sheathed in the dress jacket. His shirt buttons are very open, very Mr. Darcy. He tries to undo her jacket, but she starts to giggle.

"That tickles!"

"Well," he notes with supreme confidence, "That's just what it's meant to do."

Meanwhile, in the less formal of the two Hawker-Meade dining-rooms, Elaine presides. When she and Jonathan were married, this Regency walnut dining table was a wedding gift from his beloved great-aunt Emily. She's always thought it a happy complement to the proportions of the room, with its alabaster ceiling rose and cornicing, and the muted mauves and greys of the striped paper above the panelling.

Osborne has pressed the embroidered white table-cloth to smooth perfection, along with the matching serviettes. He's placed the candles and small sprays of roses to enhance, never to interfere.

The table itself seats six with room to spare, but this evening there are only five diners. Elliot and Camilla Thompson sit opposite each other, and their son Theodore is across from Jo. Elaine is relieved that Jo has made an effort and by comparison with her work outfits, she doesn't look half bad!

It hasn't escaped Elaine's notice that this isn't the liveliest of supper parties, but Elliot Thompson is one of Jonathan's longest-standing business contacts. And she herself serves on the Board of a local children's charity with Cammie, so there's no point giving in to social defeat. No one would be more pleased if young Teddy could somehow capture her daughter's attention. Alas! she knows how unlikely that is, and so she takes comfort in small talk with the Thompsons, memories of dear Aunt Emily, and the lasting solidity of the table.

These days Teddy prefers to be called Ted. He's the same age as Jo but already carries a trio of frown lines on his forehead, and the sagging shoulders he shouldn't expect for at least another thirty years. He's that double whammy: shy and charmless. Whatever conversation there was at the start of the meal vanished long before the pudding. Jo forces a smile of anticipation when it looks as though Ted is about to say something, but it's just a stifled yawn. There's less atmosphere in the room than on the moon. When Osborne asks permission to clear, and announces coffee in the paisley drawing room, everyone rises eagerly just for the change of scene.

No such pomp and formality grace Denny's dalliance. He moves the wine bottle and glasses out of the way and gently pulls Brynthila toward him. She's unsure when he boldly undoes the buttons of her jacket; she's even more confused when he reaches behind to unzip her dress and tries to stick his hand down the front. But she doesn't resist. Suddenly, he pulls away in disbelief and sits up.

"What the... ?"

Brynthila can't tell if she's caused some offence. "What is't troubles you, sire?"

"No way! That's weird. That's just... weird!" He scrambles to his feet. "Get up," he commands. And she does. He faces her, at arm's length. "Look," he says, "Don't take this the wrong way, but... how do I put this... where's your body?"

Totally bewildered, Brynthila touches her arms, face, and neck. "What mean you, my Prince? 'Tis my body here. Hast thou perchance gone blind?"

"No! No, yes, I mean yes, I can see that, but... lower... underneath your clothes. What's underneath your clothes?"

"'Tis nothing."

Denny tries to follow the logical illogic, the illogical logic. "Yes. Exactly. Nothing. Where's the rest of you?"

Brynthila peers down the neckline, but can't quite see whatever it is that Denny is expecting to see. "I wot not." She turns around and asks Denny to unzip the dress completely.

She eases the bodice down over her shoulders. Denny gasps. Slowly he turns Brynthila around to face him. Instead of the bust and torso of a nubile young woman, there are just blank spaces. Her arms and upper chest fade away to nothingness. Denny reaches out to poke her, but his finger doesn't connect with anything. Brynthila inches her skirt up past her knees, only to discover her upper thighs, hips, and tummy region are also absent.

"Oh," she says, somehow surprised yet somehow accepting.

Denny may also be surprised, but he just cannot accept what's in front of his eyes. "No! This isn't happening... are you telling me you really are Brynthila? Brynthila from the game? Not an actress who knows magic tricks? Jo wasn't having me on?"

"As we said, my mission is to rescue you. I am here to battle on your behalf."

"Never mind that! How are we going to... let's just say... fill in the blanks?"

"And, whereof art thou made, my liege?"

In response, Denny removes his shirt. "See? Here, look, hereof am I made!" He takes Brynthila's wrist and pushes her hand against his chest and then against her own. "Where you have empty air, I have bones and blood and skin. All over!"

"I beseech your forgiveness, my Prince." She tries to replace her hand on Denny's toned six-pack, but he re-buttons his shirt and exclaims, "Of course! This is my fault! I never designed you a... whatchacallit... an undercarriage."

Brynthila is left to contemplate her existence as Denny hurries to the computer. He calls up his paint programme, preparing to work, when the doorbell rings. Followed by Brynthila, he cautiously approaches the door and peeps through the spyhole. It's Lauren, ready for a night of clubbing. She pushes the bell again. "Denny?"

Denny backs away to the far end of the room, shoving Brynthila into a closet. "Not a word!" he warns. then calls out, "Who is it?"

"Den, it's me, Lauren. We had a date, remember?"

He answers in a strangled voice, pretending he's got flu. "Just coming." He shoots into the bathroom, emerging with a robe which he ties over his clothing. He pretends to sneeze and opens the door a wee crack. He sounds wheezy, sickly, and a few other of Snow White's dwarves.

"Hello, Babe," he croaks.

Inside the closet, Brynthila listens to the conversation with growing anxiety. Perchance this is the Treacle Tart of Temptation, come to lure her Prince away.

Lauren attempts to push against the door. "Aren't you going to let me in, tiger?"

"Best not tonight. I'm… thing is … I'm wasted." He has managed to sound like an adorable puppy… with flu.

"Oh, poor baby. You sounded fine earlier."

Denny pretends to sneeze again. "I know, right? Came on just like that. Must be a bug."

Brynthila takes this as a request from her Prince. Toting the silver satchel, she sneaks out of the closet on all fours, and scurries up next to Denny behind the front door. She reaches into the satchel and dumps something into Denny's hand. He looks down and screams. It's a huge insect, inverted in his palm, legs waving impotently. Denny flings it across the room and tries to remonstrate with Brynthila, whispering and shooing her towards the closet.

"Denny?" says Lauren. "Have you got someone in there?"

"Of course not! It's… it's the radio." He produces a feeble cough. "Please, babe. I'm really knackered, need sleep. Right as rain in the morning." He starts to close the door.

Lauren's reply promises seduction, "Well… If you're sure I can't… you know, make you feel better …"

But just as she starts to leave, Denny backs up and trips over Brynthila, still crouching on all fours. She yelps. Lauren rushes back and shoves the door open. She quickly surveys the scene. Denny is sprawled in the doorway, on top of Brynthila.

"Wait, Lauren… Babe… It's not what it looks like."

"You bastard!" she yells, her high heels clicking along the corridor.

Denny pulls Brynthila to her feet, and adjusts her clothing. He chucks her under the chin as though she were a little girl. "What are we going to do with you, eh?!"

Brynthila starts to embrace Denny, but for once in his life, he's too scared, too mystified to respond.

In another street full of semi-detached houses, in another suburb, and officially in another country of these British Isles, a forty-something woman finishes dressing. She retrieves the drain-pipe jeans from the floor where she recently dropped them, and rescues her tank top and stiletto heels from under the bed. She pulls her uncombed hair into a pony tail and applies some lip gloss with her forefinger. A naked man is propped up on the pillows, watching her. He points to the bedside table, and the woman counts out some pound notes, tucking them into her jeans pocket.

"Ta, Rhys," she says on her way out.

"Take care, Wenna," he replies.

When Osborne applied for the position of butler to the Hawker-Meades, he'd been a widower for three years and was looking to leave his tiny one-bed, all mod cons off the Harrow Road in London for a fresh start. That was more than twenty-five years ago, and he's never regretted accepting the terms and conditions of the job. He didn't so much enter into service as become a trusted employee, and, yes, a family friend.

 He settles into the comfy armchair in the corner of his living quarters just off the kitchen, studying a framed wedding photo, him and Leesa. On a sentimental journey through his past. They'd met outside a club in Kilburn, rebels in waiting, couldn't stick school, couldn't stick the dole. He wanted some real life, and Leese had enough zing for the pair of them. They were post-punk Goths. She was holding a promo for *Trainspotting*. He asked if she'd go with him.

 Couple of months later they were posing for photos outside the registry office, couple of the band as witnesses. Seemed everyone was in a band back then. You either played something, or you could drive a van and hump the gear. In time he leant his hand to all-sorts, drew the line at procurement, but could dive down on a fader and check EQ levels when needed. As a street-cred roadie, he figured he'd always be involved in the music biz. Funny, he thinks, how life throws you curves. He was always packed and ready to rave with the boys, and always glad to get back home to Leesa, but never realising how much he was taking her for granted. Loyal Leese.

 He's in a long black leather coat in the photo, hair falling over one eye, shaved up on the other side. Looking sideways at Leesa, never could keep his eyes off her. Her hair black and long under a trilby, black choker around her neck, laced-up bodice and ankle length tulle overskirt. Benj and Leese, Mr and Mrs Osborne, you may now kiss the bride. Long time ago.

 He'd had to give up the touring when she got the diagnosis. Changed their lives. Ditched the old image, bought a straight suit and got a gig as a bartender in a posh hotel just a bus ride away. And that led to a chance to fill in for some geezers at a private party in Mayfair. The lad done good, and it led to another. Then another. He was there at the end, holding her hand, glad it wasn't the hospital. Music loud and proud, in their bed, where she'd been loved. Fade out.

Till one day he met a man who knew a man who knew that Jonathan Hawker-Meade was looking for a butler at his family home in the country. And so he learned deference and became Osborne, and he's never looked back. Well, only once in a while. But he never thought his former life might be of some use to Jo. So when he hears that Max expects her and Denny to supply music for their game, he's only too willing to help. And he knows just the place to find it.

His simple but comfortable rooms easily accommodate the furniture he shared with Leese. He couldn't bear to part with that painted pine cupboard she'd decorated. He opens it, knowing just what he's looking for. Tucked away in an old shoe box he lifts out a tattered contacts book from his roadie days, safely bound to keep the loose pages falling out. Finally, he finds the name he's looking for and makes a call.

"Wotcha mate," he says. "It's Ozzie."

Meanwhile, Denny has abandoned his plan to redesign the missing bits of Brynthila's digital anatomy. Time for Plan B. He hustles her out the door and into his convertible. Sitting beside him, Brynthila is ready for the next level of the adventure. She is very happy. He's increasingly apprehensive.

"Jo was right," he confides. "We've got to get you to a place of safety." He checks the time and accelerates toward the edge of the village. About ten minutes later, Denny turns into the Hawker- Meade drive and waves to the security camera. The gates open, then close behind them. He slowly steers up to the Lodge.

In the small drawing room, Ted sits next to Jo on the settee, each sipping coffee. Jo's noticed Elaine hasn't set out the best china and wonders what the protocol is. These are things she's never paid attention to. She stopped listening about ten minutes ago to Ted's monotone recounting a promotion. Something about an engineering project for an international hydro-electric company.

Out of politeness she should offer congratulations, but she assumes the scheme will deprive people of their homes. She really doesn't want to embarrass either her mother or herself, but… and it is with great restraint… she has, up to now, refrained from expressing her true feelings on the matter. Truth be told, her inner collision of boredom and anger has brought her perilously close to blowing her cover of feigned interest.

Osborne reappears, offering a small tray of after dinner mints to Elaine's guests. "Will that be all, Mrs H?"

"Thank you, Osborne."

"I'll have the Merc ready for you in the morning."

"What would we do without you, Osborne." Elaine confides to her friends, "I'm meeting Jonathan's flight tomorrow."

Osborne nods a general good-night to the room.

Elaine catches her daughter in an undisguised yawn. She attempts to pump some air into the conversation, but they're all saved from pretence by the arrival of Denny. Jo jumps up at the sound of his car and rushes to the garden entrance.

"I'll go." She waves at Denny's car, diverting it away from the imposing front entrance to Falcon Lodge. He pulls up on the gravel drive and escorts Brynthila over to Jo. She can't help noticing they're holding hands.

Whatever explanation Denny's been rehearsing has been replaced by his silent Wow! at Jo's almost glamorous appearance. And he sure doesn't expect her greeting.

"Am I glad to see you!" she exclaims.

Denny tightens his grip on Brynthila's hand to keep her tethered, while he desperately conspires with Jo. "You were right," he whispers.

"And that's not easy for me to say."

"Was I? About what?"

"We've got to get this girl, woman… thing… whatever she is… back into the game. Have you seen her… her… nether regions?"

Before Jo can reply, Elaine appears. "Oh, here you are, darling. Don't stand there in the doorway, invite them in."

Denny leads Brynthila into the foyer. Ever the diplomat, Elaine says, "Denny, what a lovely surprise! And you've brought your… friend. How nice!"

"Evening, Mrs. Hawker-M… I mean Elaine. Bit of a situation. Can I ask a big favour… can you put Brynthila up for the night?"

And before anyone can change their minds, their wish is granted and all the arrangements made. "Now, I really must get back to my guests. Good night, Denny." From Elaine's tone, even Denny takes the hint and leaves.

"I'll show her upstairs, Mummy."

"Whatever it is you're not saying, Josephine, you can tell me tomorrow. I'll make your excuses to the Thompsons."

On his way home, Denny has stopped for a red light when his phone rings. He can't quite make out who it is, but the faint vowels of a Welsh accent allow an accurate guess.

"Hello?" he says, "… Who is this? … Wenna who? … Oh, that Wenna! Known liar and general screw-up …" The car behind hoots as the lights turn green. Unable to avoid the inevitable, Denny pulls into a small lay-by and untethers the phone.

"How did you get this number, Mam? … Yes, okay, I heard you, you've left him … Left who? I mean, it's difficult to keep up. … Rhodri? Never heard of him. Must be new … A whole three weeks.

Really? That's something of a record for you. Last before him was two days ... So what's the problem this time? ... He was a bit what? ... Whoa! Too much information, Mam!... A bit lacking in the what department? ... Huh! Tell me about it! ... No, Mam, please don't tell me about it! It was a figure of... You're looking for what?... Here?! Stay here?! No! No chuffing way!... I don't care how long for... Well, you keep on looking."

Denny switches off the phone and continues driving. I wouldn't advise going anywhere near him at the moment, whoever you might be. Instead of heading home, he checks the time. Not too late for some live music and real live women. He puts it down to research. As Max wants them to source music for the game's soundtrack, The Truck Stop is the perfect place to look.

Up in Jo's turret suite, she's changed out of her dinner dress and is zipped into a cosy flannel onesie, decorated with cartoon princesses. She's trying out different scenarios in her mind to lure Brynthila back to the game. "I think the safest is to keep you in here with me." She points Brynthila toward the bathroom. "You can borrow one of my nighties; they're in the ensuite."

"Are they locked up?" Brynthila asks.

"What?"

"The knights... are they locked up in a suite... I mean a suit...uhm, of armour?"

"No ... nightie, not knight. Just pull it over your head."

As Brynthila explores the spacious marble-tiled bathroom, her corporeal form is undergoing certain almost imperceptible changes. You'd have to look hard, but she's very slowly becoming paler and paler. She opens cupboards, sniffs lotions and potions, licks labels. She finds a stack of carefully folded night-gowns and takes one off the top. It's a long-sleeved full-length white cambric affair, trimmed with lace collar and cuffs.

She tries various ways to wrap herself into and around it. Head in an armhole. Legs through the bottom opening. Finally, she figures it out and pulls it over her day clothes. The gown swathes her from neck to ankle. As she stares at her reflection in the full-length cheval mirror, she can't help checking underneath the gown. As she pulls up a handful of cloth, lifting it higher and higher, she sees the full horror of just what baffled Denny. Entire sections of her body are just missing. Not there. Empty space. And from the progress of her fading anatomy, she could soon become quite invisible. No potion required!

She searches the room for an energy restore station, like the one she visited on Level One of the game. But she can't find anything and goes back to Jo, who's been looking for extra bedding. She glances up at Brynthila. "That's a perfect length. Like it?"

"Verily, 'tis a dainty garment. Prithee, tell me why is't to be donned at night-time?"

"You do sleep, don't you? Or do you?"

"Well, in a manner of speaking. I can force a system shut down... you know, eyes closed, sys restore. It was while I slept, those bleeping trolls robbed me of my bejewelled amulet."

"Ye-es. About that... Not one of my better ideas. Stupid bleeping trolls." Jo discovers a pillow inside a storage bag. She tucks it under her arm and keeps searching. "Right. I've always slept alone, but I suppose we could share. Do you tend to move around a lot?"

"Do you mean through the teleport? I wot not."

"Teleport? No... what do you mean 'whatnot'... teleport? ...uhm, nevermind... What about snoring?"

"Oh, yes," Brynthila says. "Yes, you do. We have all witnessed it."

"Not me, I meant you! Maybe this isn't such a great idea. Pity you can't shrink down, I could fix you up a comfy couch in the desk tidy."

Brynthila stares in bewilderment at the very untidy desk. "Desk? Tidy?" Her mission is clear; she whizzes around at an impossible speed, straightening, tidying. Meanwhile, Jo has opened another storage cupboard, and rummages through a selection of boxes.

Brynthila finds an ashtray full of Kurt's discarded joint butts. She places one in her mouth, takes an experimental chomp, likes what she tastes, and scoffs the lot. After rolling the stray tobacco strands around in her mouth, she decides they need some liquid softener. She wanders into the ensuite and swigs from a bottle of organic shower gel. Some of the ingredients elude her chemical receptors, but she recognises Benzyl Alcohol, Potassium Sorbate, Glyceryl Oleate, some kind of cyclic terpene d- isomer - possibly Limonene - and Aqua.

Jo has pulled out a carton labelled 'airbed,' and removes it along with an accompanying hand- pump. "Brynthila? Where are you?"

Brynthila returns to Jo's side. She takes the pump Jo's holding out to her, and awaits further instruction. Jo sniffs at her. "Why do you smell of oranges?" But Brynthila just shrugs. Jo attaches the nozzle to the air bed, and demonstrates a pumping action. It only takes two or three of Brynthila's super-pumps, and the bed is inflated in seconds. "How would you like to sleep on air?" asks Jo.

Denny steers the convertible down a side-street leading to an industrial estate. One of the units is lit up, coloured lights spelling out the words The Truck Stop. A roaring back-beat seeps out into the parking lot. Denny pays the door charge and filters through the dancers on his way to the bar. He orders a pint, and lets the forceful music osmose into him. One young musician in particular catches his attention, not more than a boy, really. Denny can't tell if he's Chinese or Japanese, and he wishes he didn't feel guilty that he can't. The kid's energy is only surpassed by his rainbow coloured pony-tail and his talent. He's equally at home on keyboard, guitar, and synth. Though he looks by far the youngest, the drummer and bass player follow his lead.

Denny's trying to find Lauren in the crowd, but if she's there, he can't see her. Then, he spies an energetic girl dancing on her own, and presents himself in front of her. They both continue moving to the music. It's far too loud to allow any conversation, but he points to himself. "I'm Denny," he shouts.

Which is the moment he spots a familiar figure dancing over. No, it's not Lauren. It's Osborne! He's changed from his day-job shirt and tie into a pair of skinny jeans, topped by a leather jacket with lots of zips. He approaches the woman Denny was dancing with. She throws her arms around him screaming "Ozzie! You made it!" She points to the stage, "That's the kid I was telling you about. With the rainbow hair."

Osborne nods a greeting to Denny and winks as he dances the woman across the floor. He can't believe this could be Osborne's natural milieu, but despite his age, he's certainly fitting right in. Denny decides discretion is the better part of valour, and leaves for home. It's been a long day.

Up in the turret room, Brynthila looks decidedly woozy after her snack of cannabis residue. She's not merely pale, she's verging on transparent. Jo's been making up the air bed, wrestling with the duvet cover, and hasn't noticed. Unable to control her balance, Brynthila stumbles towards Jo's own bed and collapses onto it. She starts to panic when Jo's wireless phone on the night-table starts beeping.

"The trolls!" she cries out. "The Bleeping Trolls!"

Jo is still down at floor level, adjusting a couple of pillows. But she recognises the sound. "Just my phone, nothing to fret about. It's telling me to charge the battery." Brynthila isn't sure what a battery is or how to charge it. Does she have at it with a lance yelling Charge!?

Both she and Jo are startled by the grunty sound of a belch. Brynthila giggles. "Are you all right?" asks Jo.

"Verily," giggles Brynthila, "'twas a mighty eructation!" And she giggles some more. Still down on all fours, Jo tucks a fitted sheet around the corners of the plump mattress.

"Right," she says, "I've made up your bed, so lie down and go to ... "

ScreenSaver!

She stands again to see Brynthila already sound asleep across the width of the four-poster. A grumpy Jo tries to get comfy on the airbed.

Denny lets himself into his ground-floor flat and surveys the evening's aftermath. He decides to postpone a clean-up and pours himself a glass of wine. Accompanied by a mellow Miles Davis solo, he retreats to the bedroom, undresses, and settles in under the duvet. Choosing the browser icon, he logs on to check his mail.

A message-box pops up on the screen from 'Lord Cassemar,' his cyberchess rival. It's a bit late and he should just go to sleep, but he can never resist a quick chess challenge. At the touch of a mouse-pad another browser window displays a digi-chess board, set up in mid-game. Accompanying the text choices that appear onscreen, a throaty American-accented computerised voice declares "Welcome Jazz Fiend. Choose Yes to resume the game."

Denny studies the board, then makes his move.

"Rook to King Four. Are you sure?" says the computer voice.

The phone rings. "Hello? Mam! Not again… It's late… Yeah, well, maybe not for you, but I'm in bed … Look. Mam, stop. Stop! … It's not convenient … I told you, because… I'm in bed… and I'm not alone!"

Of course Denny is correct, but only in a very specific sense. His digital bed partner, Lord Cassemar, is about to concede defeat after realising he's got no further moves. He makes a declaration via the computer voice of resignation. "Uh-oh, I'm completely trapped. Nothing to do but lie back and prepare to be mated."

"Oh, you heard that, did you?… Of course it's a woman. She's just… got a very deep voice." Denny ends the call and takes another sip of wine.

And sometime later, as the night swims into the sea of dawn, somewhere at the side of a quiet main road, a female figure is back-lit under a roundabout sign. She appears to be a teenager in hot pants over sheer leggings and a skimpy top. Her thumb is out for a lift to the motorway. A huge lorry screeches to a halt. The tubby, unshaven driver opens the door and waits eagerly as the girl gathers her bags and climbs aboard.

"You're taking a risk, ain'tcha, darlin'?" The girl wriggles into the passenger seat, then lifts her face, so he sees it clearly for the first time. You guessed! It's Wenna, Denny's mother. Far from a teenager, her wild hair and thick make-up are fooling no one. Her appearance may be ersatz, but her Welsh accent is genuine.

"I can look after myself, boyo. They are big muscles you got, isn't it." Her laugh has something of a cackle about it. The driver looks shaken; he puts the rig in gear, staring straight ahead. Wenna helps herself to the half-eaten candy bar on the dashboard. The driver flinches slightly as her fingers reach out to feel his studded leather jacket.

Level 2 - Chapter 9

The echo of last night's moon vies with the grey tints of dawn, peeking into Jo's turret room. Brynthila is drifting in and out of visibility. She shudders as far away, a hunting owl swoops silently onto a vole in the forest. From deep inside her, bubbles travel up and burst from her lips, spraying citrus mist everywhere. She moans a moan that sounds suspiciously like a hangover.

The sounds wake Jo, who hasn't yet seen her princess in this semi-transparent form. Jo props herself up on the airbed and leans close, checking Brynthila's rhythmic breaths. She whispers as though she's a hypnotist implanting subconscious thoughts. "You don't belong here."

"Mm-uhm."

Jo points at the computer with the hole in screen. "You belong in there."

"That box? You want me in that box?" Aha! Brynthila's been listening after all.

Jo tries to keep a soothing tone. "It's not a box. It's a portal. To your other world. Remember? Your old world. That world of magic and enchantment."

"Looks like a box to me."

"No, no. It's a whole world. I promise. Look… it's just like… uhm …" Jo glances at her wall-mounted television. She finds the remote and flicks from channel to channel ad nauseam. News headlines, horror movies, cooking show, amusing puppies, a sub-titled Spanish soap opera: literally hundreds of choices.

"Look, Brynthila! At the multitude of wondrous delights contained within." Onscreen is the dubbed Bulgarian version of a Jeremy Kyle type show with everyone arguing, fists flying, and the swear words heavily bleeped.

Brynthila screams. "More bleeping trolls! They're everywhere." She panics and hides her head under the pillow. Jo unzips her onesie and locates her day clothes. She needs to rethink, but she's running out of Plan B's.

An unexpected turning along the main road through town, leads to a pretty lane planted either side with young laurels. A paved opening in the hedge reveals a cluster of six new-build detached houses arranged in a star-shape, each with its own private driveway and bespoke front door.

The house with the frosted transom was bought by Max with proceeds from the international success of *Bluebell's Magic Garden*. He shares both it and the existing mortgage with Fiona. It allows them both their own space, but Fiona can keep tabs on her little brother. And it's a short walk to the office on the High Street.

At the moment, Max sits at the kitchen table, finishing his breakfast crunchies with one hand, clutching his mobile to his ear with the other. "Are you sure? We sent the cheque last … Yeah, yeah … Okay, I … Uh, abso…" Max finally gives up trying to get a word in, and submits to a long torrent of verbiage, abruptly terminated by the caller at the other end.

Calmly, almost casually, Max moves his bowl of cereal to one side and begins systematically to bang his head onto the table. The phone rings. Max stares at it for a moment, then ignores it and starts to pour himself some more cereal. Fiona's hand reaches out and picks up the phone. "Hello?"

She hisses to Max, "It's the bank."

"Can't it wait?"

Fiona holds the phone out to him. "What do you think?"

Max growls at her. She growls right back. He tosses the open cereal box over his shoulder and takes the phone. "Greg! 'morning, squire."

Meanwhile in the turret room, Brynthila is still flat out and virtually lifeless on the bed. Jo shakes her vigorously, quite alarmed by her pale complexion.

"Come on, let's get you back in that game. You want to meet your prince, don't you?"

Brynthila mumbles, "I have already met my prince."

"Who? Denny?" Jo says, gently tugging the duvet off her. "He's not a prince. He's a graphic artist - and I don't mean an artist formerly known as prince." She pulls the nightgown up over Brynthila's head, noting she's still wearing her new dress underneath. "Oh, you're meant to take off the day clothes first. Nevermind. Come on, let's get your warrior costume on. You like that one."

But Brynthila ain't budging. Jo tries another temptation. "If you step back into the game, you can design your own dress. Hell, you can design your own prince. How many girls get the chance to do that? Any shape or size within reason. Oh, what's reason got to do with it? This is a computer game. You could be a very, very, very lucky girl."

"I already am."

"Give me a break, he's just plain old Denny da Vinci. Nothing special. Trust me."

Jo goes over to the photo blowup of Denny and touches his face. It's as if she's suddenly seeing him in a new light. And she's not entirely comfortable with that. "I grant you, he's quite… attractive. If you like that sort of thing."

Brynthila moans. Jo turns, genuinely concerned by her appearance. "You really don't look at all well." She tries yet another approach. "I know! What about some breakfast. Get you fit for the challenges ahead."

Brynthila, leaning heavily on Jo, follows her downstairs. Neither of them hears Jo's phone battery bleeping its imminent death.

Across town, a tousled Denny emerges from under stylish bed sheets to answer his ringing phone. He assumes it's his relentless mother. "Listen, Mam, what part of no ... Max! G'morning ... Brynthila? Oh, you mean that woman who... No, she's with Jo, I think ... What photo shoot? ... You want us to organise a photo shoot?... When do you... Tomorrow?!... Fine, no probs ... Her dress, yes... Low cut, very revealing. Got it, no problemo..." Denny suddenly remembers Brynthila's anatomy, or lack of it. "Wait, no... I mean, revealing, of course... but not too revealing... Why? Yes, why... because... to be honest with you, Max, there's certain parts of Brynthila which really can't be revealed ... No! No, there's nothing wrong with her. She's just a bit... shy ... Yeah, hard to believe, but she is ... Yes, I will... I'll get on to Jo. Get her round to yours ASAP. Will do. Bye, Max. Bye."

Denny tries in vain to ring Jo on her dead phone. Every cell of his body beckons him back to bed. To sleep. Perchance to dream. He's really not ready to meet the day, but summoning up a strength he didn't know he possessed, he pads into the bathroom and surrenders to the shower.

The lorry has stopped at the side of the road. Wenna is surrounded by thick clouds of cigarette smoke as she descends from the passenger seat. The Driver passes her bags down. He strains against the weight of the last one.

"Cor, missus, wotcha got in here... Tower Bridge?"

Wenna coughs and stubs out her cigarette. "I only wish there was some way I could repay your kindness. Maybe stop for a few minutes, hop in the back... we could ... I could..."

But the Driver slams the door, floors the accelerator, and speeds off. With a triumphant cackle, Wenna unzips one of her bags, and pulls out the driver's studded leather jacket. She tries it on.

Osborne, showing no trace of last night's revels, has arranged breakfast in the conservatory, overlooking the rose garden. He's set three places around the glass-topped cast-iron table. A trendy shabby-chic sideboard offers a jug of juice, a choice of cold cereals, a shiny toaster, and a large cafetière half-full of coffee.

Elaine is trying to pay attention to her daughter's guest, but her mental checklist is filled with welcoming home her husband. She and Osborne have been preparing for days.

Jo munches toast, off in her own little world, as usual. Brynthila seems to move in slow motion. Elaine fingers the ceramic milk jug in front of her. "Who'd like more coffee? Jo?" Brynthila shakes her head. "I'll get it, Mummy," Jo says, making for the sideboard.

Elaine presses on her path of politesse. She addresses Brynthila. "So! We never did get properly introduced last time. My name's Elaine." Brynthila ignores her. "And you're Denny's... friend."

Jo pours herself some juice. "She's called Brynthila." She carries the cafetière to her mother. As Jo bends down to pour some coffee, Elaine whispers, "Does she speak English?" She tugs her own earlobe in what she thinks is a subtle mime. "Is .. is she deaf?"

Brynthila tries to suppress another belch. Jo returns to the sideboard. Elaine has become more concerned about the wellbeing of her guest.

"Can we get you anything, Bryth... Bryl... uhm, dear. Some eggs, perhaps. Can't have you wasting aw... "

But her sentence vanishes into the air, and Brynthila, who is already deathly pale, momentarily does the same. Instantly she re-appears. Elaine rubs her eyes, hoping she's not hallucinating. Jo is waiting for her toast to pop up and hasn't noticed.

Brynthila's in some sort of trance. Elaine speaks quietly to Jo. "Your friend does look rather peaky, darling."

Jo whispers an attempt at a reasonable explanation. "Mmm. Had a big bust up with Denny. She's in shock. Best not to mention it. Too painful."

Elaine looks over at Brynthila, who again briefly fades from view, still unnoticed by Jo. Elaine is now doubting her own sanity. "I understand," Elaine nods, not understanding anything. "Poor thing. Gracious, look at the time. Do you girls want to come to Heathrow with me to pick up your father? Lunch in town, perhaps a film?"

"Thanks, Mummy, we've got work to do."

"Well, I'd best dash. You know those morning flights. Absolute chaos!" She kisses Jo on the cheek. "Bye-bye darling. Bye-bye Brillo … Byn… uhm, dear. I hope you feel better soon."

Elaine heads out to the car, while Jo brings her second-helping over to the table and tucks in. Brynthila moans.

Denny's espresso machine has worked its caffeine magic. He's dressed and about to leave. But when he opens the door, he's confronted by the leather-jacketed Wenna. She's surrounded by her several bags and cases and smiles sweetly even as she puffs out a blast of cigarette smoke. She greets him in Welsh, "*Bore da, mab.*"

"Mam! What part of 'you can't stay here' didn't you understand?"

Wenna pushes past him, lugging her bags, exploring all nooks and crannies, calculating and planning and scheming. Denny sets his iPad in its carry-case on the floor and follows her. She chastises him, "Why won't you call me Wenna? I mean, we're not what you'd call traditional mother and son."

"You can say that again."

"More like brother and sister, isn't it. And big sis Wenna has come to look after you."

"Bit late for that, Mam."

"Let's leave the past in the past," she counters, making it almost sound like a warning.

"Besides, I don't need looking after."

"Course you do! Without my love and attention, who knows what horrible diseases you could go down with, see." Wenna goes to kiss Denny. He tries to turn away, but not quickly enough to avoid the huge cloud of smoke she blows into his face. She cackles quietly.

"Stop that! I'm late. Look, you can stay just till I come back. But certain areas are out of bounds. Are you listening? Put your cases in that spare room. You can use the kitchen. You can use the loo… if you must. Everywhere else is no go. Verboten, got it?! Especially this room and double especially my desk. Got it?"

"Got it."

"Good."

"Thanks, son."

"I must be mad," he says, reaching down for his iPad. Instead he grabs the handle of a solid wooden case containing Wenna's ancient sewing machine. He drops it back on the floor with a thump.

She cries out, "Careful with that."

"Jesus, Mam! Nearly wrenched my arm off."

"That's a genuine Singer."

"Oh, yeah, which one… Pavarotti or Demis Roussos?" He surveys the room, trying to fix in his mind every single item that isn't nailed down. "Remember, behave."

Denny retrieves his iPad and leaves. Wenna immediately steps into the no-go area of his living room. She deliberately blows smoke round the room, flicks switches on and off, then picks up a weighty bookend in the shape of a chess king, sending a row of neatly ordered books tumbling. She starts pushing buttons on her phone as she makes her way over to Denny's forbidden desk.

In her car parked on the High Street, Fiona waits for Max across the road from a bank. Through the window she sees him sitting opposite the manager, each dressed in the suit-and-tie uniform that serves as a pass to the world of finance. It's clear the manager is doing most of the talking. Max nods, shakes his head, and tries to interrupt the monolog. The manager finally shoves a sheaf of papers toward him.

Fiona feels a pang of pity as Max gets down on his knees, clasping his hands in a begging gesture. Before she can run over to save him, the manager hastily goes around the desk to pull Max to his feet. He says something, holds up four fingers, and Max embraces him. The Bank Manager accompanies him to the door, watching him cross the road to join Fiona.

She opens the passenger door as he declares triumphantly, "Stay of execution! Four weeks!"

Back at Falcon Lodge, Jo leads a faltering Brynthila up to the turret. "Are you feeling any better?"

"Faint."

Jo is trying to understand. "You mean swoon?"

"No... I am faint." Brynthila fades away, then back. "Low energy level." Jo tries to hide her complete shock.

"Oh... That's... not good. You know, I'm sure you'd feel so much better back in the game. You need restoration."

"Denny... I need Denny."

"Denny's not here." Jo races through possibilities. "No... he's... he's in the game. Didn't I tell you?"

"In the game?"

"Yes. You think you're the only one who can pop in and out of the game? Denny does it all the time. He's an expert. A regular game popper-in-and-outer." She hopes this will convince her, but Brynthila's still wary.

"I've never seen him."

"No... No?... Ah, no. That's because he's so good at it. You'll meet him on Level 12. That's where he usually hangs out."

"Level 12? I've only reached Level 3."

"Exactly. Ergo...?"

"Ergo," says Brynthila with a sigh of resignation, "I need to get back in the game."

Which is what Jo has been waiting to hear. Brynthila gets into business mode, but her bouts of transparency are becoming more frequent. They slow her down, her speech starts to slur.

"Where's the Mober... the Momo ...Motherboard?"

"Oh, she's in there somewhere," Jo says. "You'll find her."

Brynthila positions herself in front of the really huge monitor with the really huge hole. She clicks her fingers as though she's a surgeon requesting operating equipment. "Soldering iron."

Jo places the iron in Brynthila's outstretched hand and watches her crawl through the hole head first, leaving her posterior sticking out. She calls back to Jo. "We have to close up the cyber-synaptic circuit gaps."

"Cyber-synwhat?! Where did you learn all this geek talk all of a sudden?"

Brynthila pulls her head out for a moment. "Your pet."

"The dog? Lovelace taught you to ..."

"Not her, the other one ... the one you call Kurt."

"You can understand what Kurt says?" Somehow Jo finds this even more surprising than a talking dog.

Brynthila explains, "It was in one of his books. I ate it. Plug in the iron."

Jo would love to discover the intricacies of such a bizarre pedagogical process, but she knows the priority at the moment is to make progress on the game. And that means getting Brynthila safely back inside.

Jo switches on the soldering iron watching its red light glow in Brynthila's hand. As she crawls head first into the huge monitor again, she calls back, "Plug in the plasma screen while I check the chipset strips." Jo obeys, connecting her perky modern plasma screen to the computer's central processing unit. Now she can see Brynthila's digital top half on the screen, while her real world bottom sticks out of the other monitor.

"How's the dielectric layer on that thing?" Brynthila's voice is now coming from the speakers on the plasma screen. Jo doesn't have a clue about such hardware intricacies. "Well, if you mean whether I can see you or not... yes. I can." And, as Brynthila adjusts and replaces some of the tiny electronic components, her lower half gradually fades away completely.

Finally, Jo can't restrain a whoop of delight as Brynthila is completely restored in digital form on the plasma screen. "Well, I don't know what you did or how you did it, but... you did it! I'd say we're a jolly good team."

Brynthila, her energy levels back at full strength, basks in Jo's compliment. She's met this fiercest of her challenges thus far. "Onwards," she declares. "To level 12. And beyond!"

Under her breath Jo murmurs, "Eventually."

Chapter 10

Denny has joined Max in his office. They're strategy planning, exploring next steps, examining some of Brynthila's new outfits. Max strides round the office in full flow. "That's right, dude, a photo shoot. For the money boys in China. It'll be glitzy. It'll be glammy. It'll …"

"…cost a fortune!" Denny interrupts. "These supermodels don't get out of bed for less than ten K."

"Sleepy easy."

"Can you afford that? Seriously?"

"I meant the models can sleepy easy. We don't need them. New talent, dude. That's what I'm after. Natural beauties who've never held a pay cheque with five zeros at the end. And fingers crossed never will."

Max pauses at his desk and sits. Denny's uneasy. "Is there a problem, Max? Never known you to be short of the readies."

"No… well, most of my reserves are in Ethelreds."

"Ethelreds?"

"The Unreadies. Tied up. Bit short on the day-to-days, like the photo shoot and the… uhm, the rent."

Denny can't tell whether he's joking. "Long as me and Jo get paid, eh?" he chuckles. But Max doesn't reply. "Max?"

And there comes that Checkman smile. "Dude… how could you doubt it? Bank manager loves me." He flips open a ledger sheet, but on checking the balance, he decides not to share it with Denny. "That other girl," he asks, " she won't want paying, will she?"

"What other girl?"

"That loony-tune who thinks she actually is Brynthila."

"Oh, her. No problemo. Not that I've actually seen her lately, but I'm sure …"

"Because she's part of the plan." Max's desktop computer signals a new eMail. He turns the screen toward Denny. "Look. Those Chinese dudes are on my back. They need some art for the investors."

Denny's still not clear. "Art?"

"Not your kind of art. Photos. For publicity. Real live people wearing game costumes."

Denny asks, "What about the Games Fair?"

"Yes, right, that's still on. But we're going global. Thing is… some of the globals won't make it to the UK. We've got to deliver! Make them part of it. No ifs, ands, or buts. They're squeezing me where it hurts, grinding me hard. Literally. Well, no, not literally. But you get the picture."

Unfortunately, Denny does get that picture, but wishes he hadn't. Max continues, "So, let's do it. Quick and cheap. Double quick, treble cheap. Ask Jo to knock together some costumes."

"You are joking, right?"

"What? She's a girl, isn't she?"

Even Denny wouldn't venture such misogyny. "I'm not sure there is a crochet chromosome," he says. But he tries Jo's number, only to find she still hasn't plugged the handset into the base unit.

"Well, get over there. Pronto Tonto!"

"Actually," says Denny, "I've just had one of those save-the-day ideas! Ring you later."

Up in the turret, Jo's hopeful as she busily taps out lines of code. From time to time she glances at the plasma screen, where DigiBrynthila admires herself in her Magic Mirror. She presses a button on the mirror to scroll through a menu-loop of hairstyle and colour changes. Upswept redhead. Auburn with plaits. A severe black bob.

"There!" Jo declares. "I've programmed in a secret passage which lets you jump two levels." Brynthila is too absorbed in her image to listen. And Jo has failed to mention that this new 'short cut' actually leads back two levels. "It'll take some finding though. If you're up to it. Brynthila?"

But the Princess is still primping. "Hmm?"

"Feeling weak?" asks Jo.

"What thinkst thou? Should I dare a more golden look. For Denny. Men can never resist blondes."

"Is that so?"

"Yes, in my experience."

"You're a month old, how much experience have you had?" Jo shuffles her desk chair to peer into Brynthila's world.

"You don't know everything I get up to in here."

"You're worse than Denny."

"Well… Prince Denny likes blondes. You might look passing fair yourself with the golden touch."

Jo fluffs up her curly locks. She decides to share a detail. "Actually, I used to be blonde. When I was three."

Brynthila peers directly into Jo's face. "Was that before a mouse died on your head, thou lumpish gudgeon?"

Jo is genuinely shocked. "That's… not very nice. In fact, it's quite hurtful. I'm surprised at you. Where did you get that from… I never programmed in those insults."

Brynthila looks away in embarrassment. "I… I filtered some phrases from the Foul Fishes of Flooded Flodden."

"Well," says Jo, "it's not very Princess-like."

"I crave pardon." Brynthila's apology lacks sincerity. "But, 'tis true e'en so, that your blood is not royal. Like Prince Denny and myself."

Of course, Jo is aware she's conversing with an algorithmic construct, yet she can't resist some one-upping. "Technically," she says, "you don't have any blood at all." She positions the computer mouse over a digital suit of armour, and with one click sends it crashing to the floor, narrowly missing Brynthila.

"Oops! My bad."

Over at Denny's flat, the chug-chug drum-and-bass doesn't quite drown out the doorbell. Wenna opens the door to a group of middle-aged hippies. She greets them warmly, welcoming them inside, where a party is in full swing. "Drinks in the kitchen, but donations always welcome," she announces, grabbing a wine bottle from one of the guests.

Little does she know her party's about to be pooped.

Elaine manoeuvres the Mercedes to the main road into London. In the passenger seat her husband Jonathan reaches over a tanned hand to cover hers. "Good to be back," he says.

She raises his hand to her lips before changing gear. "Let's hope you don't have to zip off again so quickly this time."

"Goes with the territory," says Jonathan.

ScreenSaver!

"I know, darling. But indulge me while I try to take your mind off business. I've booked our table at Claridges."

Jonathan smiles his approval. "Excellent! Long as we don't have to order anything with chilies. Or banku! Have I told you about banku?"

Now that Brynthila's been safely contained in digital form, Jo consults a check-list of deadlines pinned up on the cork-board above her desk. She picks up the phone to ring Denny, notices the charging light is flashing, so she plugs it into the base unit. While she's waiting, she decides to accept Brynthila's golden hair challenge. Her mission is clear.

Trawling through her memory bank, Jo recalls her mother's hair-dye surprise. It was strictly a do-it-yourself procedure, and Elaine had roped in teen-aged Jo to help deliver a charity fund-raiser with a popular theme. Her former experience as junior partner in a corporate events company assured success. Coordinating with the run-up to the Oscars, everyone loved her idea for a movie-themed costume party - come as your favourite film. Her father was away on business as usual, but with Osborne, Jo, and even little Robby as assistants, they'd transformed the Long Gallery into a mock-film studio. Elaine had also transformed herself from top to toe, and was a big hit as the film *Goldfinger*.

Jo recalls being enchanted at her mother's golden locks. It was the same feeling she got when Denny first showed her the prototype sketches for Brynthila. Yet another reminder that whatever their personal differences, she and Denny are in synch professionally.

She enters her mother's copious marbled bathroom, hoping the mirrored cabinet might contain something useful in the dye department. But at first glance, there's nothing resembling hair colour. Unwilling to give up and, after a further search through a small set of drawers, she finds a likely-looking box tucked away at the back. The close-up photo on the label seems the perfect shade of burnished gold. Reading quickly through the instructions, Jo discovers its 'best before' date is out by several years. Hmm, would this stuff really go off? she wonders. She decides to risk it, and heads downstairs for some necessary equipment.

Hearing unexpected activity in the kitchen, Osborne appears in the doorway. He looks no worse for wear after his disco night out, and offers to help. She can easily manage her raid through the kitchen cupboards, but requests that for the next hour or so she mustn't be disturbed.

About half an hour later, back in her own en suite, Jo surveys the sink surround on which she's placed a mixing bowl and stirring stick, a vial of chemical re-agent, kitchen timer, and a lidded container of cotton-wool pads. Her mirrored reflection reveals shoulders draped in an old towel, hairline glistening with petroleum jelly, and head swathed in another huge towel. She lifts a vinyl-gloved hand to dab at a rogue dot of dye on her forehead. The timer ticks down. Just another ten minutes and her curls will rival Brynthila's.

Meanwhile, Denny's convertible pulls up outside his flat. He hears music blaring. It's coming from an open window on the ground floor. It's his open window! He fears the worst, and as soon as he lets himself in, his worst fears are met. In spades!

The room seethes like a sleazy disco perfumed with pot and the tang of half-naked bodies. The music could drown out a jet engine. A puddle of wine fills a dent in Denny's leather sofa. "Mam!" he bellows. And "Mam!" again. Finally, he strides over to the cassette deck and turns off the music. The hubbub fades away. "Out! Everyone ... O... U...T!" The hippies stop dancing. They stop eating and drinking and smoking and toking. A chastened yet defiant Wenna tries to hide herself among the party-leavers. "No, Mam, not you," Denny pulls her out of the crowd.

"Don't hate me, son," she pleads. "It was just ..."

"Oh, nevermind all that. Grab your sewing machine and come with me."

Over at Falcon Lodge, a bloodcurdling scream jolts Osborne from his final preparations for Jonathan's homecoming. The scream definitely comes from Jo's turret room, and he races upstairs two at a time.

He knocks discreetly at the door, but is greeted by a long wail. "Please, Miss. Josephine. Open the door."

"Go away! I want to die!"

"Now, you know I'm not going away. I'm opening the door and I'm coming in. Whatever it is, we can fix it." He inches the door open and looks around. The room is empty, but suddenly Jo rushes out of the ensuite and buries her head against Osborne's chest. He gives her a paternal pat of reassurance.

"What am I going to do?" she sobs.

Osborne holds her at arm's length and finally sees the problem. It's as clear as the tangled hair on her head. Which is a match for the shade of electric green swirling around Arctic skies during the Aurora Borealis. Although Osborne and Leesa never had children of their own, over his years of service he's grown to care very much for Jo and her brother Robert. There's no way he'd let even a sliver of a snigger or a smile betray how ridiculous she looks.

Unseen by them both, DigiBrynthila stares at them from the monitor, visibly shocked at Jo's transformation.

Seated opposite each other at their favourite balcony table, Elaine is savouring her halibut in pine, while Jonathan smothers a forkful of Galloway beef in onion sauce. "This was a great idea, darling," he says. "Perfect."

She beams, loving to get things right. "I'm glad. You deserve some de-stress time. Fancy a pudding? Or some cheese?"

Quite frankly, Denny's afraid to trust Wenna to wait in the car, which is not a very nice thing to admit about one's mother... but it's true. So he insists she accompany him to Max's High Street office. Max himself is on a business call, but it's Fiona Denny needs to see.

He introduces her to Wenna and asks if Max will give her some time off. "Why?" asks Fiona.

"You know those costumes for the photo shoot? Well, Wenna just needs a hand getting some fabric. Apparently, she's a dream on her Singer."

"That sounds a bit rude," says Fiona with a chuckle. Wenna joins her with a cackle.

"I'd go myself, but gotta nip over to Jo's."

"Not to worry, I know just the place."

"Cool!" says Denny. "I've got the sewing machine."

"I'll just let Max know. What do you think we'll need… couple of hours?"

Wenna has been uncharacteristically quiet. She'd never admit it to him, but she's impressed by this business niche Denny has found for himself. Now, how can she turn that to her advantage?

"Mam?" he asks.

"What? Oh, yes, that should do it."

"I'd better hit the road," says Denny. "Don't forget your credit card… and, keep her with you at all times!" he warns.

Back in the turret ensuite at Falcon Lodge, Osborne holds a hand-mirror to help Jo cut off her garish curls. He tries to bolster her dwindling confidence. "It's no use," she moans, "by the time this grows out I'll be a pensioner!"

"Don't be daft, this could be a good look."

"Oh, I don't know… what about a wig?"

"Very trendy, actually. Neo-punk."

"You think? You keep up with the punk scene, do you?"

"You'd be surprised," he counters.

Jo holds up the hand mirror to check the back of her head. Osborne says, "Here, give me the scissors, you missed a bit." He sees Jo is still sulking. "By the way, " he says casually. "If you're still looking for a music track, I just might be able to help." And that definitely puts a smile on Jo's face.

Over coffee, Elaine is still determined to cater to Jonathan's every whim. But she's distracted by thoughts of her breakfast encounter with Brynthila. She knows what she saw, or more precisely, what she didn't see. But she couldn't have seen it, because that would have been impossible. So, she must have imagined it. I mean, she asks herself, how can a person just vanish. Poof! Just like that? And then re-appear. Just like that. Suddenly, she's aware that Jonathan has asked her a question.

"Pardon, darling. Miles away."

"No, just saying I got Robert's letter. Did he tell you he wants me to take him on a wild-life safari."

"Yes… well, cameras, though, not big-game rifles. Actually, I'd love introduce him to photography. He's always been fascinated by my dark room. Of course, that might just be because he thinks it's very Harry Potter to be able to see in the dark."

"Could do worse. It was good enough for that Anthony Armstrong-Thingy."

"What?" she giggles, "you think he'd have a chance with little Princess Charlotte." She's pleased to see Jonathan relaxing. "Actually, he's becoming quite the environmentalist. Gets it from Jo, I think. Well, we all like animals, don't we?" Jonathan's non-committal 'hmmph' doesn't escape Elaine's notice. Keep it light, she reminds herself. "And we'll all need to be bright and shiny a week next Saturday." Elaine can tell he needs a prompt. "You remember… Robert's sports day."

"Of course, of course. Can't miss that!"

She pats her tummy. "Delicious… I won't need to eat for a week! Fancy a film, darling? Or …"

"Well, I just have to pop into the office," he says over Elaine's mock groan, "and then, honestly," he squeezes her hand affectionately, "can't wait to get home."

They're both trying hard to repress the memory of the year their son embarrassed himself in the egg and spoon relay. "Yes, home's best!" Elaine agrees. "He's developing into a fine all-rounder, is Robert. He'll do us proud."

"I'm sure he will." They pause as the vigilant waiter tops up their coffee. Jonathan asks for the bill, then lifts his cup in a toast. "To our all-rounder. It was funny, though," he chuckles. Elaine knows exactly what he means. "Balancing the spoon on the egg."

Elaine shares the smile. "But don't you dare say anything. That was yonks ago."

"'Course not. And how's our Princess?"

Elaine is relieved Jonathan's changed the subject so deftly. "You know Jo. Since she's on that new project with Denny, she spends her life in that tower. Not that she's normally a social butterfly. Unless you count going on demos to protect the environment."

Jonathan's face threatens to glower. "Hm, not sure I do. Probably just teen-age rebellion."

"Darling, she's twenty-two! Well, nearly twenty-three. Mind of her own."

"I still say it's about time she focused on something bigger than the planet." Elaine giggles, then sees it wasn't a joke. Jonathan realises what he's said. "No, I just mean… you know, place of her own, match, hatch, dispatch."

"I suppose Denny's the closest thing she's got to a friend."

"What do we know about his people?"

Elaine's slightly taken aback. "Jonathan!" He shrugs. "I'm not sure he has 'people'… well not like you mean. Mind you, I don't think we need worry. She doesn't much like him except for the work they're doing. Whatever that is! Whenever she tries to explain it to me, it all sounds like a foreign language!"

"He's certainly a clever lad, I'll give him that. I just wish he was, you know, more 'our sort'."

"Well, darling, I wasn't exactly 'your sort' when we met."

For just a mini-moment, Jonathan looks a bit chastened. Then he puts on a voice like one of those old-fashioned cinema villains; he twirls imaginary moustaches. "That's right, my pretty, and don't you forget it! I dragged you out of the gutter and I can toss you back whenever I fancy!"

Elaine plays along, tugging an imaginary forelock. "Yes, master. I am not worthy, master."

And when the waiter appears with the bill, they're both giggling like stoned teens.

At Falcon Lodge, Denny lugs the sewing machine over to the turret entrance and sets it down. The door is ajar, so, unsure of the protocol, he nudges it open and peeks in. "Hello?" he enquires of the air, and then "Hello" he says a bit louder.

Osborne has been waiting for him.

"Well, well, if it isn't Disco Ozzie!" Denny indicates the sewing machine. "You couldn't bring that up for us, could you." Osborne hefts the heavy case, and quickly sets it down again.

"Is Jo up there?" asks Denny.

"It's… uhm… not the propitious moment, sir."

"How do you do that?"

"Sir?"

"You know, come mid-night you turn into Mr Tight-leather Trendy, and next morning you develop 'turret's syndrome' and back you crawl into the 18th century?"

From upstairs, Jo calls down, "Who is it, Osborne?"

Denny ignores Osborne's protestations and bounds up to meet Jo. She clutches a small damp towel around her head. It's just about hiding most of her hair, but not quite keeping her despair in check.

"Oh, I wasn't expecting you."

"Yeah, I'm like the Spanish Inquisition. What happened to your hair? All cut off? Come on, don't be shy, let's have a look."

Before Jo can stop him, Denny snatches at the towel. He tries to joke away his shock at the sight of her bright green hair. "Well… that's an… interesting look. What do you call it, Zombie Punk?"

Jo grabs back the towel and retreats to her room in a huff, followed by a very apologetic Denny.

"No, really. It's not funny. Not funny at all." Denny looks around for Brynthila. "Where is she?"

"Oh, she's here all right."

Denny scours the room. "Can't see her."

"Can't you?"

He plugs his memory stick into the USB port of Jo's computer. The monitor displays Brynthila's tower room, her Magic Mirror, but no sign of their Princess.

"Anyway, I was talking to Max and..." He clicks on a drop-down menu triggering a scrolling array of costumes across the bottom of the screen. "About costumes."

Jo is relieved to be distracted from the disaster on her head. "What about costumes?"

"Right. We were talking, me and Max... and there's a part of him that thinks the outfits should be... how can I put this... briefer."

"Now which part would that be, I wonder?"

Denny scrolls the images back and forth. "Where's that cave girl get-up?"

As he presses keys, DigiBrynthila strides into her onscreen tower room, and with each key option, her costume changes. Finally Denny pauses on a fur bikini, but he's so engrossed it takes him a minute to register that Brynthila is back in the game, and modelling the various outfits.

"There," he says. "See? Very Raquel Welch. Very authentic."

"Authentic to what? Since when is she from the stone age?"

They're interrupted by Brynthila's voice on the screen. "Prince Denny, my liege! 'Tis you! Have I found the Portal to Level 12? Is that wherefore I need such furry nether garments?"

Denny stares at DigiBrynthila as the penny drops.

ScreenSaver!

Jo wrests control of the mouse, and scrolls through more clothing options. She tries to reassure Brynthila. "No, we have something else for you. Look. Now you won't freeze in the Ice Field of Farrah."

Like an arctic explorer, Brynthila is now clad in a thick padded tunic and leggings. On her head a fur-trimmed helmet completely covers her face. She tries to speak, but her voice is muffled and incomprehensible.

"Ta-dah!" says Jo, as Denny stares in disbelief.

"You did it! You put her back in there! She's not here because... she's... there."

"Well done, Sherlock."

"You got her back inside!"

"I thought that was the idea."

Denny's trying to understand the implications. "No... I mean... well, yes, it was, but..."

"Oh, don't bother to thank me."

"No... but we need the other one out here. The real one. The uhm, the real unreal one. For the photo shoot."

"What photo shoot?"

"You... you can get her out again? Can't you?"

"Quite... possibly."

Denny tries his authoritative best. "Get her back out here! Now!"

Jo recognises his frustration. She tries to lighten the mood with a film impression. "I'm afraid I can't do that, Dave." She waits for some recognition. She tries again. "Open the pod bay door, Dave."

Denny stares at her as though she's lost her mind. Then he bursts out laughing. "Oh, right! I get it! *2001: A Space Odyssey.* Very good." Brynthila mumbles loudly from the monitor. Which focuses the attention of their current dilemma.

Jo repeats, "What photo shoot?"

Elaine and Jonathan are on their way home with full tummies. She's been trying to bring him up to speed on their domestic life, just the little random things not included in their eMail messages and phone calls. He's listening, but jet lag is creeping up on him.

"Actually, darling, it looks like she has got a new friend," Elaine says, wondering how to explain the mysterious Brynthila.

"Oh yes? Another geek, is she?"

"There's definitely something… odd about her, but actually, they couldn't be more different."

The car stops at a red light on the High Street. Jonathan's fighting sleep.

"You'll meet her," says Elaine. "Friend of Denny's. Long story."

Jonathan's head droops, then bumps back up. He surveys the High Street. "Hm, that Denny… he's a… thieving dogoody bastard!"

"Who, Denny?!" Elaine's shocked. "What are you talking about?"

Suddenly wide awake, Jonathan points up at the building where Max has his office. "No, not him. See that, up there? Our client was all set to redevelop. Entire block. Great deal. Then one of the tenants - him, that guy up there - started up some petition. Save Our High Street or some such. What's worse, he's way behind with his rent. About as much head for business as a duck-billed platypus up a sand dune! Ruddy Max Checkman!"

Elaine gazes up at the building. Framed in the window Max is staring out into space. The light changes and the Merc drives off. Jonathan's asleep before it gets to the end of the High Street.

Chapter 11

Osborne's waiting at the main entrance of Falcon Lodge as Elaine pulls the car up. "Welcome home, sir, madam," he says. They exchange the expected polite chit-chat, while Osborne retrieves Jonathan's stylish valise from the boot. Elaine hands him the car keys, and the couple go inside.

When she sees her husband heading for his home office, she says, "Don't you want to take a little nap?"

"Ten minutes," he promises. "Just ten minutes."

She gives him a quick kiss. "Obsessed… you're obsessed!"

Once inside, Jonathan pours himself a drink and settles into the soft-leather luxury of his desk chair. He logs into his cyberchess program with his username 'Lord Cassemar,' to find an eMail from 'Jazz Fiend.' He's completely unaware that his opponent is actually Denny.

Jonathan studies the board, impressed by the latest move. So, Mister Jazz Fiend, he thinks. The gloves are off!

Upstairs, Denny and Jo are still sorting through costume designs on the computer. Brynthila watches them from inside the game. Denny wants to know which ones they can get ready for the photo shoot? The simplest? The quickest? The cheapest?

"Cheapest?" asks Jo. "He spends pound notes that haven't even been printed yet. Cheap is hardly Max's style."

"You know Max. All style, no substance. Well… apparently just at the moment there's a distinct lack of substance in the wallet department."

"You're double joking! He's in cash flow hell, and he expects us to bail him out? No way, José."

"Yeah, still, not to worry. Just get her back out here. I mean, Brynthila would even look sexy in a sack." Brynthila beams at the compliment. She waves frantically to Denny, and bangs on the monitor from the inside. "Can you sew a sack?" he continues.

Jo's overcome with suspicion. "Or am I being stitched up? I do not do sewing."

Brynthila's still waving. "Let me out!" Her digital voice is filtered and thin.

"Shut up, you!" Jo shouts at Brynthila. She's beyond fed up. This whole thing is getting way out of hand. Typical Denny is still flirting with an animated algorithm. And, when she reaches a hand up to her head, the shame of her green hair is too much. "Tell you what, Mister Arts and Crafts, how's about you do the sewing … I've still got masses of code to write."

"Oh, come on, Jo… you're not serious."

"I know someone whose idea of hard work is fiddling around with cyber images, can't appreciate the brain power needed to devise precise calcula…"

Denny cuts her off. "Yeah, with all that brain power, no wonder you had to chop your hair off or there wouldn't be room left under your cycle helmet. Get over yourself."

"How about you get over your libido before you trip on it. Apart from coding, lest we forget, I'm meant to record voice-overs for the game, and make a stab at some gob-stopping fx, let alone grab some sleep along the way."

"Well boo-bloody-hoo! It's a wonder you've got any time left to save the planet!"

Brynthila's still waving, but Denny ignores her and considers his options. "Right! I'll find my own model, if I have to audition every blonde in the county!"

ScreenSaver!

"I thought you already had!"

Denny storms out, slamming the door. Jo goes to the blowup of Denny and punches it, sending it flying. She catches her image in the mirror… her green disaster. She bursts into tears. Brynthila can't help feeling sorry for her. She has no idea she's been programmed for that. Come to think of it, neither has Jo.

As Denny rushes downstairs, he almost collides with Jonathan heading up. Denny's phone rings with its jazz ringtone, which Jonathan recognises straightaway. "Ella! *Stompin At The Savoy*." "Yes! The Birthday Concert. Great album." They listen, each tapping a foot to the beat.

"I was lucky enough to see her at the Royal Albert Hall. Before she died."

Jonathan and Denny pause for a brief a bonding moment. Denny would love to hear more, but his phone's still ringing. He answers. "Max!" he says, as Jonathan does a double-take at the name. "Yes, everything's just fine," he continues with barely repressed anger. "Everything's hunky- *gwaedlyd*-dory!"

Jonathan isn't familiar with the Welsh language, but he can tell something's very wrong. He continues upstairs while Denny heads for his convertible and speeds off. Jonathan leans against the doorjamb of the turret room, watching Jo type code into the computer. She's aware of a presence, but assumes it's Denny. An apology would be too much to hope for. She glances around.

"Daddy!" And she bursts into tears.

Jonathan gives her a big hug. "Looks like quite a rough day at the office." He runs a flat palm across her bright green head. "I bumped into Denny on the way up."

Jo would like to tell her father everything, but it all gets tangled up in her mind. Instead, what emerges are more sobs and a strangled "Don't tell Mummy."

Jonathan says, "It's not so bad, Princess. The hair. It'll grow back." He's diverted by the computer screen where Brynthila is battling Lord Cassemar. "Ooh, that looks painful! Who's he?"

"The evil Lord Cassemar. Anagram of …"

"Massacre. I get it. How did you come up with the name?"

"Dunno," she sniffs. "Denny's idea." Jo hates having to credit him with anything at the moment.

Jonathan gives her a paternal hug. "Actually, he's quite a clever lad."

Some time later, Jo, scissors in hand, stands in front of the full-length cheval mirror, trying to shape her hair into something she thinks might be trendy. It is not good. DigiBrynthila giggles from the computer screen.

"Oh, ha-flipping-ha!" says Jo, bravely trying to recover some dignity.

Brynthila tries to be sympathetic. "It's… well, it's a definite improvement." But her smirk gives her away. "An improvement on the Monster From The Green Lagoon."

Jo types furiously on the computer keyboard. "Okay, Miss Perfect, let's see how you like it!"

When the monitor clears, DigiBrynth is completely bald. She peers at herself in her magic mirror, feels her head, whimpers and hides behind the wall tapestry. Jo wishes she could savour the sweetness of vengeance, but she's now more depressed than ever.

A tentative knock on the door, and Fiona walks in with a carrier bag stuffed full of fabric. She's followed by Denny and his mother. Wenna spots her sewing machine on Jo's desk and opens the case. She blows out cigarette smoke followed by a racking cough, and her hair is wilder than ever. On the screen, Brynthila peeks from behind the tapestry, sees the Wenna-dragon and cries out in fear.

Wenna gives Jo the once-over. "Loving the hair, petal."

Jo deliberately hides the monitor from Denny, and rounds on him, partly to drown out Brynthila's cry. She gestures toward Wenna. "This is your idea of a model? Uhm… no offence, Miss… Denny, aren't you going to introduce …"

He starts to reply, "She's my mo … "

Wenna interrupts in her heavy Welsh accent. "Hello, petal. I'm Wenna. You need some sewing, is it?"

She grabs the bag of cloth from Fiona, opens the sewing machine, whips out a tape measure and starts to drape fabric around Jo's body. Fiona, usually Captain Control, is rendered speechless as the turret room fills like a bottle with the stream of visitors. She feels her elbow jostled as Kurt pushes past. He scrabbles round Jo's desk, searching for something through the mess. Jo replies as his excited, incoherent mumbles acquire increasing urgency.

"The van? Sure. Take it."

Kurt presses her for more. Only the phrase mixer-desk is audible. Jo's baffled. "Seriously? You just want to give me that mixing-desk I've been drooling over? Why? Where are you off to? … For how long?! What … Of course I like Lovelace, why? … No, I don't think that's a good idea …" Jo looks vaguely around for the dog. "… because my parents… "

And right on cue, a flustered Jonathan enters, followed by Elaine. Confusion not only reigns, it's taken up residence and it budgeth not, stubborn as a mule and twice on Sunday.

"Whose is that dog in my office? He's chewed right through my stress ball!"

"Shouldn't he be at the end of a lead?" asks Elaine timidly.

"... or a noose?" whispers Denny.

Studying the chaos, DigiBrynthila peers surreptitiously from behind her tapestry. Wenna catches a glimpse of her and approaches close to the screen. She blows a plume of cigarette smoke toward her. Brynthila coughs and hastily retreats behind a pillar, peering into the room. With a cheery bark, Lovelace bounds in, almost restrained by Osborne, holding on to her collar. "I've got him, Madam." But he's spoken too soon as Lovelace breaks free, accidentally knocking Osborne to the floor. He stands up, right next to Kurt. Osborne sniffs discreetly but disapprovingly. It's part snobbery, part Kurt's lack of personal hygiene. And he's smelled a lot of that in his day. Keeping his promise to Jo, he hands Kurt the van keys.

"The keys to your... er... conveyance, sir."

Everyone's jam packed and crammed in. Fans of the Marx Brothers in *A Night At The Opera* will have some idea of the invasion. But no one is ordering any hard-boiled eggs!

Lovelace is barking around Denny, who attempts to gently move her away with his leg. Kick? Did I say kick? No, of course not. Just a slight foot-shove. Brynthila notices, conflicted and confused. She's pledged to save her Prince, but she loves the dog. Denny turns to Jo. While unseen in the melee, Brynthila takes an executive decision. *Et voila*!

Denny's still trying to become dog free. "Can't anyone control this... arghhhh!"

Denny points, jabbing the air in the direction of the newly materialised bald Brynthila. His strange gargled scream silences everyone in the room. They all turn to stare, baffled by Brynthila's sudden appearance from nowhere. Lovelace affectionately licks her hand, then settles loyally at Wenna's feet. Denny freaks in grand style. He can barely speak as he confronts Jo.

"What did... you!... Her... What have you done to her?!"

Jo is contrite, murmuring. "She laughed at my hair ..."

"Yeah, well, your hair is hysterically funny." He points to Brynthila's bald head. "This... this is bloody serious!"

Denny tries to placate Brynthila. "No probs. We'll get you sorted in plenty of time for Max's photo shoot. Won't we!?" he challenges Jo with a slicing gesture across his throat. "Or else it'll be Game Over!"

But Jo's attention is on Kurt, about to head downstairs. "Kurt! Wait! What about the dog?"

He shrugs and mutters. Jo tries to contain her shock. How many of these can she take in one day? "Borders?" she parrots. "What borders? ... Morocco?! You're moving to Mor ..."

Wenna's quick as a whip. She chirps up a perfect solution. "No worries, petal. Denny and I will have him."

"Oh, no you don't, Mam!" he explodes. "One flea-ridden mongrel in the flat is plenty." Wenna tries not to show how hurt she is.

The room goes quiet. Everyone wants to help, but no one knows how. It's clear Denny and Jo need to work something out, but what about her green head... and that bald woman? This would be the perfect time for a soundtrack sting for a cliffhanger announcement. You know... Dah-dah-DUM! Tune in tomorrow for the next exciting episode of...

Jonathan takes some kind of charge. He starts ushering Elaine, Kurt and Osborne out. Wenna remains stubbornly ensconced at the sewing machine, Lovelace curled up at her feet. But Jonathan shoos the dog out and Wenna can only follow.

Elaine just wants Jo to be happy and senses this isn't the time to protect her daughter with platitudes. She stops Jonathan on the landing outside the turret room. She's thinking laterally, and suggests a very different solution. "What if we invite him to join us for Robert's sports day?"

"Because...?"

"Oh, I don't know. It just might... help smooth out some rough edges. Just a feeling."

Over the years of their marriage, Jonathan's learned to trust his wife's instincts. And so, as the others parade downstairs, he waylays Denny on the landing with the unexpected invitation. "Yes, true, it's a family occasion, but we'd all like you to come."

Denny's not so sure. "Even Jo?"

Jonathan drapes an arm around Denny's shoulder. "Oh, she'll come 'round. You'll see."

"Well, thanks, but... "

"We always have a good time. Osborne packs quite a mean picnic. Very good school, lots to do. Cross-country, basketball... chess club," he says pointedly. "Besides, it's jolly good for contacts. Must cultivate contacts, old chap!" This is such an alien world for Denny. "Yes," continues Jonathan, 'fiendishly' good chess team. Very 'jazzy.' They'll really 'massacre' you. Well, think about it," he says, following Elaine up to the master bedroom.

Oh, wow, thinks Denny. He turns to see Jo's been watching from the doorway. "I get it!"

"Yes, he's big on anagrams. Massacre? Cassemar?"

"No way! Cyberchess! That's what he's been trying to tell me."

Jo returns to her room. "For such a clever lad, you can be so dim, sometimes."

Denny follows her inside, confused and desperate. "Jo, I'm begging you. Max is going to murder us! Rethatch Brynthila! She looks like Captain Jean-Luc Picard from *Star Trek*!"

"I'll see what I can do" Jo still isn't ready for total forgiveness. "But just now, I need some peace and quiet."

Denny packs the sewing machine into its carrying case. "Okay, okay, we'll re-locate the costume department to my flat, and…" He hears barking and struggles downstairs with the heavy machine, calling down to his mother. "Mam! Let that dog go!"

Brynthila shyly emerges from her dark corner. Jo whispers, "So, found the secret passageway, have you?"

Brynthila nods, super pleased with herself. "Well, It was a bit obvious, if I may say so. I was expecting a true challenge."

"Were you now."

"What's my reward?" asks Brynthila.

"My eternal admiration and respect." But that winged irony flies right over her bald head.

A lightning bolt cracks raggedly across the sky just outside the turret window. Jo launches into a warning about the perils of leaving and re-entering the game. She aims the words straight at Brynthila's face. As Jo acquires authority over her creation, Brynthila sees her surrounded by a multi- coloured aura. Jo finally pauses for breath, just as a loud thunder clap echoes through the room. Ooh! Spooky!

Jo continues. "And here's something to ponder, Princess Genius… each time you escape you lose health points, and when you go back inside to top up from the Well of Wellness, you drop back a level. And… I hope you're listening… if you do it more than three magic times… it's bye-bye Brynthila. Game Over!"

Brynthila looks shaken as Jo asks,"Do we understand each other, Madam?" Brynthila nods. "Good. Now let's see what we can do about your hair. Or lack thereof."

Some hours later ensconced in Denny's spare room, tape measure draped round her neck, Wenna bites off a stray thread and adds a finished costume to the growing pile on the bed. A handful of her hippie friends do their best to help. She beckons over a particularly burly man and measures him from crotch to ankle, with much giggling and mutual fondling. To Lovelace, everything's a game as she runs around, getting tangled up in cloth and trimming.

Meanwhile Denny-the-Grumpy is talking on the phone in front of his open laptop. He's trying to concentrate as the dog occasionally invades his space. One of Wenna's friends, wearing the head of a giant insect, attempts to steal a pen from under Denny's nose. Denny grabs it back.

"Oi, watch it, you thieving bug! ... no, not you, Max ... London? What's in London? ... The venue, yes I know. But why do I have to be there? You can manage an inspection on your own, can't you? ... Well, because we're just a bit busy. I mean, as it's a Games Fair, I thought it might be nice if we actually had a game to bring along, don't you think? ... Weeks away? Well, two and a bit, but who's counting? ... Soundtrack? Yeah, yeah Max, it's all in hand. Good luck in London."

He turns back to the motley crew of flat invaders. "Listen up, everyone" he yells. "We're on the move. Grab your stuff and come with me. Pronto Tonto!"

Back at Falcon Lodge, Brynthila and Jo stare glumly at each other. "Come on, you promised. This will only work if you're back inside the game."

"You who knows all, first I have questions. Question one: who or what is this Captain Picard?"

"Just a man. A typical man."

"A friend of Prince Denny's?"

"Quite possibly. Neither of them is who they seem." Jo returns to her computer, determined she can reverse the coding for Brynthila's appearance.

"Fair enough. Second question: why would you want to shoot at photos? And why does it mean such a lot to you?" Jo continues filling the screen with incomprehensible algorithmic figures.

She attempts an explanation, but her concentration is on her coding. "No, we don't want to shoot at photos. It's a photo-shoot because we shoot photographs with a camera. And it's important to the man who's paying for everything because it's good for advertising and promotion. Right… your hair."

"You refer to Max Checkman?"

Jo is astonished that she knows the name, let alone who he is. "How do you…?"

"Yes, I'd expect it of him. But, I must say, I didn't think Prince Denny would be so petty. After all, I'm more than just a pretty face and door knockers."

Jo looks up at her. "Door knockers?

Brynthila gestures at her bosom area. "I think that's what he called them."

"Hmm, a proto-feminist in the making. There's hope for you yet. Come on, in you go." Brynthila edges toward Jo's computer. "Can't think why he's so angry about your hair. Bald is not such a terrible look, what do you think?"

"It's a bit anachronistic." A smug Brynthila notices that Jo is newly staggered by her vocabulary. "Yes, I know… I'm working my way through the Oxford Shorter Dictionary." Casually, she fingers one of Jo's baggy cardigans, draped across the back of the desk chair.

"Impressive!" says Jo, getting anxious about the time. "Uhm… wait a minute! You're… you're not eating it, are you? The dictionary." Innocent Brynthila shakes her head no, but surreptitiously pulls a piece of paper from her mouth and smoothes it out.

"Now, please, pop back inside the game so we can grow you some hair." Jo points to the huge monitor with the huge hole that still rests on the floor.

"As you command, my lady."

"Promise?"

"Yes. But you mustn't look."

As Jo starts to say, "Why mustn't I … ?" Brynthila flings the cardigan over Jo's head.

"Question three, " she counters. "What's a promise?"

Jo snatches off the cardie, but Brynthila is nowhere to be seen. Jo looks out the open window just in time to see a flash of Brynthila's cloak disappear into the shrubbery.

"Oh, no!" she moans. "Not again!"

Chapter 12

A glass-roofed exhibition hall set back from the high street is hung with a 15 foot drop-down banner illustrated with stylised graphics of boats. Max has arrived at the cavernous London venue for an exhibitor walk through. Though the Games Fair is still some weeks away, Max feels increasingly unprepared. He tries to remember the mantras of calm he learned at his management course. But confronted by all the activity around him, everything running like clockwork, he sees how much is needed to get his stand ready in time. No wonder the guidelines have mapped out a timetable covering most of the year.

He flashes his invitation to the uniformed guard at Door B. At the sign-in table in the lobby he collects a glossy folder and a name badge which he pins to his lapel. He tries not to get distracted by the current show, Marine Matters, tempting a constant stream of punters. If he's to attract similar numbers, he'd better offer something amazing. What the brochure calls his very own USP... unique selling point.

He tries to focus on fleshing out his half-formed ideas. But in every section of the hall, scantily clad models are draped over yachts surrounded by photographers. Circulating among the crowds, a bevy of teenagers in sailor suits accost the gawpers with leaflets and free pens in a marketing push. Max drools with envy at all kinds of river craft and accessories... boats, jet skis, outboard motors, etc. Someday, he promises himself.

He consults a photocopied floor-plan on which each company stall has been designated a number. While he's trying to get his bearings, he's distracted by a succession of tannoy announcements. The sound system can't always cope with the hall's acoustics, so he just catches a snippet about a video demonstration in Conference Room B. But by the time he locates the room on the floor plan, another announcement blares out. "Anyone from GoTronics to the meeting point. GoTronics to the meeting point."

Across the hall, Max spots a handful of young men and a few women, definitely not the boating crowd. They're casually dressed, many with spiky hair and backwards baseball caps, all oozing confidence. He was once considered the boy wunderkind of the video games world, but he's feeling like an old man at the sight of these entrepreneurs who surely can't yet have reached puberty. He steers a way over to join them and discovers they're clustered around an Exhibition official, whose laminated name-tag reads Gordy.

Max catches up to the front of the queue, as they stride through the large exhibition hall, clutching their freebie folders. He introduces himself to Gordy, who leads them through the main hall, pointing out each of the allocated stands. Taking up much of the central area are two enormous platforms, one displaying a fully equipped motor boat, the other a half-size scale model of a hydrofoil.

Gordy announces those stands are reserved for two of Max's fiercest rivals. He looks around, but can't see them anywhere in the crowd. Of course not, it dawns on Max... backed by international brand names, these big boys of the games world have already been given their own private walk-through. The four-year-old who lives inside Max feels hard done by. He trails after Gordy to the far end of the vast room, hoping his Asian backers are rising high enough through the ranks to sprinkle some pixie-dust over Brynthila.

Well, well, well, speak of the devil. Look... over there. Can you see her? There, behind that pillar. Yes, it's Brynthila, trying and failing to blend in among the boat show stragglers. She's wrapped in her game cloak, its hood fastened over her bald head. She hides behind sunglasses, an inappropriate outfit which frankly defeats her purpose not to stand out. Her memory bank prompts her to emulate the undercover cops she's seen on Jo's television. Walking on tiptoe, continuously glancing round, she freezes in her tracks, then follows Max at a discreet distance.

Gordy stops the group at one of the stands, strategically placed for maximum sales advantage. He addresses a young man in the group. "That's your one there." Spying from her vantage point, Brynthila scribbles a note on her copy of the floor-plan.

Max wants to ask about his own position, but Gordy sweeps everyone further and further away into the darker recesses and outer corridors of the hall, pairing stands and people. Trying to put a brave face on it, Max smiles at a fellow exhibitor, wondering what he'd have in common with this sixth- former. But the kid's up on his protocol and flips a business card toward Max. "Phantom," he says by way of introduction, and Max reads 'The Phantom Experience' on the card.

Max fishes in his jacket pocket to reciprocate, "Checkman," he says.

Phantom studies the card, puzzled by the address. He speaks with estuary vowels. "That ain't in London, is it?"

Gordy's proximity to their exchange for some reason makes Max adopt a superior tone. "Yeah, no one who's anyone is actually in London anymore. Way I see it, dude, people can chuffing well come to me." At which point Gordy points Phantom in the direction of a small alcove lined with stands.

He consults his clipboard. "You, Checkman," says Gordy, "follow me." He leads Max through a swinging door into a badly-lit scruffy narrow corridor. The sole exhibition stand has been abandoned and is littered with left-over flyers announcing a sale on foam mooring buoys. Gordy assigns it to Max.

"These guys had to pull out early, but you get the idea. By the way," he continues before Max can challenge him, "we don't seem to have received your entry fee. Yet."

Max has to say something. "In the post, hand on heart. Look, Gordy, mate… I was promised a stand slap bang in the middle of the main hall. Wuzzup, dude?"

"Oh," says Gordy, "No one who's anyone is actually in there. They can chuffing well come to you. Dude." Max fumes silently over- hearing Gordy mumble 'wanker' as he heads back to the main hall.

Have you ever noticed that when you see someone appear in a place you don't usually associate with them, you fail to notice them? Perhaps

ScreenSaver! 141

that's why Max doesn't recognise the becloaked figure of Brynthila as she deftly turns her back to him. He presses buttons on his phone. "Fiona!" he bellows, hoping to find a way to make all this her fault.

Brynthila removes her shades, and consults the floor plan. She scribbles another note.

Inside Max's office, a flustered Fiona is on the phone, trying to talk over the noise around her. She's fighting a losing battle with the rat-a-tat of Wenna's sewing machine and Lovelace's barking. Wenna occasionally filches something from a desktop or drawer, slipping it unnoticed into her capacious sewing bag.

Fiona screams into the phone: "I don't ruddy care… just get back here, Max. Now!" She hangs up, and calls over to Wenna. "I thought you were staying with your son."

"I was. He's very busy, isn't it, so we thought you'd like the company, petal."

Fiona controls her temper. "Oh, did we!" She runs her finger down a column in Yellow Pages, then throws it aside. "What's the use! I've been through every model agency West of the Urals. No- one will do it. Well, not for what we're offering. Gotta be cash on the line."

"Cash on the line… sounds like a track from *The Man in Black*." Fiona doesn't get the reference. "Nevermind," says Wenna. "I think I can save you a bundle, Fiona."

"What a tempting offer." But Fiona's expression conveys deep doubts.

It's night-time at the exhibition hall. A roly-poly guard clocks his time-sheet. He settles in behind his console of display monitors and opens a newspaper to the Top Tipster page. Resting on top of the control panel, a bag of chips, hot with grease and the demanding scent of malt vinegar, begs to be opened and consumed. The guard grabs the bag, and swivels round in his chair, studying the racing form.

Down a lonely corridor and well out of sight of the guard, a shadowy figure emerges from a store cupboard. Walking on a whisper, it stops in front of each door, peering inside, then moving on. Finally, the figure enters an office and approaches the desktop computer, typing in an access code. In no time the system reveals itself, as the figure searches its files and folders at warp speed, and finds the stand allocation plan for the Games Fair exhibitors. More typing produces an animated graphic, switching the number assignments with a platoon of red arrows. One of these switchover arrows lands on a label that reads 'Max Checkman'. As another cluster of keys is pressed, the whirr of a printer prepares the revised allocations. A hand deposits the new documents on the desk, and the figure glides from the office.

The corridor to the main exit is badly lit, but there's just enough spill to catch the swirl of Brynthila's cloak… were anyone there to notice. But back in his room, the roly-poly guard swivels his chair around to face the bank of monitors. Not a flicker, not a sound. Nothing to report. As usual.

The following day finds Jo and Denny each hard at work behind their separate computers. Both search wildly through every micro-pixel to locate the missing Brynthila. Denny calls up all the scenes they've been working on, while Jo scrolls her way through row after row of hexadecimals, but their heroine is nowhere to be seen.

Denny hits speed-dial and Jo fumbles around for her phone. "Yes?" she says, as if she didn't know who's ringing. Or why.

"Where is she?" Denny tries to control his rising panic.

"Who?"

"You know who. Brynthila." He's beginning to doubt himself, and again calls up the empty digital tower room. "She's not in the game."

Jo's evasive. "Isn't she?"

"Me mam's got everyone together for the photo shoot tomorrow… so where is she?"

"Silly me. There was I thinking you'd rung to apologise."

Denny's completely taken aback. "Me apologise? For what?"

"For being rude, for bullying ..." Her voice gets quieter and quieter. "... for generally being a not very nice..."

He's straining to hear. "Sorry?"

Her triumph is palpable. "Apology accepted."

Denny can't believe he's fallen for that silly old school-yard trap, or that she doesn't seem to realise what a serious pile of dragon dung they're both in. "Bloody hell, Jo. I'll say it again, the shoot is tomorrow. Where is she?!!"

"Don't ask me... I'm not her keeper."

"Yes, you are! That's exactly what you are!" In the messy pause that follows Denny tries some lateral thinking. "Okay, just tell me. Did you manage to get some hair back on her head?"

Jo will do anything to avoid admitting she's been negligent with Brynthila. "I notice you're not concerned with the hair on my head." She's dangerously close to pouting.

But Denny's in no mood to placate her. "Can you blame me?" he rails. "You programmed her to be everything you're not!

Jo is genuinely stung, and her voice is very calm. "Don't you have work to do?"

"Look, Jo, why do you think you have to protect her from me? What could I possibly do with a woman made of binary code?"

"I'm sure you'd think of something!" She flings the phone down, and rips a bite out of the half- eaten sandwich beside her keyboard.

Later that evening, Wenna and Denny sit opposite Fiona at her kitchen table. She pours tea into their cups. "Help yourselves to milk and sugar," she says holding out a plate of shortbread fingers. Denny takes one, but Wenna shakes her head. She rummages in her bag and produces a hip flask, pouring a glug into her tea. She half-offers the flask to Fiona, but tucks it away before she has a chance to accept.

"So, petal," she says, savouring her drink, "Max is definitely out for the evening."

"Yes, he's taken up yoga at the Village Hall."

Denny couldn't be more surprised, but they need to talk business. Crisis business. Namely photo shoot business. He explains that the star of tomorrow's main event has gone walkabout.

"Where's Jo?" counters Fiona.

Denny doesn't want this meeting to be about him and Jo's recent altercation. "She's… uhm… doing the digital thing. You know."

They don't, but they nod anyway. Fiona says, "Okay, so what are our options?"

Wenna rummages again in her bag. This time she produces a folded sheet of paper and opens it out to nearly fill the table. It features a decently hand-drawn plan of the Village Green, marked with various symbols. Denny's impressed, and so is Fiona. "Did you do that?"

Wenna flings her arm around her son's shoulder. "You didn't think his talent came from the stork, did you?" She cackles quietly. "Now, look you, here's what we have to do." They all bend their heads over the plan as she explains.

The following morning gifts the Village Green with steady sunshine as Wenna, unrecognisably dressed as a troll, gathers a motley crew of locals and her visiting hippie pals around her. They all depict characters from the game. A photographer lugs his tripod to strategic points among the costumed creatures. He positions some of them against leafy backgrounds, grabbing shots where he can.

One of Wenna's pals struggles to walk normally, encased in a suit of crocheted chainmail. He makes it over to her and lifts his visor. "It's stifling in here," he pants.

"Take a deep breath and think of the money, boyo. You lot are all on for ten percent of the profits."

"Ten per ... ?"

Wenna slams down his visor. "Shh! It's a private arrangement. Very few people know about it." She looks around nervously. "Practically nobody."

From the other side of a small pond, the photographer waves Wenna closer. Two giant lizards are standing by, and the photographer directs them to lift Wenna as if they're about to throw her in the water. At the last minute, she struggles free and pulls off her mask.

"Stop!" she screams. "I can't swim."

The lizards put her down. One of them pulls off his head-mask. It's Denny. "Pity," he says. "I was so looking forward to that."

The other lizard removes her mask, revealing Jo. She stares icicles at Denny, and wanders off down the hill. She joins up with a crowd of friendly monsters fawning over Lovelace, who's frisking about in a dragon costume. The photographer lugs his equipment around the Green, making the most of the light.

A few hours later, Max gets out of his car and walks towards the action. He spots Brynthila's cloak. She's standing alone, with her back to him, and he approaches, hoping for a cuddle.

"Come on, sexy. It's time for your close ups."

The woman turns round, revealing her flimsy dress under the cloak. But it's not Brynthila. It's Fiona, looking decidedly uncomfortable in such a revealing costume. Max releases her immediately and recoils.

"Fiona! You're not ..."

"Not what? Not sexy?"

Max sputters his confusion. "Of course you're sexy. Uhm... I mean, no, you're not... like that, I mean. You're my sister. I mean, sexy, yes, but not... I mean... uhm... where's Brynthila?"

Max turns to make a quick escape. With all these costumes, he can't tell who anyone is. Jo will know, he thinks. Gotta find Jo.

Lovelace snortles and sniffles behind a bush, then barks a greeting. Suddenly Brynthila materializes, and the dog jumps up to lick her face. She whispers into Lovelace's ear and points her toward Wenna in the distance; she's chatting to her friend in the crocheted chainmail at the side of the pond.

Further down the Green, Max catches up with Jo, holding her lizard head. He pants for breath. "Where's Brynthila?"

"Not here."

"What do you mean - not here. She should be here. She's got to be here. She must be ... " Max finally notices Jo's hair. "Wuzzup with your hair, dude?"

But before Jo can reply, a loud whoop resounds from the pond, as Lovelace runs straight at Wenna and pushes her into the water. She sputters, and gets to her feet. The water only comes up to her waist, but her knight in knitted armour jumps in to rescue her. She wraps her arms around his neck as he scoops her into his arms, wading through pond weed before he sets her down on the grass. "Let me take you away from all this into a nice warm bath," he whispers. She slides her hand down to pat his nether regions, which he takes as an acceptance.

The photographer catches every golden moment. "Perfect," he announces. That's a wrap, everyone!"

But for Max it's the last straw. After the debacle of the Games Fair stand allocation, and the less than perfect photo shoot, with the bank wanting its money any minute, his uneasy promise of solidarity with his fellow businesses to block redevelopment on the High Street, and his confidence dwindling by the microsecond, is this truly Game Over for Max Checkman?

He looks around for some support, but he's all alone. He falls to the ground and, typically, has a temper tantrum. But out from the budding shrubbery steps trusty Fiona, still in costume and undaunted by his plight, to cuddle him back to life. Proving if proof were needed that Checkman blood is thicker than pond water!

In the aftermath of the photo shoot, and with Brynthila yet to reveal herself to them either inside the game or in the meat-world, both Denny and Jo have plenty to be getting on with. The structure of the game has long ago been debated, agreed and signed off by all concerned, which means Max is legally entitled to approve each stage of the work in progress. And that means that wherever they choose to work, Denny and Jo must coordinate that progress.

Given Brynthila's absence, they've convinced Max that all the scenes peripheral to the main action need to be completed as soon as possible. One of the biggest gaping holes in their plans is finding time to come up with an integrated music and effects track. To buy more time, they've agreed to let Max think that the Games Fair deadline determines everything else. That will get them off the current hook. But not for long.

Back in his office, Max seems placated, especially when Fiona shows him the contact sheet of the Village Green shoot. Using the photos of costumed creatures and the frames of Brynthila from their demo disc, Max and Fiona piece together quite a decent mock-up publicity brochure.

"We need to get these…" Max begins. But Fiona's way ahead of him as usual.

"I've got the printers standing by," she says. "And I've arranged shipment to the money men in China. With plenty left over for the Games Fair."

They toast each other with a freshly brewed cuppa. Max hardly dares mention the gaping money-hole threatening to tow him under, but Fiona has it covered. "We're going to ask the Chinese chaps for an advance. And," she says before he can interrupt, "you are not going to spend it on any more hotel rooms. It's bread and water for you, Mister… for a while at least."

When the phone rings, Fiona assumes it's the printer, but it's a call for Max. The High Street Traders Association want him to join their demo against the redevelopment. "What, right now?" asks Max. And he's told to look out the window. An orderly gathering of well-dressed shop owners parade back and forth, holding placards that read 'Save Our High Street.' "I'll be down straightaway," Max says.

About half an hour later Fiona hears the worrying sound of glass shattering. A lot of glass. Much shattering. And some screaming and shouting. Then the sound of a police siren. Glancing out the window she sees a crowd in shock just across the street. The entire show window of the newsagents has been smashed to smithereens. A uniformed cop handcuffs a man, removes his balaclava, and forces him into the police car.

Max bursts into the office. "Did you see that?!" he says to Fiona. Prepared as ever, she diagnoses shock, leads him to his desk and serves him a cup of tea with extra sugar.

"Take a deep breath and tell me what happened." She listens as Max recounts how a couple of strangers wearing face masks crashed the peaceful demonstration, provoked fights among the crowd, and threw a brick through the shop window.

"What bullies!" declares Fiona. "Who'd do such a thing? How did they even know about it!"

"We've demanded protection," he tells his sister. "Night-time patrols. Starting tonight."

"Well, at least we have some good news. The printers will collect the brochure lay-outs, and we'll get them back in good time." She checks to see Max is really okay. "Drink your tea while its hot."

Meanwhile, Denny's taking advantage of his mother's absence with a well-earned coffee-break over a bout of cyber-chess. At least that should focus his attention away from the Princess who's gone walkabout.

Clicking a bishop on the monitor, he traces along its diagonal. He leans back smug in the knowledge he'll have won in the next three moves. His opponent also sees the inevitable and has to concede. A short pause until the computer voice remarks, "Well played, Jazz Fiend, you triumph once again. Another game?"

Denny types as the words appear on his monitor. "Not 2nite, Lord Cassemar. 2morrow?"

"Right you are, Denny. We can resume after Robert's sports day." Jonathan exits the program.

Denny's still apprehensive. He knows neither he nor Jo has any spare time before the Games Fair, but the revelation that his chess rival is Jo's father is definitely affecting his impulse to decline the family's invitation. And where the hell is Brynthila?!

Chapter 13

Robert's school takes Sports Day very seriously indeed. On display outdoors and throughout every corridor, the atmosphere fizzes with colour and bustle. Boys as young as five and up to sixteen cluster in small groups, each wearing maroon gym shorts and vests decorated with the school logo. Primed for action.

"Jo must be running late," Elaine says. She's up in the guest viewing stand overlooking the cross country event, sitting alongside Denny, Jonathan and Osborne. She passes Denny a sandwich from Osborne's picnic basket.

An area in the centre of the newly mown field has been roped off, a chalk line defining the start of the race. Jonathan frames Robert in his camera-phone and returns his waves to the family. Elaine spots Jo approaching the stand. "Oh, look, there she is." And she signals her daughter to join them.

Jo's wide-brimmed sun hat is more to hide her green hair than to acknowledge the weather. She starts to sit beside Denny - then remembers they're still not speaking, and pointedly moves to the other end of the group. She spots her brother doing leg-stretches on the field. "Robby's looking keen," she says. Jonathan greets her, then returns to his phone messages.

Denny notices that Robert's a bit smaller and scrawnier than the other boys, and he's appalled that a couple of them deliberately jostle him. The runners approach the starting line. They all give a little jump as the chubby Games Master blows his whistle. And they're off.

Each family shouts encouragement for their son. As the boys hook behind some trees, Robert streaks ahead and out of the spectator sight-lines. It's clear his size is no barrier to what a canny runner he is. Most of the others struggle to catch him up, but three of them do. Looking around to see no one's watching, they push him roughly into some brambles. Then they scarper away down a dip in the landscape.

The family get to their feet, expecting to see Robert re-appear into the open. But he doesn't. Something's wrong. Ignoring repeated blasts of the whistle, they all race onto the field toward the brow of the distant hill. Denny joins them, sprinting ahead. But no one sees another sprinter appear out of nowhere, charging in from behind some trees. It's Brynthila. She pulls off the hood of her cloak as she reaches Robert. The injured boy, covered in scratches and cuts, clutches his leg in agony. His ankle bone has dislocated. He tries not to cry as the world blurs around him.

Just before he passes out, Robert glimpses his attendant apparition. As she applies some magic balm from her satchel, she begins to fade. This is what Jo warned her about; she must get back to the game Pronto Tonto, to top up at the Well of Wellness. But, from Robert's point of view, her bald head shimmers like a halo. As the family approach from up the hill, Brynthila vanishes into thin air. Denny is first to reach Robert. The others arrive in time to see him gently patting the boy's face, helping him regain consciousness.

Seated around the table in the small dining room at Falcon Lodge, Denny and the Hawker- Meade family allow Osborne to clear their supper plates. They've been trying to fathom the day's bizarre events. "But I saw her, Mummy," Robert repeats. "She was as close as you are. Only glowy and sparkly - with a halo. An angel."

Neither Elaine nor Jonathan is convinced they should be encouraging this kind of fantasy. "Really, my darling?" says Elaine. "An angel?"

Jo and Denny try not to exchange any hint of what they actually know. But Robert pushes the point to his sister. "Your angel."

Jo deliberately chooses to misinterpret his remark. "Aw, that's sweet, Robby you're an angel, too. But what about that P. E. teacher of yours? If ever there was someone in need of a sports bra!"

Robert's confused. "My P. E. teacher's a man."

"Exactly," says Jo. "You'd think he'd keep himself in better shape."

Denny works harder than anyone to bite his tongue. Osborne returns to serve dessert.

Elaine raises her glass to Denny. "Well, I'd like to propose a toast to the hero of our day. To Denny!"

"To Denny," agrees Jonathan. But his attention is diverted by his mobile's ping of a text message.

Denny beams modestly at the approval of the family. Only Jo looks unimpressed.

"To Denny," she says. "Friend to the angels."

Denny visibly deflates, while Elaine covers the awkward pause. She turns to her husband. "You're unnaturally quiet, darling."

"Sorry… just business. You know, those dogoody retailers I was telling you about. The Save Our High Street brigade? Word from the Board is there's been some fracas involving the police, but they've got enough signatures and gone ahead and filed their petition with the council… which means we'll be counter-filing and re-filing for years in some bottomless pit of political correctness gone mad!"

Jo can't let this slide. "But, Daddy, isn't that democracy? The will of the people?"

Elaine checks her impulse to intervene, and Denny gets busy on his passion-fruit parfait. Robby also knows when to be silent.

"Will of the people?" snorts Jonathan. "The will of Max Ruddy Checkman, more like!"

That gets Denny's attention. "Max Checkman?" He and Jo have quietly begun to panic.

"Well, we're just the holding company," Jonathan explains, "but they say he's the ring-leader. I'd like to rip up his lease right now and shove him out on the street! Right out into the traffic!"

Neither Denny nor Jonathan can pass up a chance for a chess challenge, especially now their alias covers are blown. They sit opposite each other at Jonathan's desk, sipping from brandy glasses, a chessboard between them. They're in mid-game and mid-conversation about the High Street. Jonathan makes a move and leans back in his chair.

Denny studies the board, as Jonathan continues his thought. "Because it's prime for redevelopment, and I've got a line of investors as long as your proverbial all eager to snap up a piece of the action."

"Well, sure," says Denny, deftly avoiding the sacrifice of his remaining rook. "But life's about more than money. I mean, put Max out on the street and what happens to Jo? Not to mention me?"

Jonathan's beginning to understand the consequences of his assumptions in a very new way, though he's not entirely convinced. Not by a long chalk. "Oh, come on, that computer stuff's just a bit of fun. For Jo, I mean. Maybe this will kick start her back to reality... you know, husband, family. She's my princess, but she can't stay in that turret forever. I mean, you don't still live with your mother, do you?"

Which is a question Denny slides right over. "Jonathan... uhm, may I call you Jonathan? I'm guessing you've got your fingers in plenty of pies, but how much do you actually know about the global games market?"

Jonathan shrugs, "As I said we're essentially a holding company." He studies the board. "Not really my field, but I'm guessing growth is exponential."

Denny threatens a pawn and continues. "Just a bit. According to the latest quarterly reports, you know... Gartner's, NewZoo, what'sit... the industry's sitting on the fence of a hundred billion dollars, projected to reach another twenty billion in a couple of years, with China taking the biggest bite. Which is... I'm so rubbish at maths... how many pounds?"

Jonathan gives nothing away as his pawn retreats. Denny says, "Are you sure you wanted to do that?"

Jonathan realizes his error and starts to replace the piece. They both know this is against the rules. "Ah, go ahead," says Denny.

"You're a decent chap."

Denny studies his options, noting "No one knows more than me that Max's methods are unorthodox to say the least, but his deal with those Chinese investors actually seems like a great business decision. Considering most of the actual talent is right here in Blighty! Of course, I'm no expert." Jonathan's concentration wavers, as Denny continues, "Besides, that building's listed."

This time Jonathan sputters out his surprise. "Listed? That foul little mock Tudor monstrosity?"

"Apparently it's a particularly fine example of a foul little mock Tudor monstrosity." Denny makes his move and raises his glass toward Jonathan. "Checkmate in two, I think."

Remember that 'secret' shortcut lane through the undergrowth leading to Denny's flat? Trudging her way through is Wenna, on the way home from her frolics, a spliff clamped between her lips. She inhales one last puff and flicks the tiny butt into the trees. She's been swiping through options on her mobile as she walks, trying to keep to the overgrown path. Suddenly the image on her display screen flickers and she shakes the handset. When she looks up Brynthila has materialized in front of her, summoning her strength, radiating with power. Wenna drops the phone in stunned surprise, choking out a cloud of smoke. But it's Brynthila who's amazed.

"Marry, madam… How dost thou do that? Breathe fire."

"What?"

"Go to! You're the Dragon I'm to meet on Level Ten, 'tis not so?"

"No, I'm the chump you've met along the shortcut to Denny's flat. Didn't they say you disappeared."

But Brynthila wants to define her terms. "Shortcut? Is that like a secret passage?"

"Have you got learning difficulties, petal? Is that it? No shame in that." Never let it be said that Wenna's incapable of pity.

But Brynthila adopts an imperious tone. "You, who guards over Prince Denny, I command you to reveal how he should plight his troth."

"Command, is it, *cariad*?"

Brynthila mutters to herself. "Of course, gifts - I always forget they want gifts." She rootles around inside the silver satchel. "I offer you this, a gift of mushrooms." But, as Brynthila holds out her hand, it momentarily fades into transparency. And reappears again. Wenna stares in disbelief. "Magic mushrooms," says Brynthila.

To which Wenna can only observe, "Uhm… I think I may have just had some."

"Then, comest thou, madam. Weasel me not and reveal how to win my prince."

Wenna tries to recover her natural authority… something that she finds usually involves sex. "Well, that's the thing, see? He's not yours. You've got to get your own bloody prince. You're attractive enough. Got to use those natural talents, isn't it. Tricks of the trade. One good turn, as they say."

Brynthila's programming has made her better at data acquisition, not so great at random connections. She's trying hard to understand. "Good turn? Like a good deed?"

"You got it, petal!" She winks lasciviously. "Do the deed, and you can have any one of a hundred princes out there. Or men who think they are. Now, maybe I can't magic you one of them, but I can teach you to breathe fire." Wenna offers Brynthila a roll-up and a disposable lighter. "That's it. Now follow what I do."

Wenna mouths the cigarette and demonstrates lighting it. The flame startles Brynthila, but she takes Wenna's gifts, and watches her wander off toward Denny's flat. At a glance, I'd say she'd probably fail the straight line test, if you know what I mean.

Does the old crone speak true? Brynthila wonders. Can I release Denny from her spell merely with good deeds?

Brynthila sniffs the hand-rolled joint and places it gingerly between her lips. It smells familiar, just like Kurt's ashtray. She lights it, and one of the cannabis seeds embedded in the tobacco strands sizzles and pops into flame. Alarmed and coughing, she throws it away.

Glinting in the moonlight is Wenna's phone which has landed in a nettle bed. Brynthila fishes it out with every good intention to return it, but sees she's alone in the wood. She swipes the touchscreen left and right, then removes the casing to examine the electronics. With a twist here and a turn there, she sets the phone back in its case, and tucks it into her satchel. Should come in handy.

I bethought me to be wary, Brynthila ponders. That strumpet genders less faith than a stewed prune! But first things first. As her hand starts to fade before her, she knows she must get back to Jo's computer and drink a goblet from the Well of Wellness. Then, she has a plan.

Later that evening, up in the turret room at Falcon Lodge, Jo emerges singing from her ensuite after a long relaxing bubble bath.
Oh! I do like to be beside the seaside
I do like to be beside the sea!

Her spirits are up because her mirror shows the green hair slowly being pushed off her head by brown roots.

Wearing her pyjama bottoms and her favourite t-shirt... yes, the baggy one with the moth hole at the side... she tours the room, making sure some equipment is switched off and others remain plugged in. She's humming now. "Strolling along the Prom, Prom, Prom…Hm, hm, hm Tiddly Pom…" But she stops short in front of her desktop computer screen, where she's surprised by a message of ornate scrawls written in lipstick. Trying to decipher the letters, Jo reads the message aloud. 'Will return ere cockcrow. Off to do valorous deeds.'

Jo wonders when Brynthila was here without anyone noticing. And what does she mean by valorous deeds? She's about to climb into her four-poster when she spots Wenna's phone on the desk. I feel like Alice, she thinks. Curiouser and curiouser. She yawns. Maybe it will all come clear in the morning.

But deep in the middle of the night, when all the shops are locked up tight and nearly everyone in town is tucked up where the bed bugs don't bite, there's a dim spill of light along the mock Tudor High Street. It's seeping out from the window of a clothes shop, populated with a selection of male and female mannequins in various stages of dress and undress. Wait a minute! That one, over there, that's no dummy; it's Brynthila! She plucks off a wig and tries it on, admiring herself in the window reflection. No, not quite right. She tries another.

At last! It's perfect… long, luscious, golden locks almost like ocean waves cascading down her back. She strolls around, striking poses, but accidentally bumps against a male dummy, which collapses. As she grabs it, two passing police constables on foot patrol shine their torches in the window where a now-motionless Brynthila is in an amorous clinch. The cops walk on. Brynthila heaves a sigh of relief, steps backward and clatters into the whole group of dummies. The policemen, alerted by the noise, hot-foot it back to the window, torches alight. Brynthila is now buried under the entire pile of mannequins.

The men look at each other, baffled, searching for clues. One tries the door, but finds it secure, no sign of a break-in. "Maybe they have mice," he says. "Worth a report?" asks the other. But they agree to leave it and check back later.

The following morning, as the Checkman siblings arrive at the office, Max is stressed as ever. "Will you stop accusing me!" says Fiona.

"Well, where was she?" he fulminates. "I mean, everyone else was at the photo shoot. Except the one person we needed!"

Fiona has put the kettle on and is staring past Max. He's not quite blocking out a giant blowup of Brynthila in costume and wig. Fiona knows it was not there yesterday. She gestures toward the photo as Max continues.

"She could have rung, she could... What is it?"

Finally Max turns and sees the photo. Taped to the blowup is the 'revised' Games Fair stand allocation plan. If he's startled at the photo, Max is simply gobsmacked by the change for his stand. He's now been placed in one of the preferred main room spots. "How did that... ? Who... Fiona, did you do this?"

"Do what? The photo?"

"The Games Fair... they've given us one of the best stands in the place. I can't believe it. Am I dreaming?"

Fiona slaps Max... rather harder than necessary. He winces. "Doesn't look like it," she says.

After a modest breakfast, Jo has spent some hours busily working at the computer. Her anxieties of the past few days are much allayed by Brynthila's return to the screen. Like the Princess she is, she lolls on a sumptuous couch, her DigiKitten playing peek-a-boo under the bedclothes.

And she's reverted to her Bossy-Boots persona. "You, Madam... I am ready for my reward. Make me a Prince!"

Jo's so happy to see her that she plays along. "Okay, you're a prince!" Brynthila rolls her eyes. "Sorry, just kidding. Right you are, a promise is a promise. How tall do you want him to be?"

"Oh.. uhm... what is the height of Denny?"

"Right," says Jo, tapping keys. "Colour of eyes?"

"More or less the same colour as ..."

Jo's ahead of her. "No, don't tell me. Basically, you just want a Denny replica."

Her programming is interrupted by a knock on the door. She calls out, "It's okay, Osborne, I'll come down for tea in a bit."

But the door opens, and Denny sticks his head inside. He clears his throat. Brynthila peers at him from the screen. Jo glances up. "Hmm, talk of the devil."

He lingers in the doorway, his sketchbook tucked under his arm. "Hi... I wasn't sure whether you're speaking to me."

Jo is wary. She doesn't want to spoil the day. "Depends what you've got to say."

"First the good news. We've got a reprieve. For Max. For us. For the game." Denny's excitement is contagious and Jo catches it. "Well... that's... oh, Denny, that's wonderful! Why are you hovering in the doorway like a dragonfly?Come in, come in." And he does, clutching his drawing pad. "How did this...? When? I want all the details."

Denny says, "I don't know, exactly, but somehow your father changed his mind. Well, he changed the Board's mind. I mean, can you change a whole Board?" He's becoming delirious with victory. "I mean... how do you change a Bored Mind?" Pause. "You raise its interest rate!"

Jo laughs. "Did you just make that up?"

"Guilty! No, listen, Jo,they've called off the redevelopment dogs, and Jonathan... I mean your father is meeting with Max next week!"

"That's fantastic! Okay, I'm ready," says Jo. "You said first the good news. "So... what's the bad?"

"There isn't any, I don't think. But I was…"

Jo interrupts. "Well, actually, I have a slice of good news as well." Denny pauses, waiting for her to explain. But she only points to the desktop monitor. At first Denny's not seeing what she means, but then he does a classic double-take. He's truly stunned at the sight of DigiBrynthila, stretched full length on her day bed, all her luxuriant hair restored and tumbling down to her waist. She waves to Denny, but he's turned his attention to Jo.

"You did it! The hair… the … her! Jo, you're a bloody genius! I could kiss you!" At which news Brynthila narrows her eyes. But instead of amorous affection, Denny opens the sketch book and looks around for a seat. The only available place is the bed. He edges toward it, showing the book to Jo. "Right," he says, "I was having a doodle last night, and … "

"I'm very much hoping that's not a euphemism." Jo moves closer, sits and pats the space beside her. Denny displays the open page.

"Ta-da! Ladies and gentlemen, I give you… The Prince's Palace!"

Jo can't hide her approval and in her excitement, flings her arms around Denny. "It's perfect."

Before they can stop themselves, their lips meet in a kiss of joy, which surprises them both. They scramble up from the bed, as it dawns on them what has just occurred. Recovering her composure, Jo returns to the computer; Denny leafs through more sketches. They've each become formality personified, trying to be businesslike.

Jo's voice is minimal. "Yes. Right." Denny starts to say something, but the words die before they're born.

From the screen, Brynthila has been watching them avidly.

Chapter 14

With the pressure on to get everything ready for the Games Fair, Denny and Jo find reasons to work together in the same room. His excuse is to avoid Wenna and Lovelace, hers that Brynthila's safer kept on her hard drive. Jo holds up the mobile phone. "I found this on the desk. Looks like your mother's."

Denny examines the phone and agrees. "Thanks. I'll hand it over when I get home."

"Any joy finding her own place?"

"And pigs might fly," he says. By now Brynthila knows that's not an instruction.

With distractions kept to a minimum, Denny and Jo are racing clear to the deadline. If you, like Brynthila, were granted the power to peer into the turret room unseen, you might conclude it's not only the game that's showing definite signs of progress. For example, you might witness Denny leaning over Jo to study the monitor. As he stands, you'd see that his hands are slow to leave her shoulders.

Or, look, they're sharing a sandwich. While you're checking out the way Jo's hair is gradually losing its greenish tinge, you'd see her gently brush some crumbs from his cheek.

They've also resurrected one of their most productive working methods from the days of Bluebell's Magic Garden. They drag the cheval mirror near to the desktop monitor, and try out various facial expressions. Denny quickly sketches them in, and in no time at all, they're sparking ideas off each other, some rejected, but others incorporated into the game characters. And then, some which are just plain silly.

As they slide between work and fun, you're sure to glimpse a static scary monster rotating on his display plinth, posing through a range of

ScreenSaver!

expressions. Jo programs in a particularly inappropriate face, causing both Denny and Jo to succumb to a fit of the giggles. The monster in the machine rips off its horn-rimmed glasses, discards its buck teeth, and relocates the carrot nose pasted onto its forehead before storming off the screen. But up pops Brynthila, with a stern reminder that time's ticking. Tick tock.

You might follow Jo and Denny downstairs into the garden to work out the choreography of a battle, using a couple of broom handles. They parry and joust along the path, and Jo eventually succeeds in pinning Denny against a tree. They're both smiling and slightly winded by the exercise. Suddenly… and this is something you're sure to notice… they're laughing no longer and are staring into each other's eyes. You may want to avert your eyes as they kiss.

Fiona has to hand it to Wenna, she's really come up trumps, assembling a reliable crew to transform a boring display stand into a micro-land of adventure. Well, reliable is a relative term, isn't it? Max, too, has been busy. Mostly stamping his approval on each bit of the overall plan. He's become a master of the check-list. Or as he's come to call it, the Checkman List!

His P. R. plan is to present each Games Fair ticket-holder with a simulation of the experience they'll get playing the game at home. Wenna has worked to Denny's sketches designing two interconnecting levels of the exhibition stand, one featuring a labyrinth, then ending up in the turret chamber. As each person leaves they'll get a small goody bag, stuffed with a cheap character mask, a promotional pen, glossy brochure, and a demo disc of the game: Brynthila: the Maze of Life!

"You're looking very nice this evening," says Denny sipping a glass of wine.

Jo blushes. "Thanks. Uhm… you too."

They sit opposite each other at a candlelit table on a country-house restaurant terrace. She's wearing a loose silk shirt over floral leggings in an attempt to hide her muffin-top. Denny's velour v-neck strikes just the right dressy-casual note. This was planned as a working

ScreenSaver!

dinner, but somehow it's turned into a night of sheer indulgence. The waiter clears the remains of their meal.

Jo sniffs the sprig of clove-scented pinks in front of her. She's been trying to get the conversation back to business. "You know we still don't have enough Levels where she needs brain-power instead of brawn."

Denny reaches over and strokes her arm. "But she's got such a cute little brawn."

"You're incorrigible! One more week. That's all we've got. One week to get everything ready. Including a backing track."

"Yeah, how are we coming with that?"

"In the lap of the Disco Ozzie god!" They share a bonding sort of laugh.

The waiter returns with a menu. "Would Monsieur et Madame care for a dessert?"

Usually not one to refuse such temptation, Jo wants to say yes, but stops herself. Now, what do you think… is it the calories that prompt her answer or not? She replies, "Sadly *non, merci*. Too much to do."

But any plans that include either a late-night bout in front of a computer or in a more romantic pursuit are scuppered by a text message from Wenna. "Not again!" he explains to Jo. "She's only gone and locked herself out. Her and that dog!"

"Poor Lovelace," says Jo.

"My thoughts exactly!" Denny kisses her lightly on the lips. "Come on," he offers, "I'll drop you home."

Some hours later, DigiBrynthila stares from her screen, apparently attentive to the slightly wine-fuelled confidences shared by Jo. She sits, still clad in half her evening's finery, pouring her heart out.

"You know how you spend so much time with someone, that everyone assumes you're a couple. Or should be. I mean naturally, it crossed my mind. And Mummy isn't exactly subtle about these things. But in a way I didn't feel good enough for him. No, actually, I didn't feel good enough for anyone. No wonder I'm scared." She pauses for a reaction; Brynthila obliges.

"I know."

"Denny's right, I made you everything I'm not. You - perfect. Me? Sassy tongue, wobbly tum, hair like a hornet's nest. Guess who'll end up getting dumped. Well, you know."

"I know."

"I thought you would."

"I know - because you've spoken of nothing else for weeks! Borring!" Brynthila rants on. "I like so do not care anymore! Besides, what about my prince? You promised me a prince, my perfect prince, and he's still not right! What happened to 'a promise is a promise'?"

Jo sighs. "What's wrong now?"

"Well…" she reddens, as much as an algorithm can. "When we embrace, he… he just doesn't feel the same as Denny."

"He should do. His arms are as strong. I made his chest as broad."

"No, it's something else, something more… netherly… in the doublet-and-hose division. I mean… How prominent is Denny's… uhm… doublet-and-hose?"

Jo is shocked and amused in equal measures. "What book are you eating now? *The Good Princess's Sex Guide*?" Unwilling to hear the answer, Jo switches off the monitor."

The following morning, Robby's back at school, DigiBrynthila is back in the game, and Jo's still sleeping. In the conservatory Elaine and Jonathan are finishing breakfast. They each decline Osborne's offer of more coffee, and he confirms the car's waiting out front. Jonathan checks the calendar on his mobile. "I've got that meeting today with the consortium." He bends to kiss Elaine. "Might go on for a bit, so don't wait supper for me."

"You will be staying on for Jo's birthday, darling, won't you? No more sudden jaunts?"

"You worry too much," he teases.

Elaine calls after him, "Think what she might like for a present, because I'm stumped!"

Across town Max studies a spreadsheet on his monitor, checking it against a folder full of receipts. He barely looks up when there's an insistent knock at the door. Ever since the High Street altercation both he and Fiona have tried to be vigilant. Cautiously, she admits a gaggle of assorted townsfolk who pile past her. They march over to Max all demanding to be paid.

He has no idea what they're talking about and waves his folder of receipts. "Join the queue, dude."

A middle-aged man in overalls is instantly cowed and steps back, allowing Fiona to elbow her way to Max's desk. The others form a queue behind her, which she finds very unnerving. As she turns to face them with a blast of shushes, she recognises the bloke who was dressed in knitted chain-mail at the photo shoot.

"We want our money," he demands.

It's news to Max. "What money?"

"For the photos. Wenna said we'd get a percentage."

Max glares at Fiona. She glares right back. "Did she, now? Well, she told me you were doing it for nothing. As a favour to the community."

Some of the people buzz among themselves. And a woman's voice pipes up, "We were. But we want a percentage as well." This is greeted by echoes of support.

Max says, "You want nothing… plus a percentage?"

"That's right," says the man in overalls.

Max replies "Cool." And Fiona bites her tongue to stop butting in. "How does five percent sound, dude?"

The townsfolk huddle, whisper, and turn back to Max. The young woman declares, "Ten percent. Final answer."

"Done!" says Max as the crowd whoop their dubious victory. They file past Max for some handshake bonding. Until a young man pushes to the front of the queue. He's very young, indeed. His pony-tail is pulled back high on his head, and streaked with the colours of the rainbow. A stud pins his right nostril, and a tattoo of a river bubbles up his arm. He shouts louder than anyone, as he shakes hands with Max.

"Plus," he says, silencing everyone. Max takes back his hand.

"What do you mean, 'plus'?"

"We demand artistic input."

"You what?!"

The young man produces a grubby flipchart, elbowing Fiona aside. "'Scuse please, love, but this won't wait. I am just bursting with ideas. Bur-sting! Future games. Games within games. Rural ideas, global reach." Proudly he turns the pages of his illustrated presentation. Clearly this is the work of months, not moments. "Here you go," he turns the flipchart to Max. "Compost Challenge. Pigsty Poker. The Weakest Turnip. To name but a few."

Max and Fiona greet each turn of the page with bigger and bigger smiles. These are no nursery scribblings. They don't need a discussion. Fiona addresses the young man, "What did you say your name was?"

Elaine is on the phone, speaking quietly. She looks around, anxious not to be overheard, though no one is there to hear her. "... for her birthday, Denny ... Of course you're invited... So, just wondering if you know any of her other friends... Nor me!...Yes, and this year we're having a surprise... " She lowers voice even more. "A surprise party ... Oh, fairly big guest list, why?... No, actually, I haven't asked your mother. I didn't think... I mean... Did you want to bring ... Oh, that is a relief... No, I mean, yes, that's fine. Probably not her thing."

As he listens to Elaine, Denny is keeping an eye on Wenna. She's flopped on the sleek black leather and chrome sofa, wearing a fluffy pink housecoat and matching slippers, and cuddling Lovelace. It's obvious she's only pretending to complete a magazine word search, while trying to earwig on his phone call. Denny can't decide what bothers him more, her constant desire to control him, or the complete design clash of her garment with his furniture.

"Right," he says,"I'm meeting up with her later... Won't say a word... Oh, wait... don't suppose you know what she might like, you know, for a prezzie?... No, me either." Denny switches off the phone.

Wenna is eager. "Do I smell a party? When? Where? What'll I wear?"

"What you've got on now is fine."

"Don't be daft. I can't wear this. It's for slobbing about at home."

Denny's score on the losing patience metre is dropping rapidly. "Ideal then," he says. "'Cause that's exactly where you'll be. Unless by some miracle you find your own place by then."

"You mean I'm not invited, is it?" There it is... that little girl pout. How does she do that, Denny wonders. How does she make me into the bad guy?

"Honestly, Mam, it's a small do. Very small. Family, close friends.

Teeny-tiny."

"I'm family," she's almost tearful. She sighs heavily. "Why do you hate me, son?"

Silently, Denny counts on his fingers. "No, between us we don't have sufficient digits."

"So, I'm guessing this isn't the best time to tell you I took your car for a slight spin-a-rama." Denny fumes and sputters, but no words emerge. With a superhuman strength of will, he refrains from killing her on the spot. She continues, "Just a small one. More spin than rama. Teeny-tiny. And …"

"And, don't tell me, you got in a small, teeny-tiny accident," he says, hoping against hope.

"You know me too well, son."

Very slowly to delay the inevitable, Denny looks out the front window preparing himself for the worst. But he can't see the car anywhere. He adopts the calm, ultra-rational tone of a parent attempting to get the truth from a two-year-old. "Mam, where's my car?"

Wenna clears her throat, which brings on a bout of coughing. She milks the moment for all it's worth. Denny streaks past calm. "Mam!" he shouts. "Where's the bastard car?!" She punctuates her spasms of coughing with discernible words, such as police, insurance, and license. She fishes in her housecoat pocket and hands him a crumpled tissue stuck to a post-it note with a phone number written on it. "Garage," she coughs.

"You know what?" says Denny. "I'm not even giving you brain space just now. I have tons of work to do. Plus, gotta think of a birthday present for Jo. Flowers? No. Perfume? Double no."

Wenna's only too happy to make amends. "Box of chokkies? Second thoughts, with her figure, very small box. Teeny-tiny. Just one choc."

"You're not helping, Mam. No, literally, I do NOT want you helping. Besides I was thinking something more personal."

Wenna tours the room, looking for a suitable gift, but Denny's minimalist decor doesn't offer much. She leafs through a few loose prints in the bookcase - and finds a photo of Denny and Jo smiling and holding an early mockup of DigiBrynthila. She shows it to Denny. "No. I don't know. Maybe."

"It's perfect. A really smart frame. Nicely wrapped." She leers. "Intimate note."

"I said maybe. I'll think about it. Look, I've got to go, I'm meeting Jo. And thanks to you, I'll be legging it!"

"Leave this with me, boyo. Wenna knows best. I'll make a really good job of it. Promise."

Denny's reluctant to leave his mother in charge, but maybe the walk will help clear his head. Lovelace wants to tag along, but Denny points her back to Wenna. She barks her farewell and Denny pulls out his phone to ring the garage.

Denny and Jo sit at a small table in their local pub. He pops a handful of peanuts in his mouth and drains the remains of his pint. Jo sips at her soda water. The laptop is open in front of them. DigiBrynthila stares out; beside her is a DigiPrince trapped in a cage.

They've been trying to devise a new scene for the game, but Denny's also trying to discover what Jo might actually want for her birthday. "How do you like that new scarf I designed for her?" he says.

"Yeah, great. Nice touch." She toggles the screen to reveal some code.

"I mean, is that something you might wear?"

"Sorry, what?"

"No, I just asked if you want another drink," asks Denny.

Brynthila replies from the screen. "Ahem! I hate to break up this charming scene, but don't you two have work to do?"

"What are you, the Pub Police?" Jo wants to know.

Brynthila's voice and tone owe quite a lot to American gangster fiction. "Listen, Buster, I been searching dis dump all morning, and I still can't find any clues to release dis bozo into my custody."

Denny turns to Jo. "What's she been eating? Mickey Spillane? Come on, another water?"

Jo stands. "Any more and I'll turn into a fish."

"Something stronger?"

Jo's adamant. "No, she's right. Still tons to do. Besides, last time I overindulged... well, let's just say it wasn't a pretty sight."

Denny's still playful. "Jo, you're always a sight. No, I mean... always a pretty sight ... uhm... I ..."

Jo enjoys his embarrassment, and drags him to his feet. "Come on, you. Back to the salt mines."

Over at Denny's flat, Wenna scans the walls and unhooks a classy framed Picasso print. She punches it out of the frame and measures it over the photo. Whichever way she juggles it around, the photo is far too big.

It's the day before the party, and Osborne is driving the family into town. Jo tried to wriggle out of it, but Elaine has laid down the law. She's booked a mother and daughter pampering morning at a beauty spa in Kensington. Facial. Pedicure. Hairstyle. New dresses. Osborne drops them at the door, and heads east to Hawker-Meade HQ in Canary Wharf. Robert's excited because Jonathan's agreed to show him round, give him an intro to his world. Osborne doubles back up West. He has a few calls to make.

Level 3 - Chapter 15

The driveway at the front entrance to Falcon Lodge is full of cars. Osborne has taken charge and guides a small battalion of helpers to ensure all guests and visitors enjoy the evening. He ushers the chamber quartet to a raised bandstand in the garden, where they strike up a medley of familiar classics. The trees and bushes twinkle, lit by coloured lights. Bow-tied waiters circulate with trays of drinks and canapes, and a handful of uniformed staff behind a long table offer platters of tempting food. Osborne and Elaine have pulled out all the stops, but she confides, "I just wish she had more friends of her own age. Or even just one. I mean, look at this lot! Not to be unkind, but it's wrinkles-a-go-go!"

Bereft of his transport, Denny's walking to the Lodge. At the approach to the imposing building he senses he's crossing a moat of unattainability over a temporary drawbridge. Over the couple of years he's got to know them, he's found the Hawker-Meades pleasant enough, but he's forced to admit, despite the recent thorny entanglements with his own mother, it's she who formed his marrow and expectations. His anxiety climbs as he passes the classy parked cars of the shinier guests.

In the entry hall a pair of crossed silver halberds gleam against the stone walls. Denny smooths down his hair in their shiny reflection, and nods politely to perfect strangers. At least he looks good in his open-neck midnight blue silk shirt and dark grey blazer, even if he didn't commission them from Savile Row. He carries a beribboned gift-box, which he sets on the groaning present table. That's the thing, isn't it, he thinks to himself. To them that has, they just get more while the poor get the finger- pointing. He wasn't expecting such a grand do, being more a drinks down the pub lad, but he's doing his best to fit in. He can't imagine how the family would cater Jo's wedding. Should such an occasion ever arise.

As he slips into the garden through the French windows, he takes a wine glass from a passing waiter. Jonathan spots him heading toward the long buffet table where a handful of people wait to be served. "Denny!" he calls, waving him over.

"What a party!" he says by way of greeting. "And where's our birthday girl?"

"Oh, she's around somewhere. Let me introduce you." Jonathan indicates a very elderly man and raises his voice slightly. "Harold, this is Denny, who works with my daughter. Harold Mayhew, a dear family friend."

Denny knows enough not to say Wuzzup, dude, and transfers his glass to shake hands. "Pleased to meet you, sir," hoping that's the correct protocol. Jonathan expands, "Harold's got some exciting news. Wedding bells will soon be ringing." Harold chuckles.

Two women approach from the buffet, carrying modest plates of finger foods. One is elderly, the other sleek and glamorous. The younger woman stops to chat, while Jonathan's attention is diverted by Osborne, signalling him to take a phone call. "Back in a moment, Harold," adding "Ah, here they come now, Harold's daughter and fiancée."

Denny greets the older woman, assuming she's the bride to be. "Congratulations," he says. "Never too late, eh?"

But her reply is stiff as two boards. "I'm the daughter."

And when Denny looks up at the younger woman, it's none other than Lauren. She sidles up to the old man and pops a *vol-au-vent* into his baby-birdlike mouth. "Hello, Denny," she says.

He's never been so conscious of his social class. Only people in the upper bit claim it doesn't exist. He bumbles out some words of startled congratulations to Lauren and beats a hasty retreat. More than ever he needs to find Jo and squeezes through the crowd in search of her. He catches a hint of Elaine's unmistakable tones coming from somewhere near-by, greeting a few late-comers. Denny deposits his empty glass and corners her in the rose garden.

"Elaine, hi... uhm... great party. Have you seen Jo?"

"Oh, she's - now where did I see her?" She's holding a small plate of food and offers it to him. "Do try this pheasant pâté? Scrummy!" She waves to a woman through the crowd and hands him the plate. "Caro!" she calls. And to Denny, "We'll catch up later."

Denny looks around for somewhere to dump the plate. Suddenly a pair of hands cover his eyes.

"Guess who?" says a whispered voice.

Denny spins round. "Jo!" he declares. But it isn't Jo... it's a very flirty Lauren. Denny tries to recover. "Yo-jo-Jehovah! Lauren!"

"Hi, again. And, before you ask, yes, it's true. I am marrying the old goat." She pulls him closer to her. "But, after the honeymoon, I'll have scads of spare time. Spare time to, you know, pick up where we left off... "

From a vantage point at the far end of the garden, someone spies Lauren holding Denny in a tight embrace. That someone is Jo. She's been waylaid by a trio from one of Elaine's charities, and has been trying desperately to get away. One of the women is just concluding an anecdote. "So Binty Clark whisked the child to Paris for the weekend!" The other women laugh behind their sandwiches as Jo plots her escape.

Why is it, she wonders, that relative strangers who don't really know what to say to you, start talking about other people you don't know... as though that might actually be interesting.

She doesn't know the answer, but she does know she's never looked better. Refusing desserts and junk food lately has proven effective in the weight department. Elaine has helped her choose a pair of stylish glasses, and her hair has been coaxed into a curly gamin style with no visible green patches. The filmy tunic over her new dress not only helps hide hippo hips, but brings out the slate blue of her eyes, and pairs well with her strappy heeled sandals. She was hoping to find Denny, but the sight of him in such close contact with that woman throws her into despair.

She plucks an open champagne bottle from the buffet table and wanders away. "Happy birthday," calls out one of her mother's friends. Jo hardly recognises the woman, but smiles back politely. She's not close enough to witness Denny's resistance to Lauren's persistence, and she wanders off before he can extricate himself from her embrace.

"Sorry, Lauren," Denny says, "I can't do this."

"Yeah, right!," she retorts. "You're just like me, you know you are… only interested in that dumpling to get at her daddy's dough."

On a very quick learning curve of social grace, Denny suddenly acquires some dignity. "Excuse me. I need to find Jo." And he wanders through the guests, but Jo is nowhere to be seen.

And that's because she's gone walkabout. Despite her party finery she tackles the overgrown shortcut through the woods, clutching the champagne bottle and mumbling to herself. She swigs from the bottle, which almost throws her off-balance, and she stumbles on some stones in the road. Take off your shoesies, she says to herself, and she plunks herself down on a tree stump to do just that. She speaks and gestures to trees and shrubbery as though they were people. Tipsy? She left tipsy about half a mile back.

Stupid! Stupid, stupid girl! You are a stupid girl, Jo, what are you?! Stoo-pid! Typical man! Typical Denny! One minute it's 'Oh, darling, I'd walk through fire for you,' next minute it's 'What's your name, again?' Have the past weeks meant nothing, you… you… Just you wait, going to find you, going to give you a piece of my mind. Never want to see you again, not ever, not even one more teeny-tiny time. First piece of mind, next, never see again. Who's that? That you?! Can't fool me… Hah! Think you're a tree! Can't fool me.

Jo continues barefoot to Denny's flat. Inside, lights are blazing, Lovelace is barking, and loud rock music blasts through the night.

Throughout the neighbourhood, residents are seriously considering moving house. A few have rung the police. Inside, Wenna and a friend belt out a disco number. Not invited to Jo's party, is it?! Well, hah! she can make her own fun.

Jo is about to ring the doorbell when a shrill siren announces the imminent appearance of a police car. Jo whirls around, holding her hands up. Her sandals dangle from one, the bottle in the other. "I'm innocent, I tell you!" she announces to the night air. "You'll never take me alive, copper!"

As a police car pulls up, Jo crouches down and duckwalks around the house, hiding underneath a ground-floor window. She swigs from the champagne bottle but it's empty. She tries to stand the bottle on a small patch of grass, but it keeps falling over. As she reaches down for it again, she falls over as well, leans against the wall and closes her eyes.

While his colleague waits in the car, an officer bangs on the front door and rings all the doorbells. He finally gains entry. In the hallway, some of the residents hover on the stairs, all directing the cop to Denny's flat, as if the music weren't clue enough.

Wenna opens the flat door and tries in vain to charm the constable over the back beat and Lovelace's barking. Her party outfit consists of frilly miniskirt and stilettos, with a teased and towering hairdo rivaling The Bride of Frankenstein. She puffs away at some kind of cigarette, batting her false lashes. "Come in, why don't you, officer… let your hair down and have a bit of fun."

"I'll have to ask you to turn the music off, Madam."

Wenna gestures to someone inside, and the music stops. Lovelace continues to bark, until she's silenced by Wenna. "Madam, is it?" she counters. "You think I'm a Madam, boyo? Well, come inside and find out."

It starts raining. Underneath the window at the back, Jo tries to brush the drops from her face as though they're spiders.

A loud thunderclap surprises the copper. Wenna cackles. "Best come indoors. Don't want to get wet all over."

"Just keep the noise down, or we'll have to interview you at the station." The policeman retreats and the car drives away. After a few minutes, Wenna's party continues. With music.

The police car hasn't gone more than a few hundred yards onto the High Street when it responds to a radio call. The driver hooks a U-Turn back to Denny's place and exchanges looks of resignation with his colleague. "Have we got a spare cell at the shop?" he asks.

What was light rain has become a downpour. Jo staggers to her feet and tries to peer through the window, but she's just a bit too short. She tries to jump up, and catches enough glimpses to confirm it's Denny's bedroom. After a failed attempt to strap on her high heels, she falls backward into some ivy and a pile of dead leaves, where she promptly falls asleep.

She's out for the count when a gaggle of party guests spill out onto the street, and relieved neighbours watch the police car pull up. After a few minutes, they watch it drive away again. Could that be Wenna in the back seat?

Over at Falcon Lodge, Jo's birthday party is starting to wind down. After searching for her high and low, Denny wanders upstairs to the turret room, and gingerly knocks on the door. A familiar woman's voice says, "Come in." Denny enters, but there's no one there. Then he sees DigiBrynthila peering out at him from the desktop monitor. Despondent, he sits at the desk. "Where is she?"

"You really do care about her, don't you?" she says.

"Funny, isn't it? You spend so much time together, everyone starts to assume you're a couple, and then, one day, you wake up and realise …"

Brynthila interrupts. "Oh, for Thor's sake! Not you as well! Let me stop you right there, Prince Denny. Now, buck up, stop moping, get your act together and …"

"Oh, shut up! Do you know where she is or not?"

A chastened Brynthila turns away to search for something in her digital room. When she turns again to face Denny, he can hear an electronic beeping. "Well?" he says.

"Well, perhaps I did hear her mumble something about going round to give you a piece of her mind. Though I can't see how cranial surgery is the answer."

Denny kisses the screen, and starts to rush out. Brynthila blushes. Denny returns to the screen. "What's that beeping?"

"Tracker. I put it in your mother's mobile. Looks like she's on the move."

A few minutes later Denny braves the overgrown path toward home. He guides his way with the built-in torch on his iPhone, and is surprised when he hears its jazzy ring tone. "Hello? … Who? … Do I know a Wenna?… Well, who wants to know?… Yes, all right, put her on… Mam?! What are doing at the police station? … Well I reckon you'd better just stay put! … Sorry, can't help you there, petal, my car's not working. Remember?!"

By now Denny's reached the path alongside his house. In his haste to find Jo, he completely misses her, curled up asleep in the undergrowth.

Inside, Denny is surprised to find his door ajar, guarded by Lovelace. The dog growls softly, but lets him in. He surveys the aftermath of the party, including a man with a ring of flowers on his head and not much else on his body, passed out under the glass coffee table.

Lovelace trots over and licks Denny's hand. He says, "Nevermind all that… a watchdog is supposed to do a bit more than just watch!" The dog lowers her head, tail still wagging. The eternal optimist.

Denny shakes the man, pulls him and his clothing from under the table, and escorts him outside, closing the door. He starts to tidy the mess of party remains, but gives up, exhausted. He can't see Jo anywhere, and heads for bed. The room stinks of smoke and strangers. He opens the window, undresses down to his Calvin Kleins and falls into bed.

He's still sleeping a few hours later when Lovelace jumps up next to him, whining. Denny turns over, as the dog jumps through the window. She wags her tail with delight at the sight of Jo, shivering from the night's rain. Lovelace encourages her to her feet.

She's dripping wet and not nearly awake. She sneezes and, nudged into place by the dog, gets some purchase on Denny's open window. It's enough to hoist herself up, legs hanging down and butt in the air. Lovelace helps push her into the room, where she lands as delicately as she can onto the bed, next to the sleeping Denny. The dog joins them, curling round Jo's bare feet.

The trilling of the dawn chorus gently rouses Denny and Jo who wake with their arms around each other. Lovelace balances herself awkwardly on top of them. Denny's still in his underwear, and Jo's crumpled but fully clothed. She opens her eyes and mumbles, "G'morning."

They both sit up abruptly, sending the dog flying. Jo starts to get up, but sinks back, clutching at the Hangover Monster lodging in her skull. "Ooo, my head!"

"I'm guessing you won't want a breakfast fry-up," Denny teases. She moans. Her face takes on a greenish tinge. With super-power determination, he swings his feet to the floor. "I'll fetch some aspirin."

Jo stops him. "Wait a minute, I thought I wasn't speaking to you."

"Why not?"

"Can't remember." She sees he's in his underwear, and asks, "Denny? ... Uhm... last night... did we? You know..."

He's quick to reply. "No! At least, I don't remember. And if I don't remember... then either we didn't... or it's not worth remembering."

"Because the last thing I remember... Urgggghhhh!" She tries again to get up. Her face is now the colour of a praying mantis with jaundice, and her gutteral cry alerts Denny that he'd better help her find the bathroom if he values his bed-sheets. Like some Knight in Shining Boxer Shorts, he scoops her up and deposits her in front of the toilet.

Leaving her to it, he finds his phone. He yells out to Jo between her bouts of sonorous spewing, "I've rung you a taxi."

Later that day, wearing her flannel onesie and receiving the solicitous attentions of Elaine and Osborne, Jo lounges on a chaise in the small lounge. Fragile, feeble, but feeling somewhat better after her purge at Denny's, Jo has been opening the scores of gifts from the night before. Her nostrils are blocked, and she's achy and feverish. She pulls up another tissue from the rapidly emptying box beside her and succumbs to a bout of sneezing, which starts her nose dripping. Elaine perches beside her on the chaise and feels her forehead. "Still a bit warm."

"I think I'll dhlive," Jo says, in a stuffy-nose sort of way. She tries a bit of levity. "I think if my nodz runs any faster I'll enter it in the Grand National."

Osborne chuckles, glad to see her fighting spirit. Within arm's reach is a tooled leather waste paper basket overflowing with used tissues and ripped open wrapping paper. He hands over another gift, collects the wrapping and goes to empty the basket.

Jo holds up a hideous cardigan, and Elaine reads out the card. "From your Aunt Aurelia... "

"I didn't even know I hab an Aunt Aurelia," says Jo. She blows her nose and finds it blocked even more.

"Mm," says Elaine, "nor did I. Well, I'm sure it will be... useful."

"Right, we could unravel it and sell the wool back to the sheeb."

"Far be it for me to pry, darling, but you haven't actually said where you spent the night."

Jo clutches her head. "Please, Bumbby, bust you shout."

"I'm not." Osborne returns and exchanges knowing looks with Elaine. "Did I mention, darling, you know my friend Gabriella..." Jo shakes her head. "Well, she and her husband saw you and Denny in the pub the other day, and thought you made a lovely couple." She laughs lightly, unsure whether she finds that idea absurd or not.

Jo ignores the implication. Osborne gestures toward another gift. "Looks like a book." Elaine hands it over. The wrapper reveals a bodice-ripper romance, and Jo tosses it onto the floor. "Really?" she's close to sobbing. "Someone really thinks that's whad I'd want for a presendt?" And the tears begin to flow in earnest. "Oh, Bumbby, why don't I have any friends?"

Osborne proffers the box of tissues, and Elaine dabs at her daughter's cheeks. She hugs her and whispers, "Shh, my Josabunny. Don't cry." Jo feels too weak even to protest the dreaded childhood nickname.

Osborne averts a crisis and hands over a nasal spray with the next present. "Who's it from?" Elaine asks.

"Dno card." Jo shakes the box and unties the ribbon, wincing at the deafening crinkle of the wrapping paper. "Looks like a phot..." She interrupts herself with a muffled wail. "That's whad he thinks ob me, is it?"

Osborne and Elaine peer over at the present Jo's holding. It's a picture frame containing the photograph, altered by Wenna to fit. But instead of Jo, Denny and Brynthila, Jo's been completely cut out, except for a part of her arm.

"Dhovely couple?" moans Jo. "Oh, yes, what a dhovely couple!" And, as she throws the frame against the wall, "What a very nice dhovely couple ... ob dhlosers!"

ScreenSaver!

Up in Max's High Street office, Fiona opens the door and admits the impetuous young man who interrupted the recent impromptu meeting of disgruntled locals. His rainbow pony-tail is set off by a spiky black circle around his right eye. He wears a kung-fu smock. Fiona takes the large portfolio he hands her. "Thanks for stopping by. Max and I were talking about you just last night."

Suddenly nervous, he shakes hands with her, and holds out a DVD. "Didn't know what format you prefer…"

Fiona takes the disc. "So," she teases, "you reckon you can make our new game more exciting, do you?" She leads him through to Max's desk and offers him a chair.

Making himself seems busier than he is, Max pretends to end a phone call. He half rises to shake hands. "Zac, isn't it?" He knows perfectly well that's the man's young man's name, but his management course advised not to appear too eager for something desired.

And both Max and Fiona are particularly eager at the moment. Neither has been able to contact Jo or Denny, and the Games Fair deadline looms above them like a gigantic alien space craft, blotting out all light and hope for the planet.

"You got it!" Zac replies, regaining his bonhomie. "Also known as Wacky Zacky. Or just The Big Zed. Call me what you like, long as you don't call me late for tea, eh?!"

Fiona and Max really need to get Zac on side and are willing to suffer his infernal ebullience and cornball jokes. "So," says Fiona, opening his portfolio on the desk, "let's see what you've brought us."

Chapter 16

After a long restorative sleep and a day of herbal tea and sympathy, Jo feels well enough to tackle some programming for the new game level she and Denny have been devising. For hours, she's been in what she calls coding prison, oblivious to her ringing phone, letting the answering machine do its thing.

Jo's blocked up nose lends a pitiful tone to her new message. "Sorry, dhere's no-one here. Except I ab here and I'b dnot sorry. You can contact be for work batters by eBail. But only work batters. Because only work batters and dnothing else does. So eBail only. Dhat's E for Empty, E for End ob, E for Ex-boyfriend. Please don't leave a bessage. 'Cause I don't give an F for … "

And the answer-phone bleep-bleeps out the rest.

Upstairs, in the master bedroom, it's packing time again for Jonathan. Osborne has set an open valise on the three-metre long upholstered bench at the foot of the emperor-sized bed. Both pieces of furniture are easily accommodated within the room, once the sleeping quarters of visiting monarchs. Its oak-panelled walls blend well with the deep-pile area carpets set onto wide polished floorboards, and the full-length tapestry curtains reproduce an Elizabethan garden.

Jo certainly approves her parent's choice of a rail journey. Instead of a quick flight to clients in Edinburgh and Inverness to discuss a possible North Sea investment and bish-bosh home again in time for supper, her father's office has arranged a smooth ticket combo to do the biz and still give him and Elaine a special treat. Far less effect on climate change, thinks Jo, though she may not entirely be aware of the damage such investment may trigger in the longer term.

Jonathan ticks off items on the itinerary his secretary prepared. She and the company travel agent have put together a perfect package. Just one loose end to tie up. He's promised to meet with Max and the Save Our High Street lot before departing the next day. He messages his office to courier over the paperwork, and, he smiles to himself, that's that! He squeezes Elaine's shoulder on the way to his dressing room ante-chamber.

She's curled up in her satin dressing gown on one of the matching armchairs; she's checking through a leather-tooled camera case, making sure she's got all her lenses. A brochure announcing The Rail Journey of a Lifetime is open on the floral marquetry table beside her. She calls out to her husband, "I'm glad you booked that cabin. Looks lovely… a home away from home."

Jonathan emerges in his underwear. "You'll manage with just the one case, won't you, darling?" he asks, tucking his wash bag into an appropriate compartment.

"I think so! It's only a Highland week-end, not a month in Melbourne!" Her own case has already been packed and ready for loading in the Merc. "Don't forget the dinners are black tie."

"Yes, remind me to fire whoever came up with that rule!"

"Oh, you!" she teases.

"I think I'll go down and have a relaxing chess game before supper. You don't mind, do you?" But Elaine has been watching him walking around the room, doing this and that, and she's suddenly aware of her heart-stopping attraction to him. Funny, she thinks, how it just surprises you after all these years. "You know, I'm really excited about this trip - it's just so perfect for my book. Thank you, my love." She rises to kiss him.

He returns her kiss with more passion and guides her over to the bed. "On the other hand, I guess chess can wait."

"I've packed that little chiffon number you like, remember?"

"Mm," he nuzzles her neck. "I even remember how to take it off."

Some hours later, Denny has shut off his phone. He can't contact Jo and won't even contemplate speaking to Max. On the glum scale - glum, glummer, glummest - he's hit glumissimo. Unshaven and uncharacteristically rivaling Jo for scruffy, he settles back behind his open laptop and tries again to work. But he just can't concentrate. Onscreen is the horned Chicken Chimera due for the next level of the game, but he just swipes past it. Suddenly a chessboard pings up on the computer screen. Denny regards it blankly as the familiar digital voice greets him. "Welcome Jazz Fiend. Click Yes to resume game."

But he shuts the laptop lid and walks out of the room. Which tells you everything you need to know.

Later still, DigiBrynthila scans the turret room from within the large monitor screen as Jo busily types out a page of code symbols. She sips from a mug of herbal tea. They both look up as Osborne knocks and enters bearing a huge bouquet.

Jo teases, "Oh, Osborne, you shouldn't have." Her blocked nose has cleared, and her pale cheeks seem pinker, less like lard.

"Glad to see you feeling better, Miss." They both know who's sent the flowers.

DigiBrynthila pipes up from the computer screen. "For me?" she enquires sweetly.

But Jo dumps the bouquet onto a pile of several others which now litter a corner of the room. She returns to her coding then notices Osborne is lingering in the doorway. "Sorry, was there something else?"

He clears his throat for a small announcement. "I think we've found our musician."

"Oh, Osborne, that's wonderful!"

"Just call me Disco Ozzie," he says modestly. "He'll need some rehearsal time, though. Him and his musos. Time and space. I don't suppose…" he pauses, "your parents would mind them using that stone gazebo, you know, down behind the lake. Should be far enough away for a bit of volume."

"Oh, yes, I know. I used to take Robby down there to play, remember? Screamed our heads off! Sounds perfect. Can't see why they'd refuse. Besides they're away all week-end."

"Exactly! I'll get it cleaned out."

And, unable to contain her smiles, Jo thanks him and asks, "When can we meet him?"

The following day, Fiona raises the painted blind in Max's office to let in the crack of dawn. She's set up an oval meeting table and distributed a small stack of stapled papers to Max and three fellow members of the Save Our High Street campaign. On the table are a teapot, cups, spoons, some paper napkins, chocolate biscuits, a milk jug and sugar bowl. "Help yourselves," she says and retreats behind her dividing screen.

The two men and a woman busy themselves pouring tea and passing the biscuits around. Max addresses them. "I think you'll be very interested in what he's offering." They all consult the paperwork in front of them.

"Devil's in the detail," says one of the shopkeepers.

"Yes," another replies. "I've heard he's known as The Devil of the Deal."

"He is actually coming, is he?" asks the woman.

"Yes, of course," Max tries his best to sound reassuring. "Just running a smidgeon late. Biscuit anyone?"

Which is the moment Fiona ushers Jonathan into the room, introduces everyone, and leaves them to it. No one's quite sure how to begin. Of course they've all read about Falcon Lodge; it's part of their communal history, after all. But, apart from Max, none of them has ever actually met the lord of the manor. Talk about different social circles! But they're all aware their business futures may be at stake. At first glance, he seems nice enough.

Max recovers enough to play the host, motioning for Jonathan to sit, offering him tea, and graciously handing him the initiative as though it's a baton in a relay race. "Over to you," he says.

Jonathan checks his watch and holds up his copy of the presentation paperwork. "Exactly. So. Bit pushed for time I'm afraid. What did all of you make of our little quid-pro-proposal?"

Fiona knows to hold all calls.

Down a turning off the High Street is a small collection of service buildings, including a garage and MOT station. Denny's precious convertible waits gleaming and dentless on the forecourt. He emerges from the garage office, pocketing his wallet, and executes his Starsky and Hutch leap into the car. He pushes some buttons on his SatNav, and speeds off.

"Merge left with dual carriageway ," suggests the pleasant mechanical voice, and he does. He continues for a few hundred yards until he comes to a small rural cop shop. You'd miss it if you weren't looking for it, as it appears to be a domestic residence, and the police logo in the front yard is overhung with shrubs. But Mrs SatNav confirms, "You have arrived at your destination."

As Denny is about to enter the building, he sees a uniformed police constable leading Wenna outside. He spots her skill at relieving the officer of the notepad in his back pocket, and calls out a warning, "Mam!" Sheepishly, she hands the pad back to the surprised man. Denny opens the passenger door. Only one word is spoken. "In," he says.

They drive in silence for a while, before Wenna dares: "You don't have to say it. You want me gone, isn't it. I know." She drops her head, as though she were headed for the gallows. She's trying her best to melt his heart of stone, but it's hardened to permafrost.

"Let's get something straight, Mam. I'm only letting you back to the flat to pack up your things. Got that? No pals, no parties… in fact, I don't want you anywhere near the kitchen. I'll buy you lunch, and then it's bye-bye Wenna. Double got that?"

"Yes, son." Denny snorts. He has no faith at all in the word 'yes' and even less in the word 'son.' She continues, "I'll just ring my friend Rhys to come pick me up. *Hiawn?*" Denny knows that means Okay in Welsh, but he refuses to engage with her.

And somewhere in the mystic realms of cyberspace, DigiBrynthila responds to the tracker signal she's installed in Wenna's phone. She's very proud of the embellishments she's made, and longs to show off to Jo. Or Denny. Or someone. For on her own mini-monitor, she can see right inside Denny's car. She can see Wenna speaking to someone. She can hear Denny's iPhone ringing, and see him turn it off without picking up. What she can't see is the message that Fiona leaves for him to attend a meeting the following day at Max's office. But she definitely can hear the same message that Fiona leaves on Jo's answer phone on the desk in front of her. It's a message delivered in a tone of frightening command and brooks no excuses. "Be there!"

And so, while Jo steels herself for tomorrow's summons to Max's office, her parents are settling in to their luxury cabin racing north of the border. The bright tartan throw on their spacious double bed presages a week-end of cosiness with a Highland burr. Jonathan's studying a bundle of legal paperwork spread out on the table. Elaine hands him a glass of complimentary champagne and asks, "That for your Edinburgh meeting?"

"No, I'm up to speed with that. No, this is the fine print I got from the lawyers to get control of Checkman and Co. Contracts and codicils."

"That definitely sounds like a law firm!" She holds up her glass to be clinked. "To us. And our gorgeous long week-end."

"I'll drink to that." Jonathan says, going back to his documents.

"Darling?"

"Mmm?"

"What do mean by 'get control'?"

He looks up. "Sorry… what?"

"You wouldn't do anything to hurt Jo…"

"Elaine! Please."

It doesn't take long for Denny to help Wenna collect her things and stuff them into her rucksack and a veritable convention of carrier bags. She hands over the spare door-keys, and Denny pockets them.

She sighs, "Yes, it's me gone. Out of your life. Never have to see me again." She reaches down to stroke Lovelace, who can sense something's up, and follows her around the room.

"And you'll definitely take that mutt with you. Agreed."

From force of habit, Wenna attempts to steal a small figurine on his shelf, in full sight of Denny. Lovelace whimpers. Guiltily, she replaces it as Denny shakes his head in resigned despair.

DigiBrynthila watches them from inside the game.

"See, here's the thing, Mam. You show up out the blue, you're here… what? a minute and a half and already I've lost my girlfriend, my flat smells like a tobacco farm, the local coppers think I'm a mother-beater, I've spent a year's wages fixing the car… Shall I go on?"

"No. Sorry." Wenna bows her head, the closest to contrite anyone's ever seen. "I'm sorry, Denny. You know I can't help it."

"I know. But that doesn't help me. Help us."

"I'm glad you didn't turn out like me."

"Yeah, must take after my dad - whoever he was."

"Mr da Vinci?"

Denny waits for some explanation. Some context. But his mother is silent. "There never was a Mr da Vinci, was there, Mam?" She shakes her head. "Unless," he continues, "unless you shagged one of the TeenAged Mutant Ninja Turtles."

"I should be put away somewhere."

Denny lugs another of Wenna's bags near to the door. "Not a bad idea. When's your friend coming." She shrugs. He turns to face her. "I do love you, Mam, just not close up. I'd give anything to know you were living the good life, only not able to hurt yourself. Or anyone else." He reaches over to the display shelf and presents her with the carved statuette she's tried to steal.

She hugs him. He hugs her back. She steals back the keys.

Brynthila takes it all in from Denny's laptop screen. She adjusts an unseen micro-component and Wenna's phone starts whirring. Stops. Continues. And latches onto a laser tracking device. Both Denny and his mother remain blissfully unaware. In the road outside a van toots its horn. All the words have been spoken. Mother and son wave farewell.

Later that night Denny's asleep in his bedroom, content in the knowledge Lovelace, Wenna, and her belongings have been collected and are heading back to Wales. He wouldn't be so content to learn that her hippie pals have only driven a few streets away to a spacious old caravan parked up in a field next to a generator. It's only taken Wenna to plug in her kettle to declare it her new home. Denny may not know where she is, but Brynthila's plotted the exact coordinates.

The following morning, Jo parks her motorbike outside Max's office and removes her helmet. She spots Denny's convertible at the end of the road, but deliberately doesn't hold the door when Fiona buzzes her in. Ever the good hostess, Fiona sets down a couple of mugs of tea in front of them. It doesn't escape her notice that they're pointedly facing away from each other. They assume Max has commanded them here for a lecture about deadlines and delays. Except he's not actually there. Well, not yet. But they've barely finished their cuppas, when in he waddles, a bit breathless but overflowing with bonhomie. His arm is draped around Zac. Denny and Jo stand up, but are waved down by Max.

"Sit, sit. Dudes," he declares, pushing the young Asian man forward like a proud papa, "meet Zac. He's joining the team."

Zac beams and greets them warmly. Jo and Denny are not quite so enthusiastic, but they've yet to discover they're his heroes. Denny, whose usual patina of confidence has been, like his car, somewhat dented by Wenna, would love to whisper his thoughts to Jo, 'I thought child labour's been outlawed.' But he can't because they're not speaking to each other.

Max yells over to Fiona, "Tape." She appears with a portable cassette machine and turns it on. "Listen to this, dudes," Max says.

They do listen, and I must say, what they're hearing makes them smile and shift their shoulders to the beat. Suddenly Denny says, "Hang about… I know you. You're that kid from The Truck Stop. Nice one!"

"Yes, sir!" Max agrees. "And he's not just a pretty face. Look at these." He opens Zac's portfolio lying on his desk. "Talk us through your ideas, Zac." Which he does, not daring to believe his luck. The gist of his bigger picture is to introduce a series of opt-in/opt-out game-puzzles that can either enhance Brynthila's story or become a brief diversion from it. True enough, some of his ideas have been nicked from other games, but some are truly original.

Even before he's finished his presentation, both Jo and Denny have set aside their private tension and are interrupting, bombarding him with questions, discussing alternative solutions, but finally, finally thrilled Max has brought them someone who not only totally gets what they're doing, but can actually help.

"I know," admits Zac, "my artwork's not a patch on yours…"

"Hey, kid," Denny says, "you're doing just fine. Thing is, we just don't have time to program this stuff in before the Fair." And Jo can only agree.

"No biggie," Zac replies. "I can code."

Denny and Jo look at each other with dropped jaws. "When did you learn that?" Jo asks, "In the womb?"

"Dunno. When I was four or five, maybe."

"I think I might adopt you!" says Jo.

"Now… all we have to do is find a good place for his band to rehearse and lay down some funky tunes," says Max.

To which Jo modestly replies, "No problemo!" And Denny murmurs, "Who says 'funky'?"

With Jonathan's meetings done and dusted, and the future of the North Sea hanging in the balance, he and Elaine retreat to the Observation Car and the visual joys of Loch Lomand. Elaine has been making the most of the lingering afternoon, planning out in her head the best presentation for her book. Now their biggest dilemma is whether to join their fellow passengers for supper in the dining car, or order a more informal meal in their suite.

True to his word, Osborne has morphed into Mr Clean and worked his magic on the stone folly in the grounds of Falcon Lodge. With Zac's help, he's run some cables, set up Kurt's abandoned mixing desk, dug out some klieg lights, and borrowed a selection of mics and amps. Sorted! All they need now is the rest of the band.

With so much to do, Max has devolved the music session to Jo and Denny. So when Jo pops over to check out his progress, Osborne calls Zac over to introduce her. But he doesn't get the chance. "Hi Zac," she says.

Which certainly surprises Osborne. "You two know each other…" Not so much a question as a moment of confusion.

"Oh, yeah," Zac says. "Long story, Ozzie."

"Okay. That's cool," says Osborne. And to Jo, "Have you met the band as well?"

"Not yet. What are they called?"

"Zac on Blac. Sort of eco-metal. Hard to explain."

And right on cue, in marches Denny leading a couple of androgynous figures carrying musical instrument cases. One wears a knitted wool cap pulled down to the eyebrows, and the other's head is completely shaved. Zac introduces the drummer and bass player as Lady and the Tramp, but no one thinks he's serious. Though Jo and Denny are still a bit cool toward each other, she brings him up to speed. Without too much further ado, the trio take their places behind the mics while Osborne plugs them in. "What have you got for us, Zac?"

"Right. So we're working up tracks for an album, maybe couple of ideas might be good for the game. Some digital metallica, some analog found sound with drop-out degeneration…" The drummer fills the pause, joined by a short riff from the bass. Zac continues, "We want to… you know… crowd source the production. Couple of ideas so far … *Young Blossom's Screaming. Invasion In Vision.* We put that one on YouTube, lots of 'likes.'"

"*Don't Forget Wart Hole*," says the drummer.

"I won't!" laughs Zac at what's clearly the band's in-joke. And the impatient bass player explains to Denny, "No, see, that's the title." And adds, "*Blade of the Heavy Metal Fan.* Title track, two, three." They launch into a thrilling intro that seems to promise one musical path of development, then subverts itself. A kind of irony in sound.

It's not what either Denny or Jo would normally choose to listen to, but they both know these tracks are perfect for the game. With some editing, of course. They send thumbs up to Osborne. "Let's rehearse on tape," he says, flipping some switches.

It's a busy day on the High Street, and the ad hoc committee of retailers has taken over a table at the local coffee shop. It's the first time they've all met together since Jonathan put forward his company's proposal.

"So let me get this straight," says the owner of Si's Cycles on the corner. "We'd be bona fide members of a consortium, and all I have to do is service his daughter's motorbike whenever?"

"And all our leases will be extended for a thousand years, capped at today's rates. Plus I get full comp for the smashed window. Provided I get the morning papers delivered to Falcon Lodge every day. What's not to like?"

"Mm," says Tansy, the owner/manager of her eponymous boutique. "I've got to admit, it all sounds good. I'm just wondering what it is he's not telling us."

"Well, he's not telling us, at least not in so many words, that he's virtually buying out the entire High Street, bar the post office. In exchange for some helpful perks for us, and some insignificant kick-backs for him and his family. What's your deal, Max."

"Oh, just that his company's expanding into Leisure, but nothing's set in stone. We still have to work out the details. You may have heard we're working on a new video game, and his daughter's part of my development team."

Cycle Si says, "Sounds like a lot of wriggle room."

"Yes, true enough. But to be fair," says Max, "at the moment we've all got freeholders to answer to, and some of us don't even know who that is, I mean, if they're holding companies, or off- shore scammers or whatever. Am I right?" They all nod. "Tony," Max addresses a grey-bearded man in a Sikh turban at the head of the table, "remember how much hassle you had trying to get that leak fixed? You had to close the tandoor kitchen."

Everyone commiserates with Tony, agreeing how much they all love Indian food, and recounting similar anecdotes. "Why don't we run the proposal past, you know, what's their name, solicitors just past the fire station?" And Tansy adds, "Actually, we should invite them into the consortium."

"Great idea," says Max. "Jonathan's due back on Tuesday, we can let him know then. Agreed?"

With the music all but sorted, and Zac's help programming in some bonus mini-games, Denny and Jo tackle the main game development with renewed determination. They're counting on the Checkman touch to arrange everything else in time for the Games Fair.

They might make even more progress if they'd patched up their personal differences, but when each of them regards a new scene for Brynthila, it's clear why they're such a great team. Their intention was always to push the boundaries of character and story-telling with the surprise of silliness and suspense for game players. And their latest efforts prove how sophisticated their ideas have become.

Max would still prefer them to work in the same room, but he's just glad they're working at all. His progress reports to the Money Men no longer rely on false optimism, and their encouraging replies feed everyone's ego. He's waiting for the right time to tell Jo, Denny and Zac that a Chinese telly crew will be covering the Games Fair launch. And Fiona knows how hard it is for Max to keep a secret. Up in the turret room, Jo fills the screen with code. While across town, Denny's screen responds with a series of action moves. The images are interrupted by an eMail from Jo which reads: Starting Level 12. Need more designs.

When he's granted access, Max peers over Denny's shoulder, approving the new work. But when he peers over Jo's shoulder, he's completely baffled by coding gobbledygook. As for his access to Zac, frankly there isn't any. The lad's a law unto himself. "Like Mozart," notes Fiona. "Or Billy the Kid," counters Max.

When Zac was little more than a toddler his parents, both secondary school teachers, encouraged him in his ambitions, be they artsy or techno. His lad-flavoured bedroom grew with him as he learned more and more of matters beyond the school curriculum. But when the volume of his music began rattling the plates on the kitchen shelf, and the force of his laser-based experiments threatened to turn their house into a Home Counties subsidiary of NASA, they set up a large shed in the back garden, blocked from prying eyes by hedging.

 It's sound-proof, fitted out with a work station, and houses his collection of physics textbooks, sharing space with a Bert Weedon manual and an enormous mixer-desk . The only bit of decor is a framed letter from Brian Eno in reply to the one he sent when he was six. If you're ever looking for him, here's a clue not even his band knows - he'll be in the shed. Which is where he is now, putting the finishing touches to his latest sock-knocker-off. A prototype Augmented Reality Hood. He tries it on and gropes around the room. But without any virtual worlds, he's just a bloke in a weird headpiece. He turns his attention to the synth and picks out the melody line of a new tune he's been working on.

 With the Games Fair deadline galloping apace, the team pushes themselves past the limit. Sleep has become a distant memory, a land beyond the hills of anxiety. Osborne's installed a coffee machine in Jo's room, keeping her wired in to caffeine, while Denny fights Morpheus with a jazz track and periodic slaps of his own cheeks.

Jo receives Denny's latest mail attachment and clicks on the image. It's Brynthila dressed in a strange outer-space bikini and shoulder-length fitted gloves. She's posed in a grand dining chamber, in the midst of a chess game. Her opponent is her DigiPrince, still confined to his cage. Jo virtually attacks the keyboard and presses 'send.'

Her message, screaming in capital letters, reads WHY NOT JUST HAVE HER NAKED?!! Denny starts to ring Jo's number, but ditches that idea and immediately starts work on a new design, covering up more of Brynthila's flesh. Fighting will get no one no where no how.

Jo reads her latest eMail from Denny. She reaches for her phone, but changes her mind. Her screen now shows Brynthila in the same chess scene, but now wearing a still sexy, but much more sophisticated and regal garment. The message reads: 'My bad! Let's just nail this, okay?'

After a few days of this intensity, it's clear to Brynthila whether they know it or not, Jo and Denny yearn to be together. This is her destiny, to bring peace and harmony. Surely she can outwit their resistance to the inevitable. She sees her chance when both Denny and Jo have given in to sleep in front of their screens. DigiBrynth reaches into her satchel and throws a handful of sparkly magic dust that somehow transcends their monitors and lands on each of them as they slumber. *A Midsummer Night's Dream* moment. And when they wake…

Time's ticking. Zac on Blac, carrying their instruments, hover around Fiona's desk waiting to see Max. He's on long distance with the money guys, giving some last minute reassurance that everything's ready for the Games Fair launch in a couple of days. He's taking them through his Checkman Check-list, trying to rein in the clown-crazy excitement he feels.

Finally, Fiona allows the band to enter the inner sanctum. They take out their instruments, and Zac gets straight to the point. "This is the new track. Denny thinks it could be a single, but he wanted you to hear it first." Max can't help but be flattered. He leans back, ready to amazed. "What's it called?" he asks.

"*When The Fox Weeps In the Forest, You Will Wither And Die.*"

"Catchy," says Max.

Whatever her irregular sleep and eating patterns over the past week, Jo's been all-but ordered by Osborne to attend the family meal to welcome home her parents. Actually, she's really missed them and listens with genuine interest to their encounter with the Highlands.

Elaine's fairly buzzing about the prospect of her book. "Honestly, Jo, I've seen photos of that landscape, of course, but I never expected to be quite so blown away. Even your father couldn't stop looking!"

"Why wouldn't I? It's stunning!"

"I got some super shots. Adorable baby Highland calf wandered right up to the train. I'll show you when you've got a moment."

"Cool," Jo says. She swallows a modest mouthful of green beans. "And is the North Sea safe in your hands, Daddy?"

"Don't you worry about that. Max has told me what a sterling job you're doing. You and Denny. And that new kid."

"Zac." She's impressed. "Didn't know you were keeping such close tabs."

The following day, Jo, Denny and Zac are in Max's office. This is the first time Jo and Denny have met up in person since they got a faceful of Brynthila's magic dust. They try to face away from each other, but can't help sneaking looks over their shoulder. With a mixture of excitement and anxiety, they've just handed over the completed demo disc for the Games Fair. Max takes great glee in opening and closing the plastic case. He fusses over the inanimate object as though he were a brooding bird adjusting its incubating eggs.

Zac asks permission to hang onto his copy. "Me and the band need to do some tweaking."

Fiona comes in and sets down some papers for Max to sign. She announces, "We've got the goody-bags, now all we need is to pop a demo disc into each one. You're all hereby volunteers." No one dares object. She turns to Jo, "Will you be travelling up to London with your father tomorrow?"

"I hope so, fewer cars the better."

"No, the rest of us are getting the train," she says. Which is news to the to others, but no one can find a reason to object. Max walks around the desk and opens his embrace to include all three of his team. "You did it again, dudes. I knew you would. *Brynthila: Maze of Life* is a triumph... what is it?" Jo and Denny repeat in dull unison, "A triumph." They know that with more time and less hassle there's so much more they wanted to do. But Zac's response is far more enthusiastic; he waves his arms over his head while making a series of unvoiced sounds by varying the position of his tongue and teeth. It's a very passable imitation of a beat-box.

"What's that?" Max wants to know. "Mouth popping," explains Zac. But Max doesn't get it. He turns to his sister. "Fi! get this disc copied, ready for... "

Max reaches for the disc case and opens it - it's empty. He panics. "Where's the disc? It was just here! You saw me put it down, where ...?"

But Fiona has already loaded the demo disc into the source drive. "Don't panic, Mr. Mainwaring."

Max is relieved, but chides Fiona. "Nearly give me a heart attack!" He pushes play. Zac's music proves the perfect intro to the opening of the story. Max bounces up and down in his swivel chair. "Wicked! This Games Fair is going to kick ass! Top stand. Top game. And top team!" Again, Max rises to hug Jo, Denny and Zac. His grin might be permanently painted on. Zac tries to be uber- cool, while Jo and Denny simultaneously try to smile, fight sleep, and acknowledge the strange force taking control of their gaze.

"Righty ho, Top Team," Max commands. "Short break, do whatever you have to do, then all back here for a glorious afternoon of disc packing. We're all in this together - isn't that what they tell us on the telly?!" But, as everyone gets ready to leave, Max says, "Sorry, not you, Fiona. Get the discs copied and rustle up some empty cardboard boxes somewhere. I think there's a sandwich in my desk."

Fiona sighs with resignation, regretting she ever encouraged her brother to attend that Village Marketing Seminar. She says, "*Jawohl mein führer*, and dare we ask what you'll be doing for the common cause?"

"I'll be at yoga class, aligning my chakras, of course." He turns to Denny, "We okay to store the boxes at yours overnight? Wouldn't want to breach our insurance." Denny nods.

Just outside town in the caravan Wenna's made her HQ, she's convened a handful of the disgruntled locals and a couple of her hippie pals. Some are packed together on the pull-down bench attached to the caravan wall, and the rest budge up on the seat at the far end.

Lovelace circles on the spot, trying to find a space to lie down. She doesn't like it when they all talk at once and covers her head with a paw. Wenna takes charge, listening patiently to their grumbles about pay and percentages. She spots her chance to parlay the obvious discontent into direct action.

One bloke isn't quite getting it. "He said ten percent of nothing is nothing. I say we ask for twenty percent!" Some other voice their agreement, but Wenna shushes them.

"Looks like that Max is pulling a fast one," she says. "Well, anything he can pull, we can pull faster! Now, here's the plan …" They all lean forward into a conspiratorial huddle.

Chapter 17

There's only silence along the High Street. The last car rolled by a while ago, and the only light seeps out from the Checkman window. No one on Max's top team anticipates sleeping tonight. Even Max. They've been at it for hours. All hands to the pump, in a mini-production line on the office floor. Fill each plastic disc case, pass it to the next person who slaps on a numbered label, and hands it over to be dropped into a goody bag, and finally piled into a box with the others.

Every time Denny looks over at Jo, he's fascinated by the shape of her profile. When she catches his eye, she immediately looks away, but can't help noticing how sweetly his hair sort of swings a bit when he moves.

Headphones are clamped over Zac's pony-tail, and he's set up a rhythm in his head. I wouldn't be surprised if he's composing a work chant.

Everyone appears to be absorbed in their tasks, until Fiona notices that at the far end of the line, Max has slumped down and the goody bags are collecting just outside the box. She rushes over, full of concern. Everyone gets up, ready to help. Tentatively Fiona feels Max's cheek and shakes his shoulder. Denny can't resist brushing away a stray curl from Jo's eyes. She smiles her thanks.

Suddenly, Max opens his eyes. "I'm awake, I'm awake," he says with sleep in his voice.

"Get packing!" orders Fiona.

The new morning is still hovering beyond the dark horizon when the team are finally done. They all help load the full boxes into Denny's convertible, and wave him off to store them in his flat for safe-keeping. Jo buckles on her motorbike helmet and takes off for the Lodge. When they look around for Zac, he's already gone. And Max and Fiona trod their weary way down the path to home. She's booked

ScreenSaver! 201

one of the Games Fair service vans to pick-up at Denny's at six. That's AM!

If ever a group of people deserved their long-awaited sleep, it's Max's Top Team. Their pillows throughoutd runs to join them.

In the security lobby they sign in and collect their laminated badges, pinning them on each other in a kind of bonding ritual. Zac is particularly thrilled to be part of it all. He thanks Fiona and assures her that Lady and the Tramp will be along later. "They don't do mornings."

Everyone pitches in, even Max, putting finishing touches to the display stand - checking and double-checking everything from amplifiers to brochures, pinning up posters, positioning the giant photo-cutouts of laser-eyed monsters, armoured mastodons, dragons, and space warriors. 'Eat your heart out, Comic Con,' thinks Max, metaphorically patting himself on the back.

"Mind the cables," warns Fiona, indicating a gang of sockets, most doing double duty. She kicks them out of the way under a table. A huge plasma screen overhangs the stand, featuring a static image of Brynthila from the game. Zac flips the switch to set her on an action loop, accompanied by his intro track. Jo and Denny are still sneaking looks at each other.

Max volunteers Zac to help him get coffees for the team. While they're gone, Fiona arranges the box full of goody bags, ready for the big giveaway. She corrals Jo and Denny to help with the inventory. They're also assigned to keep a daily record of potential customers and list likely distribution companies and other contacts. As she shows them the small blue metal box for collecting business cards, Jo tells her, "Daddy's got an early meeting but he'll drop by later."

"You think he's the one who swung us this great location?" asks Fiona.

"Oh, I think he would have said. Don't you, Den?" Denny has been gazing at the curve of her neck, but manages a murmur of agreement. If you happen to be looking at the big display screen, you just might catch Brynthila glance away from her battle and smile her approval at him.

"Honestly," continues Fiona, "I thought we'd been consigned to the murky depths of corridor hell." She senses their anxiety, though misreads the cause. "Oh, don't be nervous," she says. "We made it through Bluebell's launch, and this one's definitely got …"

But she's interrupted by Zac's arm holding out a takeaway coffee. Max pulls a chair up next to the demo computer. He clicks his fingers towards Fiona. "Disc," he commands. Fiona passes a CD case to Max. He opens it and tosses it aside.

"Very funny. I said disc. Not empty case." Fiona sighs and gives him another case from the display pile. Max opens it. "Fi… What are you playing at?" He throws this second empty case aside and picks up another for himself, opens it, tosses it aside. Soon all five of them are frantically going through the cases and chucking them over their shoulders.

"Who packed these? Fiona?"

She's in no mood for this. "You know full well who packed them. We all packed them. Including you! When we left last night those cases were full."

Max knows there's no one to blame. At least no one right here, right now. The others try to find something logical to hold onto, but they're grabbing shadows. Jo looks straight at Denny. "Who'd want to sabotage our work?"

"Sabotage is an ugly word."

"Passing the buck is two ugly words."

"Three!"

"I wasn't counting the definite article!" And they march off to opposite sides of the platform. Uh-oh! Brynthila's frown and furrowed brow might be a reaction to a troll attack, or a fear that Jo and Denny are resisting the magic. And she was so sure it was working…

Zac's been on the look-out for his band, but he spots a two-man Chinese camera crew scanning the main hall. He hops down from the stand to guide them over. He's delighted to discover their English is terrible, and he can be a useful interpreter. He absolutely loves being useful.

Max regards the empty plastic cases littering the display stand, and sinks to his knees in despair. "This is like maybe the worst day of my entire life!" He sits cross-legged on the floor, attempting the lotus position, despite being unable to get his chubby legs down. Intention, he believes, is as good as execution.

When he looks up there's a lad scribbling on a notepad. He points a camera-phone at Max. Click click. His official badge identifies him as a reporter for the daily *Exhibition Newsletter*. "Can I quote you?" asks the tyro.

Max growls at him. He flees. Max rocks back and forth, trying to get to his feet. He looks like one of those bottom-weighted toys that always rights itself, but in his case, try as he might, he can't haul himself up. He yells, "Fiona!" But his sister has deliberately turned her back, ignoring his plight. Is Max at last learning she can't be the solution forever?

He's desperately trying to remember the best yoga tips to keep calm and carry on. Breathe, he tells himself. Breathe in, two, three, and out, two… But a klaxon jolts his calm into sudden panic. It's the signal the doors have opened to punters and players and games pros. Calm, Max repeats to himself. Calm. Calm.

Denny helps him to his feet, and shares an idea. "Look, why don't we turn this around?"

"How, dude? Everything's going tits up and I don't see how it could get any worse. So how's it going to get better?"

"Well, we strategise." Max recognises that word from his seminar and pays attention. Denny continues, "If anyone looks interested, and they take a goody bag, why not say the empty case entitles them to fifty percent off the retail price when the game's officially launched. Then we make a note of their contact details, and voila, ready-made database for publicity and that."

"Denny, that's double brilliant! High five, dude!" He goes off to explain the plan to Fiona and Jo. Good old Denny!

The first rush of Games Fair punters tours the main hall, and some stop at the Checkman stand. Brynthila's action loop seems especially popular, and Jo is especially pleased to see so many tween- aged girl gamers… definitely their target market! She fields questions about the game and official launch date, and explains the discount offer, while Fiona collects business cards and keeps the paperwork updated.

Meanwhile, Zac has brought the TV crew onto the display stand where they wait politely to be introduced. He taps Max on the shoulder and consults with the men in Chinese. Both Denny and Max are more than impressed. "They're from China Global," Zac says, adding their audience is in the billions. As the men offer their hands to shake, Max and Denny bow their heads in what they assume is a traditional greeting. Zac translates the slight mix-up, which breaks the diplomatic ice. Happily, no one's lost face, and there are smiles all round. "I said they could plug in here, okay?"

Max, of course, is the wrong person to ask about technical matters, but he knows he mustn't risk causing offence. "Sure," he agrees. Zac and Denny help the crew adjust lights and find some spare sockets for their equipment. The plan is to interview Max, get some quotes from the top team, and record some excerpts from the demo disc. Except, of course, there are no demo discs.

They clip a tiny microphone to Max's tie for a Q and A, and start the camera rolling. There's a fizz hiss from one of the sockets. On the huge screen overhead, Brynthila's scream is drowned out by the crowd. Nooooooooo! Zac translates the first question to Max, but before he can answer, the air blooms into an arc flash which explodes with a deafening Ka-boom! It shoots Max clear across the floor and shorts out the entire stand.

No spotlights. No Brynthila display screen. No demo hard drive. No Chinese telly. Max's face is charred and his dreams shattered. Fiona can't abandon her sororal duty and runs to his side.

A flurry of Exhibition stewards cordon off the area, directing the public well away. At which point Jonathan makes his belated appearance. He's missed the excitement and bounds up to Max who's giving in to catatonia.

"How are we doing, partner?" says Jonathan.

Max completely loses it. "Help!" he shrieks.

Denny is driving Jo home. They sit in silence for a while, till she says, "It wasn't me. Stealing those discs."

"'Course it wasn't. Why would you? Wasn't me either."

"No. I know."

"I still have no idea why we aren't speaking."

Jo says, "We are speaking. This is us. Speaking."

"Give me a clue. Please."

"Try starting at my party," she says.

"Yeah, I spent the whole time trying to find you. To tell you…"

"… that you'd rather be kissing that - what'shername woman."

"Who, Lauren? You saw that? No," he tries to explain, "that wasn't what it looked like."

"Well, it certainly looked like what it looked like. Oh, and what message exactly were you sending me with that… so called present?!"

"What? That photo of you and me? I thought you'd like it."

She's confused. "You thought I'd like a photograph of you and Brynthila and my arm?"

"Hang about. It was supposed to be that photo of you and me with Brynthila in the middle." Denny's trying to add two and two and suddenly getting five. "Actually, I had some help. But that person promised to put it in a lovely frame and wrap it nicely. And if I ever see her again, I'll wrap her very nicely in a cement overcoat before I push her off the nearest pier."

Jo realises exactly what he's saying. They pull into Falcon Lodge. Neither of them moves. Jo ventures a suggestion. "We could copy the discs from the master. Won't take that long. We'd be back in time for…"

Denny considers the practicalities and checks his watch. "The fair closes in half an hour. Besides, the whole stand is wrecked."

"Oh. Maybe not, then."

"Maybe we should wait to hear from Fiona. I think your father drove her and Max to the hospital."

"Probably right. Poor Max. All his plans." She's about to get out of the car. "Speaking of plans, I think your plan for the discount demo is inspired."

Denny takes the compliment with good grace. "Thanks."

"Like to come in for a minute?" Jo says.

"Maybe another time. First I have to talk myself out of matricide."

She smiles. "You're going to murder your mattress?"

ScreenSaver!

He leans over and kisses her on the cheek. She watches him drive off.

Wenna, swigs from a lager can, Denny's laptop open in front of her. She's attempting to play the game. The irony is that for all her expertise in daily life game-playing, she's totally unfamiliar with the video version. She takes a long drag on her ciggie and drops it into the empty can. Brynthila fades onto the screen.

Wenna hasn't a clue how she managed to summon her up. She presses her palms over random keys, like a two year old at a piano. DigiBrynthila reacts by skipping all over the monitor display, fast-forwarding through the game levels until her limbs fly off, and she disintegrates in a muddle of colour. A warning siren accompanies the dreaded screen message: Game Over. Lovelace barks. The game logo fades in with a 2D image of Brynthila's face beside a Replay button.

Wenna confides to the screen. "I don't get this game. Tricky enough when you've got the disc," she cackles. "Must be a whole lot harder without." She lights another fag and clicks Replay. As she waits for the game to load again, she flicks cigarette ash over the keyboard.

Suddenly DigiBrynthila appears unbidden. She leans forward, her golden hair falling down out of the monitor into the 3D world. Her digital arm passes through the plasma screen to become tangible as she brushes away the ash from the keyboard. There's no doubt her words are directed straight at a very mystified Wenna. "Thou baggage! Thou evil bedswerving driggle-draggle!"

"What did I press? What did I press?" Wenna says aloud, looking round at the sound of the front door being unlocked.

Denny's voice bellows long before we see him enter. "Mam! I could smell you from the next village." He is fury redefined. Trying to shoo the smoke away, he storms in to see Wenna cowering in a corner. As he goes after her, he trips over one of the plastic carrier bags which go flying, spilling their contents all over the floor. You'll have guessed by now that those are the missing demo discs.

ScreenSaver!

Denny glares at his mother. "I knew it! I knew it was you! Why? Why would you do that?"

Wenna sinks to her knees, pleading, trotting out every excuse in the book. But Denny's read the book too many times to be fooled again. And still she tries it on. "I told you, boyo, it's that Max, isn't it? He's a crook. He'll bring you down. And that Jo, she's a bit of a gorgon, as well."

Suddenly Denny's voice becomes very calm. "A touching tale," he says. "And now we come to the part where I render you inoperative. Stay right there, I'm just going to fetch a sharp implement." He heads for the kitchen.

Unseen by Denny, Brynthila materialises completely from the laptop. This will be her last time out of the machine, and she knows it. But she musters enough venom to declare, "Gorgon is it? Hold fast, harpy... thou shan't 'scape, vile scullion."

As Wenna looks for an exit, Brynthila and Lovelace foil her every move. Brynthila confiscates Wenna's mobile for safe-keeping. Then she reaches into her silver satchel and flings a handful of immobility dust over Wenna and the dog. They immediately fall into a trance while she produces a tiny cage from the satchel and shrinks them down into it. She tucks them both back into the bag and leaves the flat.

Meanwhile in the kitchen, Denny clutches a small butter knife. But instead of committing murder by dairy spread, he's speed-dialling Jo. "Hiya... only me. Listen, don't worry about the discs. They've turned up ... Where? Funny you should ask... just lying about in a witch's cauldron... Cool, I'll check them now and ring you back."

Denny, knife still in hand, tiptoes into the next room. It's empty. The flat door is ajar. Denny peers down the corridor. Nothing. He steps into the street, glancing right and left, and calls out, "Mam?" But it's all quiet on the western front. Deciding his mother has legged it, he retreats to the flat to inspect the digital damage. But when he calls up one of the turret scenes, all he can see is an empty castle room.

ScreenSaver!

Realising how silly it is but unable to stop himself, he calls out to the screen. "Hello? Brynthila? Oh, bugger! where have you got to now?" For safety's sake, he knows he'll have to check through every disc and accepts the challenge. This calls for a caffeine boost. Provided Wenna's left him any beans.

While he's in the kitchen, the doorbell rings. Denny assumes it's Wenna with more excuses. Should he just ignore her? Let her wait, he decides, weighing up the options. Maybe till the coffee's brewed. The bell rings again. Maybe he should answer but leave the security chain on. After all, his car's outside and he hasn't forgotten the last time she got her paws on that! Speaking of paws, where's the dog?

At last Denny decides to see who's ringing the doorbell. But instead of buzzing them in, he walks cautiously to the front door trying to peer through the frosted glass. Nobody… there's no one there. He steps outside and sees a packet about the size of a basketball, all wrapped in brown paper and scribbled with his name on front and back. He takes it inside and removes the paper. It contains a woven metallic fabric fashioned into a hood. Inside the hood is an audio option and a viewing system attached to a standard usb cable. Denny is uber-intrigued. He searches the package for some kind of note or message.

Chapter 18

Jo stares up at the tapestry tester over her four-poster bed, trying to make sense of the long day's ups and downs. An empty mug of hot chocolate residue rests on the bedside table, lovingly prepared by her mother. She's drifting off to sleep when she hears a noise, and sits up to find Brynthila materialised in front of her.

"What are you doing here?!"

"I know everything seems to be going wrong, but we can fix it. I just need more information."

"Why? More information for what?" She notices Brynthila fading in and out of view. "Uh-oh," she says, "you're going all faint again."

"I know. 'Tis as you decreed. This is my last time… out here. In your world."

"I'm sorry," Jo says, and she genuinely is. "But it's too late to reprogram you. What else can I do?"

"We've got to save Denny, of course. Oh, and you as well. And the game."

"But… the Games Fair… you saw what happened…"

"By the Rood and verily, that Fair was foul, but the game can be saved if you work together." She seems very confident.

But Jo's reluctant to believe her. "By a miracle, maybe." She starts to get up from the bed but Brynthila sprinkles her with immobility dust and she freezes. "Verily," Brynthila says, "a miracle from my world." She pulls out Wenna's phone and calls Denny's number.

Denny sees the caller ID, and steels himself to confront his mad mother. But it's not Wenna after all. It's Jo! Well, let's just say if you had Jo in front of you and that voice on your phone, you'd be mighty confused. It's an exact replica... who's real, who's the imposter? She tells him that she's been sent one of those Augmented Reality hoods and asks if he has one as well. He confirms that he does. "Well, plug it in and load up one of those discs, and we can meet up inside the game." Denny agrees that's a great idea.

Back onscreen, DigiBrynthila smiles and transports herself to the grand hall. She reclines on a bench that appears to be made of solid silver, but gives under her weight as though it were the softest down cushion. Beside her are two cages. In one is her DigiPrince, asleep in the corner, and the other contains DigiWenna and Lovelace, shrunken to game size. Their cage rests on wheels that look strangely reptilian. Yet a third cage, strewn with meadow flowers, houses a tiny DigiJo. Striding into the vast chamber comes DigiDenny, navigating under the AR hood.

DigiBrynthila claps her hands to summon two striped Guard Lemurs with particularly muscular arms. The first Guard asks, "Hood on or off, Your Highness?" She gestures for them to remove the Augmented Reality hood from shrunken-down Denny and pops it into her silver satchel.

He blinks against the fire-torches fastened to the walls. When he tries to look up, he's all-but blinded by the intense blur of light bordering the ceiling. The Guard Lemurs manoeuvre him into the cage with Jo, and ever so slowly she emerges from under a mound of blossom so relieved to see him. As they hug, Denny wonders, "Did you program those creatures to speak?" She shakes her head.

Brynthila dismisses the Guards. "Welcome, little poppet people, to The Maze of Life," she announces. Denny and Jo pinch each other to check they're not dreaming.

Out in the meat-world, Zac rings the band with the bad news about the Games Fair, and ensconces himself in his shed. He loads up the demo disc he's been hanging onto, but he still can't quite figure out the best configuration for his AR invention. After an hour or so, he make some final electronic adjustments, checks and re-checks that everything's ready, and activates the hood.

"Excellent fair and timely!" exclaims DigiBrynthila as Zac drops down at her feet. No wonder when his mum knocks on the shed door to tell him supper's ready, there's no reply.

Instead, he can hardly believe his eyes as he pivots around for a three-sixty view of the rendered royal hall. The vaulted ceiling overhead appears miles away, great curtains of gleaming light dropping the full height to the ground. He greets Denny and Jo, together in their cage, both trying to control their sense of terror. Zac is now as small as they, which doesn't appear to concern him at all.

Brynthila confiscates his AR hood, and hands him a furled parchment. She pats a jewel-encrusted ottoman beside her. "Thou art the chart, good my fellow, and wilt map the journey that follows." He hesitates. "Sit!" she commands, and down he plops.

"Zac… mate," pleads Denny. "You've gotta get us out of here."

In the corridor of a hospital ward Jonathan helps Fiona question the doctor on call. "He's a very lucky man," he tells them. They're both relieved to learn, despite his char-grilled cheeks and blurred vision, Max will suffer no lasting effects. They glance over to him through the ward window. His bed has been raised slightly at the head; he stares into space, breathing through an oxygen tube in his nostrils. "We'd like to keep him overnight," the doctor says, "just for observation. Why don't you go home, and we'll ring if there's any change." He checks his wrist-watch. "Please excuse me, I'm due downstairs."

Fiona is reluctant to leave, but Jonathan gently guides her to the lift. "I'll drive you home," he says, but he's already plotting how to turn the Games Fair debacle into an advantage for the consortium.

Brynthila presses a shard on her mail and leather forearm bracer. It produces a strident chord, not unlike a rutting moose, and the cage housing Wenna and Lovelace shapes itself into life. The front end develops four pairs of unblinking eyes on either side of a crocodilian face. Two tapered tails swish together at the opposite end. The bars of the cage interlock like curving rib bones, and the whole contraption rolls away on its lizard wheels. Brynthila ignores Wenna's faint protests and instructs Lovelace to keep her in check. She'll deal with them later.

First, she addresses Denny and Jo, who are trying in vain to understand what's going on. She serves them a goblet of refreshing liquid. "Cold enough?" she asks. She takes back the goblet and adjusts a temperature valve at the base, before handing it over to Denny. "You'll have to share," she explains. "We're a bit low on supplies."

Jo has no idea how she got here nor how this intra-game works. She assures Denny she never programmed it. He denies it's his design. "Zac?" she asks, but Zac shakes his head. Denny is diverted by the effects of the strange drink and offers Jo the goblet. It's like nothing they've ever tasted, and with each sip they feel new power coursing through their veins.

They hear Brynthila reel off a set of tasks, designed to explore the missing game Levels. She stresses Zac's neutrality, and repeats over and over that the couple can only succeed if they join forces. Wit, she says, not weapons. As she speaks, the map flies from Zac's hands and pins itself to the air, making visible the sections of the game that require their attention.

A series of inter-connecting caves is traced out in laser-light, each leading to a different era of human history, from the first Dmanisi hominid trek out of Africa right up to yesterday. Zac's amazed. "Hey, dude!" he crows, "those are my caves!" He looks over at Denny and Jo for a sign of approval. "I just designed those yesterday; how did you…"

"Awesome!" says Denny. And Jo agrees. Zac rises from the ottoman and high-fives them through the cage. But an unseen powerful force pulls him back down.

Brynthila interrupts the self-congratulation with a recitation of rote. "Heed well, my friends of petty size. This is a game beyond play. Heed well if you value your very lives and the breath therein." From her

ScreenSaver! 214

trusty silver satchel she flings a filigreed wand to Zac. He examines its composition... a set of inter-relational rotating disks. They all recognise the principle as a standard games fare problem-solving challenge. Altering any of the disks also affects the others. But none of them has any clue for the correct code.

Jo asks, "I don't suppose we have time to reverse engineer it, do we?" Zac consults Brynthila, but she's looking up, up to the far away roof of the grand hall. Soundlessly, the entire ceiling opens out like a camera iris, revealing the incalculable pattern of swirling galaxies, ever on the move. Through the star-beams a blazing light forms itself into the gigantic Goddess Gevreen. Brynthila drops to her knees, and the others find they cannot stare at her directly but must avert their gaze.

The Goddess beckons to Zac, who rises up in the air to her huge face. "You hold the Chrono Crater Creator," she tells him. "It is the salvation of you all." They watch in amazement as the map bulges like a bas relief with a hidden sector of the landscape. "But you must tread the Maze path in the proper order, for Time waits for no man. Or woman. Or... oh, you know... those other genders. So difficult to keep up with these evolving life-forms... Sorry, what was I saying... oh, yes, Time." She releases Zac, who falls back down just near Denny and Jo. Only their hands outstretched through the cage bars prevent him from landing with a bruising bump.

The Goddess lifts Brynthila's bowed head. "Thou, brave warrior, thou knows't thy fate. If they succeed you will die." She nods, accepting her lot in the game.

But when they hear this, Jo and Denny scream "No!" And Zac dares "Whoa, are you for real, lady?" Jo simply cannot accept this news, which she takes as an attack on her programming prowess. "Why do you need to sacrifice her? I mean, she's not perfect, but..."

"Yeah," agrees Denny. "She's just been trying to help."

"And so, at last," decrees the boom boom of the voice of the Goddess. "At last you see the meaning of true power in the Maze of Life."

ScreenSaver!

Their dejection is palpable. But Zac asks, "Come on, there must be something we can do. You seem like you might have a decent bone in your body. I mean… does your body have bones?"

"Silence, and listen well. Your Final Level Task is hidden in one of the caves, and do not imagine we will reveal which one, however passionate your orisons. Clues abound if you but sense vision over mirage, and attune your auditory canal. Not to mention closing tight the dominion of your tongue and trachea. Do not get silly with your cilia, and try for pity's sake to refrain from farting. What can break can also mend. With every cave you conquer, the Chrono Counter will rotate, and the Crater will be filled. When all are filled in the right order, your path will become clear." And before they can stop her, the Goddess rides a beam of light up and up to join the stars overhead. For those of you who know who Scotty is, I can tell you, he ain't here!

The three can't decide whether to come up with a strategy to comply with such bizarre, draconian rules, or to figure out a way to subvert them. Suddenly Jo calls out, "Yo, Brynthila! Seriously, are you just going to sit there and take all that… that…"

"Bullshit!" Denny finishes her thought. Zac agrees. "Totally, dude!"

"Yeah," Jo continues. "Games may need rules, but life's not like that. Nobody can tell you how to live… I mean so long as you don't hurt anyone along the way. Otherwise it's just tyranny."

"How 'bout it, Brynth… you up for some rebellion?" Denny asks Brynthila, "or would you rather be a pawn?"

She fixes her gaze on Jo. "You! Wench! What do you mean I'm not perfect?!" It takes them a moment to realise she's made her first joke.

"Does that mean you'll help us?" asks Jo. She's still wary, but willing to play her part.

"You'll have to do the legwork," says Brynthila. But if I were you, I'd start with that handy clue."

Jo and Denny try to remember what that might be. Zac knows. "What can break can also mend," he declares. "Cool! Who's going to help get me back up that light beam?"

Zac explains his plan, hoping that the item about to be broken is the rotating Chrono Counter, and not himself! Jo and Denny are very concerned for his safety. They want to do something... anything, but considering they're confined to the cage, there aren't a lot options. They're at the mercy of Brynthila to help and protect them all. There's a lot at stake.

Have you ever heard of the Chinese rope trick? It's also known as the Indian rope trick and its variations support a staple con in magic circles since the ninth century. In case you don't know, a magician takes a coil of rope and throws it high into the air. Instead of falling back down, the rope stays upright. At that point either the magician himself or a young assistant climb up the rope and disappear and then reappear. The whole thing is, of course, a hoax; no one's ever proved such a trick could work.

So why am I telling you? Well, you remember that Brynthila has promised to help Zac rise up to the top of the beam of light. That help is rooted on her head. Since Jo reprogrammed her to grow back her hair, it's been sprouting at super-speed and reaches down to her ankles. She gathers the loops and bunches of golden hair and throws them higher and higher still to the top of the grand hall. And, just like in the ancient rope trick, instead of falling back down, the pillar of hair remains rigid and sturdy.

Without a moment's hesitation, Zac executes a kung fu leap onto Brynthila's shoulders and begins to climb up the rope of gold. Jo and Denny hold their breath in anticipation as Zac reaches the top. "Now!" he shouts, and Brynthila's hair collapses, leaving Zac holding on to thin air. The Chrono Counter slips from his grasp, and down, down he plummets, with nothing to break his fall.

He lies face up on the ground, unable to move, unable to speak. Denny turns to Brynthila. "Is he..." but he can't bear to finish the thought. "You've killed him!" yells Jo. "How could you believe that so-called Goddess?! And how could we believe you?!"

Gradually Brynthila focuses on the Chrono Counter. Yes, it's smashed to bits and is scattered all across the huge slabs of the floor. But now, ever so slowly, all those bits are moving together, slithering along the stone. They head for the area just next to Denny and Jo's cage. But instead of reforming, the pieces line up as individual tools, each intricately crafted in silver and gems. A kind of screwdriver. A serrated blade. A trowel and hand rake. And a beautifully rendered key. As Denny and Jo collect the pieces, they see there's a codex rolled up around the rotating gears.

Jo reaches for the key as Denny feels around the cage for an appropriate lock, and soon they're free. First they kneel beside Zac, trying to discover whether he's breathing. It's not looking good.

Denny approaches Brynthila, while Jo positions herself on the opposite flank of the cushion. "Hang about," he says, "you've just conned us into sacrificing Zac to take your place." He signals to Jo to move in closer. "Well, you self-appointed princess, let's see how you like it!" And they grab hold of her, spin her around so that she's bound by her own hair, and bundle her into the meadow-filled cage.

Denny embraces Jo, and they share a pretty passionate victory kiss. "Ahem," Brynthila interrupts before the literary censors send in their storm troopers. "Aren't you forgetting someone?" And they run over to Zac.

"Didn't that light-beam bint say something about auditory canals?" Jo nods, adding, "... and what would he want to hear right now?" They begin searching for Zac's AR hood, hoping he's programmed in his music for the game tracks. But it's a fruitless search. Until they glance over to the meadow cage.

Brynthila has managed to wriggle an arm through a loop of her hair, and she holds out the hood, just beyond reach. Denny and Jo decide not to risk opening the cage; they understand all too well that Brynth's powers of deception can work for good or ill. There must be another way.

"I'll tell you what," Brynthila says. "Here are my terms."

"Terms? We have you locked up with the magic key, lest you forget," says Jo. "Do you really think you're in any position to lay down the law?"

"Yes. I do. First of all, I will accept any genuine apology."

"For what?!" Jo and Denny say together.

"'Twas no deception of mine that you're all in this thribbling mussy muddle. I am trying to help. I am still trying to help. I know I owe you my very existence, and whether or not the Goddess Gevreen is a truthy-soothsayer or a strike of ball lightning, the rules of the game cannot be codified in every nook and granny-knot. So, yes, I am trying to help you, but not to save myself."

She purses her lips and fashions a whistling sound sending its aural curlicues reverberating deep into every wood, copse, forest, and jungle in this and all neighbouring lands. The chamber fills with all the characters that Denny and Jo have designed for each level of the game. They wait in attendance, head bowed. "Not to save myself," repeats Brynthila, "but to bargain on their behalf."

Jo and Denny share looks of baffled amazement. Can this exemplar of altruism truly be their selfish Princess? Brynthila waves the AR hood temptingly and asks, "Well?"

Denny says, "Okay. What are you all demanding?" The game creatures congregate in a huddle, a purple-eyed troll in between a pair of winged unicorns, Grandpappy Growler Goat hosting the Chicken Chimera on his forehead horns. A banded SnowSnake slithers down from the ceiling, piggy-backing a flapping Treader Fish which clings on with its opposable fins. Finally they clear a space and a small gryphon steps forward, lit by its luminescent beak. Its voice is deceptively deep for such a tiny thing.

"The most important is Health and Safety," he announces, and the rest all agree. "No more slippy surfaces on heights over four trolls, and all thorn-work to be accessible with at least one glove to be hidden no more than one Level down."

"Okay," agrees Jo. The SnowSnake whispers something to the gryphon.

"Yes, of course," the gryphon continues, "we want an inclusion rider. Equal pay for gender and species. And," he adds before they can interrupt, "we require a better health care plan. And we want it in writing, added to the Official Rules."

"Sounds reasonable," says Denny. "What else?"

"No more crop spraying on any natural surface. Fruit only plucked with permission."

"Permission?" asks Jo. "Whose permission?"

"The tree's, of course," the gryphon says. "It's all explained in the Environment Plan enclosed for your convenience."

Denny teases, "Are you sure you didn't write this, Jo?" She shrugs, but is delighted by these requests. "Is that it?" she asks.

Morbo, one of the Pentangle Monster heads leans down to the gryphon and whispers, "End credits." "Right," repeats the gryphon. "End credits… we want acknowledgement on the packaging, and…"

It doesn't take long before Brynthila and the game creatures negotiate a deal that satisfies them all. A bit of give and take, a bit of take and give. True to her word, Brynthila holds out Zac's AR hood as the cage is unlocked and she can unwind herself from her own hair.

Jo gently lifts Zac's head as Denny fits the hood. Brynthila explains how to connect the auditory channel to surround him with the game's sound track. After a few minutes they see Zac's legs begin to twitch in rhythm and soon he's conscious and standing there with them. "What a trip!" he enthuses. "Good to be back, though." He embraces them.

"The Three Musketeers!"

"Four," corrects Jo, indicating Brynthila.

"True," Denny says. "Couldn't have done it without her." Brynthila blushes.

"Okay, then," Zac asks, "Are you going to help us explore those Chrono Caves?"

"Don't be silly," laughs Brynthila. "The caves are red herrings to keep you from getting out to your meat-world."

"You mean we can go home? Right now? You're going to let us get out of here and go home?" Jo is desperate to believe her. So is Denny. He asks,"I don't suppose we'll be able to remember any of this, will we?"

"Don't be silly," she repeats. She directs them to lie back on the ground. "Now, where would you like to wake?"

When Zac opens his eyes he's back in his shed, examining his Augmented Reality hood. It seems as though he's been away somewhere for ages. He's trying to remember an idea he had for coordinating the electronics, but a knock on the door blows the idea away with a soft breath. "Zac," calls his mum, "Supper's ready."

Across town Jo's lying under the tester canopy of her four-poster. She's almost naked and a naked Denny snoozes beside her. She stares across in admiration of his nether regions. A modest knock on the door and Osborne's voice asking "Jo?" has her reaching to pull up a bit of the coverlet. Which wakes Denny. He kisses the smile on her lips. "Be down in a minute, Osborne," she tells him. Denny stretches and yawns and embraces Jo to meet the next kiss on her agenda.

They're interrupted again by a familiar voice from Jo's huge computer unit. Brynthila emerges, coughing discreetly. She's fading in and out of transparency. "Put some clothes on," she says. "We need to talk and there isn't much time before I'm back inside for good."

Once they've explained that they've got to find a way to recover from the Games Fair explosion and meet their launch deadline, Brynthila helps them see the bigger picture. It's time, she tells them, for some hard truths, for a reality check. They must re-plan the launch, think way outside the box.

"Listen," she says patiently. "I have lived my life in a castle. So has Jo. The castle is where the game must be. Anyone who owns a castle has money. And anyone with money can make more money. That's the way it is in your world."

"You got that right," agrees Denny.

"I know," Brynthila say, adding, "it's pretty obvious. And that is all I will say."

"Yes. Of course!" Jo says. "You mean Daddy! You mean Falcon Lodge! You really are Princess Genius."

Brynthila fades out and in again. Jo says, "Try to hang in there… I'll be right back."

She grabs Denny's hand, racing downstairs. "With Max out of action, we need to get Fiona here. Pronto Tonto." She calls down, "Mummy!" and pulls Denny into her father's office. He's behind his desk speaking on the phone. He holds up his hand for them to be quiet as he completes the call.

"Daddy, we have something very important to ask you."

"Okay."

"Can you send Osborne to pick-up Fiona. Please."

Elaine comes in and sits on the sofa. "What's all the fuss?"

"Well, Max is in hospital, so we need Fiona to…"

"Hold on, hold on," says Jonathan. "What's all this about?"

Denny tries a slightly calmer approach. "Are you and Max still in that, you know, business arrangement, sir?"

"Yes. That was the Chinese guys on the phone just now. We're trying to find the best way to salvage everything."

"Great! That's great, isn't it, Jo, because…"

"Because," Jo takes over, we have the Lodge, which is sort of a castle, and Brynthila has a castle, and she's our Princess, and she's trapped. See? In a castle, see? So why not have the launch here? In our castle. See?"

Jonathan considers the prospect as Jo continues. "But Max is in hospital, so we need Fiona."

"Sir. Jonathan." Denny says. "Aren't you always telling me to capitalise on contacts, parlay the assets."

Jonathan looks over at Elaine. "Sounds fun," she says.

"Well, I hear everything you're saying. And …" They all lean forward to hear the verdict. "Yes, it's a great idea! I'll run it past the Chinese team, and we can discuss details with Fiona tomorrow. She's had a pretty rough day, after all."

Bonus Level

In the months that follow, Max makes a full recovery. Both he and Fiona love the idea of the castle launch and Jonathan flies them out to Shanghai to plan the deal. Both the Chinese team speak excellent English and regale them all with tales of Brynthila's appearance at Comic Con. Seems her image is going viral on YouTube. "Over a million Likes in the first hour!"

"Okay, Max," Jonathan says, "let's map it out. Launch next month, distribution before Christmas, set up a global sales team. Now, let's talk percentages. The guys here and I have agreed our deal. So, for Checkman, we were thinking…"

"Fifty-fifty?" Max tries to pretend he's joking. They all laugh, trying to pretend he is, too.

"Now, now, don't be greedy. Let's say seventy-five twenty-five. Shall we?" By now Max knows that's a great deal. Unless the games market suddenly gets sucked into a black hole, he and Fiona will be set for life. He shakes hands with everyone.

"Excellent, Max. Good call," Jonathan says.

After the paperwork's been signed, Max uses some of the insurance money to take Fiona on a luxury cruise of the Yangtze River.

"This is it, Fi. It's finally it! Isn't it?" They're leaning against the top deck rail, marvelling at the magnificent gorge bounded by the high cliffs dwarfing their ship.

"Yes, Maxi," she says. "I'm very proud of you."

He turns and kisses her on the cheek. "Wherever would I be without you." And she thinks that she could certainly get used to this new version Max.

On the day of the official world premiere launch of *Brynthila: The Maze of Life*, the grounds of Falcon Lodge are set out like a medieval village fair. Elaine has contracted the events company she used to work for and has put herself in charge of photographing the whole shebang for the official press pack.

The whole village has been invited, along with the national and regional press and television coverage from around the world. With a handful of A-list celebrities, they're having a field day. No expense has been spared to recreate Brynthila's game world, including creature costumes made specially by a well-known cinema supplier of wearable animatronics.

If anyone on the planet requires bunting today, they're out of luck. A large plasma screen in the garden plays loops of the game while Zac on Blac blast out the tracks from their new album.

Robert and some boys from his school chase each other around the grounds, reenacting scenes from the game. Max is there, too, of course, in medieval garb and acting the grand lord. He encourages a group of locals to chase him, and when they get close, he throws handfuls of cash at them.

The music wafts up to Jo's turret window. Denny and Jo peer down to the bustling garden, their arms around each other. Her main monitor unit reproduces the huge plasma screen outside. Brynthila smiles at them from inside the game. She turns to her Prince and they, too, embrace.

Jo catches Brynthila's eye and returns her smile, giving her the thumbs up. Brynthila does the same.

Downstairs, Denny and Jo wander around enjoying what they've created together… funny how it starts with the tiny seed of an idea, and now look… all the costumes, the atmos, music and excitement. They're stopped occasionally to give short press interviews. As they look up at the giant plasma screen where the game is being played out, Jonathan and Max approach them.

"Hot off this press, you two. We just bagged the Indonesian rights!"

Jo exclaims, "Brynthila in Bali! I guess she can have her bikini after all!" she teases Denny.

Max is keen to look to the future. "So what's next? Mustn't rest on your laurels. Zac tells me he's bursting with ideas."

"Whoa!" Jonathan says. "Give them a chance, Max."

"Mind you, next time maybe we can adjust those percentages."

"Oh, yes, I quite agree. Say eighty-twenty?"

Max chuckles, but knows when he's bested. "And you call me greedy!"

Denny and Jo leave them squabbling. They turn to survey their domain, and see a woman in Brynthila's dress, abseiling down from the tower. She's attracting a lot of press attention and a small crowd has formed around her.

Elaine waylays Jo as Denny edges in closer. He's eager to see how Brynthila has managed to escape from the game yet again. He tries to hug her. "Well done," he whispers. "We couldn't have done any of this without you. But the woman pulls away from his embrace. It's definitely not Brynthila, and she's double-definitely uncomfortable being hugged by Denny. He springs away.

"No!" he mumbles, "I mean... the agency. We couldn't have done it without your agency. Well done. You're from the agency, aren't you?" Suddenly very formal, Denny shakes hands with her, and walks off.

Elaine hugs her daughter. "I am so proud of you, Josabunny."

"Mummy, please!"

"Sorry, but you'll always be my little girl. And look at you... positively glowing!" Jo gives nothing away. Elaine says, "I thought

Denny would have brought his mother… she's so keen on parties."

Jo inspects the garden. "Oh, I expect she's around somewhere."

Now, if she and Elaine happened to glance up at the giant plasma screen, they'd be able to catch an excerpt from the exciting Action Levels. There's DigiBrynthila, aided and abetted by a barking DigiLovelace, and, look, they're deep in battle with a horrid fire breathing troll. Look closer… can you see? You guessed, that troll is none other than DigiWenna, trapped forever in the game. Let's see her get out of that one!

Denny and Jo, holding hands, walk further and further along the drive and onto the path through the woods. Like Zac, they can't keep their thoughts off the future.

"Right," Jo says, "What about a male hero next time?"

"You're just trying to make me jealous. I know! A mermaid."

"No, a muscley man. Brain. Brawn. But in touch with his feminine side. Very 21st century."

"What does that mean?" asks Denny, "he uses moisturiser? I dunno… it just doesn't speak to me."

"Sometimes I think the only thing that speaks to you would be a pair of talking tits. And I don't mean little birdies!"

"Shocked! I am shocked, Josephine Hawker-Meade! Okay, how about a couple. A heroic couple."

"What about a wombat. A heroic wombat."

And their voices fade into the foliage as the trees close around them.

The End.

About Beth

Once upon a time I spent 6-months in a cage with two baby orangutans at the LA Zoo. This is true, but has nothing to do with my professional career. Read on!

New Yorker Beth began acting professionally at age 12, coming to prominence as part of the award-winning LaMaMa Troupe. She was part of the Greenwich Village scene during the culturally-amazing 1960s. With her Scottish husband, she co-founded the Troupe's UK branch, touring throughout Europe. Her successful solo career in films & television includes starring roles in Woody Allen's *Love & Death; Tales of the Unexpected; Hitch-hiker's Guide To The Galaxy*; and ITV's hit series *Rock Follies*.

Acting segued into media journalism as London Editor of *Film Journal International;* writing fiction & drama; being appointed BBC-TV development executive; & working as exec producer of corporate websites for an international web-house.

Intellect Publishing brought out her book *The Net Effect*, a socio-cultural account of the internet, with a foreword by David Lord Puttnam. Resident Aliens: stories of NYC in the 1960s was her first solo collection of short fiction.

In September 2014 Beth published *Drama Queen*, a collection of her original scripts and screenplays, and in April 2016 she published her autobiography *Walking On My Hands: how I learned to take responsibility for my life with the help of Woody Allen, Barbra Streisand, Greta Garbo, Harvey Milk, Idi Amin, Guy the Gorilla, & Frank Sinatra among others*. Its foreword is by Shane Connaughton, award-winning novelist and screenwriter of *My Left Foot*.

In 2016 Beth published *Settling Beyond The Pale*, her 2nd collection of short fiction, followed by *Feeding the Twins*, a horror-novella and *ScreenSaver!* her first novel.
    All are available as eBooks on Amazon.
Beth's Wikipedia page   http://en.wikipedia.org/wiki/Beth_Porter
Beth's book promo site   http://www.bethporterbooks.womenstuff.org

ScreenSaver!

Pre-Publication Reviews

"The characters are appealing and what-happens-next kept me reading on and on. I was happy in the castle. I learned there to appreciate your good humor, kindness, child-likeness, imagination, and persistence."
Jean-Claude van Itallie
 multi-award-winning dramatist, author of the acclaimed *America Hurrah!*

"Imagine Evelyn Waugh in computer graphics. Imagine animated Don Quixote. Then imagine the offices of *The Guardian* after a night on the tiles. Now you are approaching the surreal flavour of Beth Porter's satirical high jinks! Its outrageous high-spirits make it required reading for those who used to be 'hip' and can no longer remember just how to do it."
David Benedictus, much-lauded novelist, including *The Fourth of June* & *Return to the Hundred Acre Wood*

"...what a romp! I enjoyed this band of kooky characters."
Marshall W. Mason, seminal stage director, educator and author; elected to the Theater Hall of Fame; 2016 Tony Award for Lifetime Achievement in the Theater.

"Imagination, tech and an original voice: my kind of story."
Robbie Stamp, Chair of Bioss International Ltd; Executive Producer of the *Hitchhiker's Guide to the Galaxy* film.

Printed in Poland
by Amazon Fulfillment
Poland Sp. z o.o., Wrocław

Printed in Poland
by Amazon Fulfillment
Poland Sp. z o.o., Wrocław